PETER FAUR

The Heretic Hunters

A Parable for Our Time

ASH & CREED
PRESS
Bold Stories. Sacred Questions.

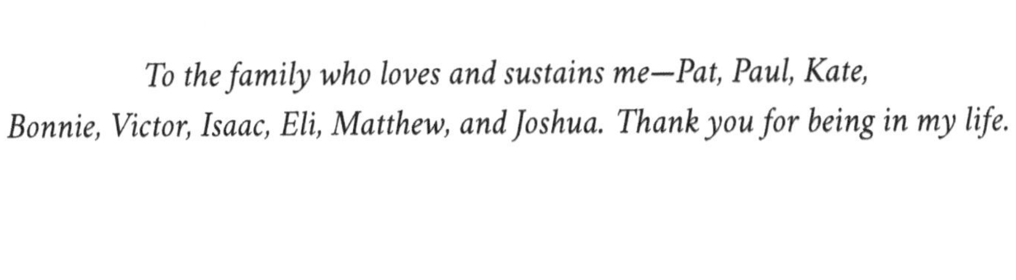

To the family who loves and sustains me—Pat, Paul, Kate, Bonnie, Victor, Isaac, Eli, Matthew, and Joshua. Thank you for being in my life.

Contents

Acknowledgments

I am an accidental Lutheran. Chances are I might never have been a church member if not for the deaths of Jane and Jill, two of the triplets born in 1952 to my mother. I suspect my parents decided then that they wanted to be part of a church community. We became Lutheran because my father had belonged to the church growing up, and he liked the music.

Dad died in 1957, when I was seven and my sister, Joan, was four. The church stepped up to take care of my family and me, especially Betty Paul, my teacher through third, fourth, and fifth grade. I became strongly attached both to our congregation, Trinity Lutheran in St. Louis's Soulard neighborhood, and to the denomination, The Lutheran Church-Missouri Synod. Until I pursued my master's degree in journalism at Kansas State University, all my education had taken place in synodical schools.

During my years in Lutheran education, I met many teachers and administrators who were among the kindest, brightest, most Christian people I have encountered. They include Wayne and Phyllis Lucht, Tom Strieter, Hillman Fischer, Ralph Gehrke, Martin Koehneke, Carl Halter, Robert Hausman, Steve Schmidt, Walter Bouman, Robert Bertram, and Ed Schroeder. The denomination almost always disagreed with my assessment, but even so, I am indebted to each of them for their kindness and inspiration.

During my newspaper years, I greatly appreciated the work of my fellow religion editor, James Adams of the *St. Louis Post-Dispatch*. His book *Preus of Missouri* is well worth your time.

A number of people have supported me during critical points in my career. Special thanks to Frank Starr, Allan Merritt, Tom Rami, Al Akerson, Jim Morice, Barbara Abbett, Doug Wolfe, Dave Pulatie, Bob Peirce, and Elaine Patterson.

Cast of Characters

In Alphabetical Order

Andy Detter, Ashley Detter's father

Ashley Detter, editor, Oberhausen University's *The Spectator*

Hillman Gehrke, world religions professor at Oberhausen

Caleb Haller, Otto Haller's son

Martha Haller, Otto Haller's wife

Otto Haller, pastor, heretic hunter

Harold Kreiss, public relations executive

Frank LaRussa, high-powered labor lawyer

Jeremiah Marquardt, mentor of Otto Haller

Betty Neeb, Otto Haller's administrative assistant

Kurt Richter, political consultant

Ted Robertson, dean, University of Chicago Divinity School

Lucy Rosenkoetter, education reporter, *Des Moines Register*

Ed Schroeder, Martha Haller's father

Robert Storck, president, Oberhausen University

Carl Walters, president, Confessional Lutheran Church in America

I

Part One

*"The best lack all conviction, while
the worst are full of passionate intensity."*
-W. B. Yeats

Caleb Sets the Trap

On the last day of fall semester, 2024, Hillman Gehrke invited any final questions from his Religions of the World students. One of them, a senior who sat in the back row and always wore a clerical collar despite not being ordained, raised his hand.

"So, Dr. Gehrke, you believe people other than Christians can be saved. Is that right?"

Gehrke suspected ulterior motives of his questioner. The professor knew who the student's father was, but he didn't care. Gehrke trusted his God, was confident in his beliefs, and besides, he had tenure. He wasn't about to pull punches with some brash undergraduate. He had something to say, and he saw no reason not to say it.

He walked to the whiteboard at the front of the room. He paused for a bit, wanting to make sure everyone focused on him. Then, with a flourish, the Oberhausen University professor drew a line that spanned the board.

"Okay, this line represents all the people who have ever lived on earth."

Next, he made a mark about ten percent in from the line's starting point.

"Everything to the left here, that's all the people alive today."

The next mark fell about a third of the way along the remaining segment.

"This third here, that's all the Christians in the world today. About 2.6 billion in all."

His final mark left a microscopically small segment.

"That's all the members of the Confessional Lutheran Church in America, which runs your university. If you think only CLCA Lutherans are saved, however you define that word, you're nuts! If you think only Christians are saved, you're nuts!

"What does 'saved' mean, anyway? I know, most people think it means you'll die and go to heaven, and okay, I believe that too. I say it every week in church. 'I believe in the resurrection of the body, and the life everlasting.' I do. I believe there's hope, and truth, in the promise that death doesn't have the final say over us.

"But 'saved' means so much more than that. It means you're set free from having to live in fear. It means you're redeemed to live beyond yourself, to do what you can to make life better for those around you. It means you're given grace, power, and humility to love and be loved.

"Some people in the CLCA think the way to salvation is through pure doctrine, as if you can trade your intellectual understanding and your affirmation of Christianity for your ticket to heaven. But isn't that saying your salvation depends on something other than God's love for you? I tell you, most people don't have a clue about doctrine, or even Christianity, but God loves them, regardless. And if they can live for people and things other than themselves, then yes, I'm willing to say they're 'saved.'

"Take a look at I John 4 sometime. 'Everyone who loves has been born of God and knows God. Whoever does not love does not know God, because God is love.' I think that's a strong indication that God knows and loves even those who haven't heard of Jesus, and they know and love him too, even if not by name."

The student in the clerical collar wasn't satisfied.

"But Dr. Gehrke, Jesus himself said no one comes to the Father except through him. Are you denying that?"

"Not at all. But we Lutherans say people don't find God, can't find God. God finds them. And scripture says God is love, and God was in Christ reconciling the world to himself. Did you hear that? The *world*!

"Jesus also told the story of the shepherd who had ninety-nine sheep in the fold and went back for the missing one. Who are we to say God isn't trying to bring everyone to himself now, despite the religious traditions they're born into or follow? And who are we to say he won't succeed, on this side of the grave or even the other side? I don't think it's our business to judge God's relationship with anyone else.

"And I'll tell you this. I have friends who are secular humanists, downright atheists, not religious at all. Most days I'd rather spend time with them than with some of my fellow clergy. I'd encourage you to seek out people who've lived life outside the confines of the CLCA. Be in the world, and despite what they tell you, don't hesitate to rub shoulders with the world! You'll be much richer for it, more thoughtful, more useful, more complete.

"Now, before we call it a day, let me leave all of you with a question. If Christ took a week to live among you today, would he spend his time sorting out complicated doctrinal controversies, or would he try to teach people more about how to love and help one another? What did he do when he lived among us? Cogitate on it for a while, and send me an email once you have your answer. I hope you all have a great Christmas vacation."

With that, the 54-year-old theologian donned his tweed sportscoat, gathered his papers, and left the lecture hall to walk into the frigid December air of Des Moines. He had introduced yet another semester's worth of students to the thirteen principles of faith articulated by Jewish philosopher Moses Maimonides, the Hindu notion that truth must be sought in multiple sources, and the Buddhist understanding of life's four noble truths. A sizable number of his colleagues in the CLCA would have characterized those religions as fatally flawed, but Gehrke didn't countenance that kind of talk.

An eavesdropper on the murmuring he left behind would have seen a microcosm of the CLCA itself. A few students stood fully behind Gehrke's comments. Most, those who came from the small Midwestern towns that embraced a quiet, conventional Lutheranism, knew they'd heard something outside their experience, but they resolved to cogitate on Gehrke's thoughts, as he would counsel them to do. Some disagreed with Gehrke but saw no reason to cause trouble. And one, Caleb Haller—Mr. Clerical Collar— smirked as he pocketed his iPhone. He had just videoed a storehouse of evidence for his father, the Reverend Otto Haller, who was rapidly building a reputation as the CLCA's premier heretic hunter.

* * *

When Caleb left Oberhausen for Christmas vacation, he was still wearing his collar. Day after day, some of his professors challenged him to take it off because he wasn't a clergyman, but Caleb refused.

He thought of himself as clergy in training and as part of the "priesthood of all believers." After graduation, he planned to enroll at his father's alma mater, Martin Luther Seminary in Cape Girardeau, Missouri. He told his professors there was nothing saying he couldn't wear a collar. He maintained it helped him strike up conversations with people about the faith. If anything, he said, maybe his professors should encourage all their students to put one on. By which he meant all their male students, because scripture said only men were allowed to be ministers. Or so he believed. His denomination's official declarations agreed with him, but many members were starting to support inviting women into the clergy.

"Come here and give your mother a hug," Martha Haller said as Caleb came down the bus steps at the combination Amtrak/Greyhound station in St. Louis. He was his father's son, but even more, he was his mother's son, and he gave her the long, warm embrace she wanted. He adored her. As a child, she woke him each morning with a hug and a smile. She cooked delicious breakfasts, taught him checkers and Scrabble, and took him on walks through the woods. Martha doted on him. After he came along, any further attempts to have children ended in miscarriages.

"I want you to drive us home," she told Caleb. "It's dark, and I'm terrified to drive even one more mile in this snowstorm."

"So, why didn't Dad come?"

"You know how he is. He just couldn't tear himself away, what with having to write his Christmas sermon, obsessing over his website, and insisting he had to take some crazy run. In the middle of winter! Those things always come first, right? I've just resigned myself to it. He's controlled by his obsessions. I know he'll be happy to see you. He's talked about nothing else but you and that video you're bringing him.

"I have to tell you, though, I'm a little embarrassed that you did it. I don't think it's right to ambush a professor." She didn't mention that she had known Gehrke during his seminary days.

"Mom, would you want this man to go on misleading people about how they're saved? I'm just exposing him for the heretic he is."

Martha buckled her seatbelt and sighed deeply.

"I don't want to talk about it anymore. Let's just get home and have a pleasant Christmas together."

Caleb pointed the beat-up, 2009 Honda Civic south on Interstate 55 toward tiny Frohna, Missouri, population 245. Powerful winds nearly blew them off the road near Perryville. His mother said a desperate prayer, and Caleb got them home safely. When they came through the parsonage door, Haller, who sat entranced by Sean Hannity's nightly rant on Fox News, stood up and gave his son a quick, stiff hug.

Caleb nodded in approval at the Christmas decorations, smiling at the real tree and the nativity scene the family had used since he turned two. He felt at home among the shabby furniture, which came mainly from congregants who otherwise would have taken the pieces to the Cape Girardeau Goodwill or the regional landfill.

After a couple of cups of hot chocolate, father took son to his windowless church office. The minister had converted it into command central, with filing cabinet after filing cabinet filled with what he deemed as evidence about individual CLCA heretics. Magazines, books, thumb drives, and even old VHS tapes were scattered willy-nilly around the room, but Haller knew the exact location of each item. From here, he ran his website dedicated to unveiling the heretics inside the CLCA, GodsTruthIsMyTruth.com.

If he needed to meet with a church member, Haller did so at his home or at Virgie's, the local breakfast spot. It wasn't exactly a secret, but it might be unsettling for some members to see just how passionately he pursued his heretic-hunting.

"Welcome to my unholy mess," Haller said to his son. Caleb was taken aback by how much his father's mounds of evidence had grown.

The younger Haller pulled out his iPhone to show the video of Hillman Gehrke. As they watched, standing side by side, Otto Haller nodded with pleasure, sometimes pumping his fists in celebration of the damning heresies he heard.

Caleb bragged to his father about how he had set up Gehrke. He knew the aberrant professor would fall into his trap.

"So, with Gehrke, it's still 'all you need is love,'" Haller said. "I'm not surprised. He's been preaching that rubbish since our seminary days."

"And people lap it up. He's a showman, all right. I swear if he wanted, he could have each and every woman in his class," Caleb said. His face scrunched up in disgust. "And these days, maybe a few of the men too."

Otto Haller nodded. He had memories of a younger Hillman Gehrke, the one in his seminary class thirty years earlier, the one who took weekend trips from Cape Girardeau to Memphis to sample the barbecue and frequent the blues clubs on Beale Street.

"He can be earthy and charming, even hypnotic," Haller said. "Just like the devil himself. Back in seminary, he'd come back from his weekends in Memphis urging us all to go with him. He'd say he wanted us to hear the pain in B. B. King's voice, the soul in his guitar. He wanted us to see how people party when they don't have a broomstick up their … well, you know. I know what he's capable of. And I know just how far he's strayed from the Bible. I've been waiting a long time to take him and his kind down."

"Did anybody go? To Memphis, I mean," Caleb asked.

"Not me, but yes, a few did. Most decided once was enough. They thought it was better to spend their weekends studying Luther and Jesus than it was to check out the fleshpots of Memphis."

Caleb asked his father when he would post his video to the internet.

"Not during the holidays," Haller said. "No sense getting people all riled up when they should be focused on celebrating the birth of the Savior."

And besides, he said, no one will be paying attention to the internet when they're traveling and spending time with their families.

Soon after Caleb returned to Oberhausen, the video would be viral, Haller predicted, at least in the little world of the CLCA. Then, he told Caleb he had some good news.

"I think of you as a Truth Force of one. But I've been working on recruiting some counterparts to you at the seminary. Starting next semester, two students will be gathering information on seminary professors. We're just getting this thing rolling. In a year, maybe two, we'll be a long way toward cleaning up the denomination. And who knows, maybe someday, I'll get to claim my rightful spot on the clergy roster, complete with health insurance and a pension. A man can dream, right?"

An Encounter with Ashley

On the spectrum of Christian belief, the whole of the CLCA was center right. No matter where a CLCA pastor or professor fell within his church body, left or right, almost all of Christendom would consider him to be a vanilla, orthodox Christian.

Haller, however, didn't see it that way, and in the early 2020s, he sent shock waves through the placid denomination by mastering the internet and social media. Singlehandedly, from his perch atop tiny Ebenezer Lutheran Church in Frohna, he developed an online following of 130,000 and counting. He also drew fervent followers to GodsTruthIsMyTruth.com, where he ranted against CLCA clergy and professors he deemed to be teachers of false doctrine.

After his daily morning ritual of a three-mile run followed by black coffee and a Lender's onion bagel, he would settle into his office to post a YouTube tirade. His performances could have landed him the lead role in *Network* or *Elmer Gantry*.

"There are at least eight heretics teaching at Oberhausen and Martin Luther Seminary, maybe a dozen, and I've got the proof," he claimed, although he rarely offered any. "Every year, these heretics send pastors into the church who are trained to teach our families false doctrine. They have to be stopped! Won't you help? Click below to send whatever you can—$5, $10, $25, whatever—so we can drum these false teachers out of our church body. And if you can't donate, then pray for our cause."

During his early social media experiments, the pastor-crusader found ways to expand his reach beyond the CLCA, most notably by insisting the

Holocaust never happened.

"I'm not anti-Semitic," he declared, "but Christians must always stand up for truth, even in matters not tied directly to the faith, and the truth is the Holocaust is a hoax." Haller said he was always ready to talk with people who believed the Holocaust happened. But in reality, he was not open to what most considered to be clear evidence that it did, most notably the millions of bodies of Jewish people slaughtered in Nazi extermination camps and concentration camps.

He was never clear about why he pursued "truth" about the Holocaust so fervently when there were so many other areas ripe for the picking. But by pushing his Holocaust beliefs, he found several individuals willing to provide seed money for his enterprise. Unlike most CLCA members, several Holocaust deniers had money, big money, enough to indulge in causes they appreciated.

Other regular topics included criticisms of various Christian denominations as too liberal, critiques of the world's fascination with "wokeness," and screeds condemning trans, bi, and gay people and their defenders.

Mainly, though, Haller carped day after day about the growing number of heretics in the CLCA. He did his fearmongering well.

"What's really being taught at our seminary in Cape Girardeau and our university in Des Moines? Do you know? I've been sending questionnaires to professors at these schools. I ask them whether they believe in a literal, six-day creation, whether Noah really existed and whether he piloted an ark, whether they think the resurrection of Jesus really took place. Some of them send it back, and I can vouch for their faithfulness to the Bible and Christianity.

"I never hear from most of them. Why do you think that is? What do they have to hide? I'll keep asking questions until I get to the bottom of what these men really believe and teach. I'll fight for your church for you until the day I die, and I ask you to join me."

Haller's congregation knew about his web-based activities, but most members ignored the controversies he aimed to stoke. His only other passion, they came to learn, was long-distance running, a torture that seemed entirely fitting for this severe-looking rail of a man. The members sometimes wondered about Haller's relationship with his wife and son, but his family seemed content, and there was no reason to pry.

*   *   *

On the first day of spring semester 2025, Otto Haller posted the Hillman Gehrke video along with some commentary. Gehrke had been a heretic since his seminary days, Haller said, and the CLCA must put him on trial for it. All it would take would be for some clergyman or some congregation to file charges with the board of regents of Oberhausen University. Within a week, more than a hundred thousand people had seen the video, and a coalition of pastors from small towns in Indiana, Ohio, and Kentucky banded together to file charges against Gehrke.

For his part, Gehrke played down the video when asked about it, but he didn't let it slide. In an email to Caleb Haller, he said, "Mr. Haller, we need to talk. Meet me in my office at 9 a.m. tomorrow. I've checked your class schedule, so I believe you're free."

Caleb showed up the next morning at 9:05 a.m. No sense ceding all the power to Gehrke.

The professor asked Caleb why he had enrolled in Oberhausen.

"It was an easy decision," the young man explained. "A couple of members of my church graduated from here. They said the education was excellent. My mother thought the school would be good for me. Also, since my congregation is a member of the CLCA, I get a fifty percent reduction in tuition. And Des Moines seemed safe enough. Not a lot of crime, not a lot of liberals."

"Not into liberals, huh? So, what do you make of me?" Gehrke asked.

"You're liberal, all right," Caleb said. "Your kind can't be avoided in a university, I suppose, but you shouldn't be at Oberhausen. You're a good enough teacher, a showman really, but I'm not sure you're a Lutheran or even a Christian. You'd fit in better somewhere back east than in a place like Iowa. I don't think there's room for you in the CLCA either."

"It seems to me it's not your place to decide how good a Christian I am. One thing we know for sure, though. There isn't room for your dad in the CLCA. He's the one who was never ordained, not me."

Caleb scowled. "Maybe that's an injustice we can fix down the road. And now that there are heresy charges being filed against you, maybe you'll be out before long too."

Gehrke said the filing of heresy charges wasn't widely known yet, but he wasn't surprised Caleb knew about them.

"Yes, I've seen them, and my father will be posting a full copy of the charges on his website tomorrow."

"Which brings us to the reason you're here," Gehrke said. "The video your father posted of me came from you. Is that correct?"

Caleb hesitated, then said, "You can't prove that."

"Just answer the question, yes or no."

"Well, yes, it came from me. No sense being coy about it."

"Right. Well then, President Storck asked me whether I wanted you expelled. Oberhausen's policy says you needed my prior permission to record me, and any such recording would be for your personal use only. The policy also says it's never permissible to post or distribute such recordings on the internet."

"So, what's going to happen?" Caleb tried his best to put on a brave front, but his hands shook slightly, his heart pounded, and his stomach flopped around like a catfish out of water.

Gehrke said he was being pressured by some faculty members to call for expulsion, but he would not do so if Caleb agreed to two conditions. First, the student would have to write a public apology for the print and online versions of *The Spectator*, Oberhausen's student newspaper.

"Apologize? For exposing your heresies? Forget it."

"Okay, then you can head to the registrar's office to pick up your expulsion papers. You should be receiving your tuition refund in about two weeks. Not even your dad got expelled from the seminary, so if you two are having a race for infamy, score one in your column. Good luck, Caleb. I sincerely hope you have a good life."

Caleb protested that a forced apology from him could never be sincere.

"I can't control what's in your heart," Gehrke said. "And I'm not forcing you to apologize. I'm giving you a choice about whether you'll do so or not.

"I'm not asking you to disavow your allegations and your father's that I'm a heretic, even though I thoroughly disagree. I'm right, though, in seeking an apology from you for violating university policy and posting my remarks online. I'll stand behind what I said in class, and I'm confident I'll be vindicated."

"We'll see," Caleb said.

"Look, the university and I would not be in this position if you hadn't recorded my remarks and distributed them publicly. The case against you is clear cut. The university has every right to expel you. I'm offering you a second chance. If Oberhausen means anything to you, you'll take advantage of it."

Grudgingly, Caleb came around to Gehrke's point of view. He said he thought he could craft a narrowly drawn apology along the lines Gehrke suggested.

"What's the second condition?" Caleb asked.

"That your father come to Oberhausen, at his expense, to meet with me and the university president face to face. And he has to agree never to say, publish, or preach a word about our meeting to anyone. We will do the same. This will be a private conversation, not fodder for GodsTruthIsMyTruth.com. He can, of course, let you know what happens, but you'll be bound by the same conditions."

Caleb said he couldn't make commitments on behalf of his father. Gehrke instructed him to make the request. If his dad wouldn't concede, Caleb's time at Oberhausen would be over.

* * *

Caleb immediately called his father to ask him to make the trip to Des Moines. Otto Haller balked at the thought.

"I won't. I don't care if you get expelled," Haller said as he lingered over a cup of coffee and thumbed through a new batch of allegations against more CLCA clergy members. "If you want to be a pastor, do it in some other denomination. The CLCA has never had much use for us Hallers anyway. Pack your bags and come home. We'll figure out something."

Caleb said he cared, he didn't want to be expelled so close to graduation. He couldn't think of another church body he'd want to be in. He still remembered how good the congregants at Ebenezer Lutheran had been to him, even when his schoolmates treated him badly. He wanted to be in a church like that. Sure, there were a few ne'er-do-wells like Gehrke, but the CLCA was still generally conservative, still a good fit for Caleb. Besides, he'd always thought he could get some measure of satisfaction and payback for his dad just by going through Martin Luther Seminary, graduating, and getting called to a congregation. He didn't want to let go of that dream.

"They're not going to let that happen, not after this," Haller replied.

Caleb told him about Gehrke's other condition, the public apology. It would be impossible for the church not to forgive him after an on-the-record apology.

"You really believe that?" Haller asked.

"Them's the rules, right? If you repent, you're forgiven. And Gehrke said I don't have to disavow any thoughts I might have about his heresies, just admit I violated school policy in recording him and distributing the recording."

"I distributed it, not you."

"Dad, even for me, that's cutting the issue a little too fine. You couldn't have done it without me. In any event, I helped in the process, and I'm guilty in the university's eyes."

Haller suggested another tack: Challenge the policy altogether as an infringement of First Amendment rights.

Caleb said he had no idea whether that would work, but even if it did, he could lose years of his life waiting for the case and the appeals to be resolved.

"I'm close to graduating," he said. "I just want to get this over."

Haller said he couldn't believe a son of his would make a public apology to a man like Gehrke.

"Sometimes you just have to do what you have to do, right?" Caleb asked. "Like in grade school and high school, when I answered on tests that Earth is billions of years old when I know it's only 6,000. To me, apologizing is just a small, distasteful action to reach a bigger goal. Politicians do things like this all the time, and my take on things is we Hallers are all about politics. Church politics. So, I'm okay with making an apology. It's just a steppingstone to get me into and out of the seminary."

Haller protested that he was all about standing up for the truth, not about playing politics. The best step his son could take, Haller said, would be to quit and come home. But he conceded that sometimes compromises must be made when church becomes a blood sport.

As far as making the trip to Des Moines, Haller worried he'd be walking into a trap, but Caleb asked what more could happen to him. The denomination had never ordained Haller. He had no pension and no health insurance through the national church. They couldn't shut down GodsTruthIsMyTruth.com. What would Haller have to lose?

"I'd have to live with knuckling under to those scoundrels," Haller said. "And if anybody recognizes me, it'll get out that I acquiesced to a summons for a command performance for people I can't stand."

"And that's going to stop you from helping me? Well, excuse me for thinking you cared more about me than that. Fine! Just do what you're going to do."

After a long silence, during which he vacillated between resentment and guilt, Haller relented.

"Okay, okay. I'll grit my teeth every second I'm there, but I'll come."

* * *

Caleb worked most of the afternoon on his apology, trying to concede as little wrongdoing as possible while sounding sincere enough to get Gehrke and Oberhausen off his back. Once Caleb had it where he wanted, Gehrke reviewed it and deemed it acceptable. Caleb then emailed it to Ashley Detter, editor of *The Spectator*.

The small-town boy knew the basics about the young woman from Chicago. They'd had several classes together—American History, World History, Introduction to Psychology, and most recently, Gehrke's Religions of the World. No matter the course, she came prepared, made insightful comments, and carried herself with a confidence Caleb admired.

The first time he saw her walking with friends through the quadrangle, the fall wind toying with her dark auburn hair, he was intrigued, curious about her manner, her laugh, and the easy way she maneuvered through life. She was such a contrast to the rigidity that kept him anchored to his straight-and-narrow world. She mesmerized him, and he fantasized about asking her out, just to see what a woman like that was really like.

But of course, she was Ashley Detter, the Chicago sophisticate, and he was Caleb Haller, the Frohna nerd. She probably dated all the time, he thought, while he hadn't been on a real date since his high school senior prom, and only then because his mom brokered the date with another mother in the congregation. He doubted the gap with Ashley could be bridged, not even for coffee, much less anything more serious.

Ten minutes after he sent his email, Ashley replied.

"Caleb, come up to the *Spectator* office. I have some things I want to discuss with you."

The office sat atop the campus's oldest building, three-story Lucht Hall. It was a trek, but Ashley and her staff didn't mind. The climb up the stairs kept them in decent shape, and the office gave them the isolation they needed to brainstorm and write in peace. The university provided several computer terminals, but the student reporters rarely used them. They preferred their personal laptops.

Caleb, who like his dad ran regularly, had no trouble with the stairs. But when he entered the office, he gasped just a tiny bit, only because he was taken aback by the beauty of the young woman before him.

Ashley was alone. She sat behind her computer screen, wearing a navy-blue sweatshirt, chewing on a black licorice twist, and shaking her head slowly as she frowned at the story she was editing.

Caleb had daydreamed about talking with her, but he never had, and now he realized she scared him. He worried he would become tongue-tied, but he soldiered on. He tugged unconsciously at his clerical collar, trying to loosen it just a bit.

"Hi, Ashley. I'm Caleb Haller. You said you had some questions?"

As he stood, she peered over her computer screen, pausing to survey him from head to toe before speaking. The odds were slim, but he wanted to believe she might be flirting.

"Caleb, I know who the hell you are." She seemed slightly annoyed. "Damn it, we've had classes together. You're hard not to notice with that collar you wear all the time. I don't have any questions, but your piece can be clearer and tighter. Writing's not your strong suit. Come over here, I'll show you what I mean."

Within ten minutes, with Caleb looking over her shoulder, Ashley cut about a quarter of his apology while keeping his ideas intact. He wasn't used to women using words like "hell" and "damn," and he'd been somewhat put off. But watching her edit, and taking in the scent of her hair, he decided he could overlook her language, at least for a while. He couldn't stop thinking about what it would be like to have dinner with her.

"When you write, you have to be willing to kill your little darlings," she said. "You know, those words and phrases you think are precious, but they're really just wasting people's time. Dr. Gehrke might think your apology is fine. I think you can get to the point more quickly. This revision is something I'm willing to run."

Caleb said nothing. He stewed just a bit inside, entertaining a notion ingrained into him by his father, that women shouldn't have authority over men. He had enough sense to keep the thought to himself, though, and he had to admit Ashley made his writing better.

"Caleb, is this okay with you? Don't just stand there."

"Uh, yeah, sure, it's good. Go ahead and run it. Thanks. I'll let you get back to work now. See you around."

He walked toward the door. Then, mustering all his courage, he turned around.

"Ashley, how would it be if I, uh, if I . . . if I took you to dinner sometime?

I've always wanted to get to know you."

"You're kidding, right? After our classes together, you have to know you and I don't exactly line up on a lot of things. This Gehrke thing, for instance. He's amazing, and you're screwing with his life. I don't see how I could ever get past that. And I can't believe you see me as anything but 'woke,' to use a word you probably throw around like confetti."

She was right, Caleb realized. But she was also Ashley Detter, and he wanted more time with her.

"Look, it won't mean anything to you, in fact you'll probably forget all about going out with me ten years from now. But it would mean a lot to me. I've never had an opportunity to talk to someone like you. You know, smart, refined, and yeah, I suppose with a much different view of the world than I have. I'm going to be a pastor, you know. I'm going to need to understand how to relate to people like you."

"People like me? What the hell does that mean? You think I'm some kind of heathen, some kind of party girl? I don't know what kind of thoughts you have about me, but they don't sound good."

"That's where you're wrong. I think you're fascinating. I don't know you well, but I do know you're bright, you're gutsy, and yes, you're pretty. I really want to get to know you, even just a little, before we graduate."

"Well, I don't want to get to know you. I can't imagine why I'd want to."

"Tell me this. What do you want to do after college?"

"I'm planning to be a journalist. I've wanted a journalism career ever since grade school."

"I'm sure that doing that, you're going to be running into all kinds of people as sources, including a lot of conservative ones, like me. You might think I live in a bubble, but so do you, I'll bet. Why not spend an evening with me just to understand my kind a little better?"

Ashley protested that she might encounter conservative types, but she wouldn't have to socialize with them.

"And as I told you, I can't get past what you did to Dr. Gehrke."

"I'm apologizing for that, you know. So how about we just forget about all that for an evening? Maybe I can show you I'm not all bad. Small-town, maybe, a little unsophisticated, a little 'un-woke,' but not all bad. How about giving me a chance? I promise we'll go someplace really nice."

It had been a long day, and Ashley was battling fatigue. She couldn't think of a reason to indulge Caleb, but she couldn't think of a reason not to, and maybe she could talk some sense into him.

"Will you get out of here if I say yes?"

Caleb nodded, unable to believe she actually might.

"Okay, then. Yes. On one condition, though," she said.

"What's that?"

"Lose the collar, at least for the evening. It looks ridiculous."

He started to protest, but then he didn't. It was Ashley Detter, after all. Slipping off a collar for an evening wouldn't be too great a sacrifice.

The Heretic Hunters Convene

Otto Haller and the Reverend David Bohnert, a friend of his in Paducah, Kentucky, wrote the charges against Gehrke together and recruited several other pastors to co-sign and file them. Haller couldn't affix his name because he had no standing in the CLCA.

"Let's make the list of charges as long as possible," Haller said. "We don't have to prove them all. Just one should be enough to take Gehrke down and get him ousted. Surely, we can make one stick. And once we do, we can go after the other heretics."

The laundry list of allegations included denying the inerrancy of scripture, seeing other religions as being equal to Christianity, advocating the ordination of women, believing in evolution and the notion that Earth was billions of years old, supporting homosexuality and other deviant sexuality, and communing with non-CLCA Christians, which was forbidden because the denomination said members could commune only with other members of the denomination.

By the time Haller walked into the office of Oberhausen President Robert Storck, the charges had been seen throughout the church body. Such was Haller's reach on social media. Gehrke chose not to address them publicly, saving his comments for the panel who would sit in judgment of his case. His silence created a vacuum his opponents used to make him something more than a run-of-the-mill, misguided heretic. In their portrayal, he was an outright agent of Satan.

Until the meeting in Storck's office, Gehrke and Haller hadn't seen each other since their seminary days a quarter century earlier. Because of their time together, Gehrke was well acquainted with Haller's biblical literalism and his heretic-hunting ways.

Shortly before their graduation from seminary, Haller charged seven faculty members with heresy. During their hearing, the facilitator said he had to read the charges only once. The reason was simple: they were exactly the same for each man.

"How about that! Cookie-cutter heresy!" a student observer at the hearing called out, causing many in attendance to break out laughing. Haller sat fuming because the comment made him look ridiculous. Even worse for him, the men were exonerated.

After the hearing, the president of the seminary, the Reverend Dr. William Bayer, had a word with Haller.

"We don't bring heresy charges in the CLCA," Bayer said. "It's vulgar. We get rid of ministers for having sex with their parishioners or skimming money from the collection plate. But for heresy, or so-called heresy? No. We discuss our theological differences in academic journals and symposia. If we disagree, we keep the conversation going. It's the collegial thing to do, approaching each other with respect. I'm going to ask you to apologize to the men you charged. Show a little humility. Show a little graciousness."

"Never!" Haller declared. "Your way of doing things is allowing heresy to take root in the church. Things need to change, radically!"

The seminarian was allowed to graduate, but because of his contentious spirit, the CLCA refused to recognize him as a minister. Still, tiny Ebenezer Lutheran Church in Frohna hired him, or "called" him as they say in church circles. His aunt and uncle belonged there and vouched for him, as did one of his professors, the Rev. Dr. Jeremiah Marquardt, who traveled to Frohna to install him.

This early-morning meeting between Haller, Storck, and Gehrke was not about heresy charges. It was about Haller's son, Caleb, and what the future might hold for him.

As the administrative assistant ushered Haller into the nicely appointed president's office, Storck and Gehrke sat in a cluster of furniture containing a couch, a coffee table, and several upholstered chairs. They situated themselves apart from one another to avoid intimidating Haller. They rose to shake Haller's hand. They had decided to be cordial, not contentious, although their visitor quickly tested their resolve. They offered him coffee, but Haller declined. All three men chose to wear their black suits and clerical collars; no one wanted to be one-upped.

"So, Gehrke, we meet again," Haller said. "I guess you've made a pretty good life for yourself. Enjoy it now, before your heresy conviction. And I might add, I don't think you'll be having such a great afterlife. I'll be surprised if I see you in heaven."

"Actually, Otto, I don't think I'll be convicted of heresy. And when we're together in heaven, I think you'll be happy to see me, and I you. I'm sure we'll move on to better things. But we're not here to talk about the afterlife. We're here to talk about Caleb."

As the three men sat down, Storck picked up the conversation. He chided Haller for sowing so much strife in the church, not just the CLCA but the church at large.

"The biggest scandal in all of Christianity is how divided Christians are," Storck said, "and you're not helping matters by being so publicly ugly to your fellow believers. Churches are struggling because people are souring on organized religion, and it doesn't help to have you slinging your mud. There's a process for charging heresy, and it doesn't include airing your grievances on a website. Do you really think you're setting a good example for Caleb by doing what you're doing?"

"I'm teaching him to live with integrity. I'm teaching him not to be afraid to call out false doctrine. I'm teaching him to stand up for truth and his beliefs. So, yes, I'm setting a good example for him."

The conversation went silent for a bit as Gehrke thought about what he wanted to say, and then: "Otto, sometimes I wonder how much you're waging a war for truth and how much you're simply trying to seek retribution for being kept off the clergy roster. We knew each other in seminary. I have no doubt you believe the things you believe, but if you truly do, why not just go find a church body that will make you comfortable? Why not leave the CLCA alone? And why not show Caleb what it means to be supportive of a church? This campaign of yours, I think, is making you uglier by the day. If you're not careful, it's going to do the same to Caleb."

Haller crossed his arms, seething as he looked away from his two hosts before turning back toward Storck and Gehrke.

"You'd be telling Martin Luther himself to stop questioning the pope," he said. "I expect that someday, I'll be in the history books for calling the CLCA back to the truth. You'll see. Besides, it's my church, not yours, and most people in the church are on my side. You and your kind are the ones who should be out, not me."

First of all, Storck said, you're the only one in this room who's not on the clergy roster. But let's set that aside and say, for purposes of this conversation, you're part of the CLCA as a pastor of a congregation. And here's the thing. It's not just your church, not just my church, not just Hillman's church, it's our church, all of ours, and if you won't stop, there might be no church left. Like just about every other church body, the CLCA is in decline, and you aren't helping. It's no secret that Oberhausen's pre-seminary program has been shrinking for the past decade. But enough of this. The subject of the meeting is supposed to be Caleb.

"We gave Hillman the power to demand Caleb's expulsion or give him another chance," Storck said. "Truth is, Hillman's the one who's been wronged here. I wouldn't have blamed him a bit if he had told us to send Caleb packing, but he didn't. He told me he believes Caleb has a lot going for him, and he's happy to give him another chance. I run this school, though, and you should know, if he pulls something like this again, he will definitely be gone from here."

Haller protested: "Caleb did nothing except exercise his First Amendment rights, and I don't think you'd have a leg to stand on in trying to expel him. If you'd tried, I would have sued you. But we've met your conditions. Caleb wrote his apology, it's been published, and here I am. So, are we done here?"

"You wouldn't win that suit. Our lawyers say our policy is bulletproof, and hundreds of universities throughout the country have policies identical to ours," Storck said.

"Otto, what you say is true," Gehrke conceded. "You've met the conditions.

But I was hoping you could clear up a couple of things for us. Well, me, really. I asked Caleb why he came to Oberhausen, and he gave me an answer. A good education, a tuition discount, Des Moines seemed like an okay place, et cetera. I have to ask: Did you and he talk about Caleb's coming here? Did you want him to come?"

Haller scoffed before answering.

"It's really none of your business, but I had mixed emotions about it. It's a church-affiliated school, and I know many faculty members here are not like you. They're orthodox. I trust the teaching of most of the religion department, and I think I've taught Caleb how to recognize false teaching when he sees it. I don't worry about him falling prey to it. Obviously, he could spot it in you, Gehrke.

"After the way the CLCA treated me, though, I'd have been fine if he had just gone to Southeast Missouri State. It's about forty minutes from us and, as you know, practically next door to the seminary. But he wanted to live further away from Frohna. The truth is, his mother played a big role in pushing him toward Oberhausen. Like me, she grew up in the CLCA. She sees Oberhausen as a good school. I think it will be a much better school once people like you get exposed for the heretics you are."

Storck had had enough.

"You toss that word around rather freely," he told Haller. "I brought Hillman to Oberhausen. I'll defend him to the death. He's one of our best professors and one of the most decent people I know. What's more, we don't tolerate 'heresies' here, even though you think you see them. I've been biting my tongue since you came into my office, but I have to tell you, you and your whole crusade, your 'GodsTruthIsMyTruth' rubbish ... it's all despicable. What right do you have to spread your vile accusations and your lies throughout our church body? You asked if we're done here. We are indeed. Please leave."

Haller got up, but he had one more question. Could Caleb count on graduating from Oberhausen, and would this incident affect his chances of getting into the seminary?

As long as Caleb followed the rules and completed his studies successfully during his last semester, there's no reason he shouldn't graduate, Storck said.

"I can't speak for the seminary, but we both know young men aren't exactly beating down the doors to enroll. I would think he'll get in. He's made his apology. That should be enough. As long as he doesn't rock the boat, as long as he doesn't start accusing his professors of heresy, as you did, he shouldn't have any trouble."

I doubt he will, Haller thought. But as for me …

"One final thing, Haller. You obtained the video you posted in violation of our policy and without our permission. Take it down, or you'll be the one getting sued."

The video came down a couple of days later. Instead, Haller posted a written summary of Gehrke's beliefs about world religions, incorporating this quote: "If you think only CLCA Lutherans are 'saved,' however you define that word, you're nuts! If you think only Christians are 'saved,' you're nuts!" He tweeted out a link to the summary several times a day.

"We were threatened with a lawsuit unless we stopped making the Gehrke video available to you," Haller told his followers. "We will never fail to find a way to let you see the truth. We wonder, though, why Oberhausen is afraid to let you see Gehrke in action. We also wonder what else Oberhausen doesn't want you to see. And we believe it's time to unmask the other heretics at Oberhausen and the seminary in Cape Girardeau."

* * *

Two miles away from Oberhausen, at a Hampton Inn, a gathering of CLCA ministers waited until Haller arrived. They had filed the charges against Gehrke, and Haller had summoned them to Des Moines, church headquarters, to plot out strategy and tactics for the heresy trial. Until Haller could join them, they killed time by eating bagels, drinking passable hotel coffee, and catching up on church gossip. The CLCA was a tight subculture, and gossip traveled quickly, far, and wide. The conversation covered topics as mundane as whose son or daughter was getting married and as consequential as which pastor had been caught embezzling funds.

Everyone quieted down when Haller walked into the room, although they continued consuming their coffee and bagels. As Lutherans always do, Haller opened the meeting with a prayer.

"Dear Father, we offer ourselves to you as warriors for truth. Give us the power and the drive to stand up for your word and rid the church of those who no longer hold fast to the truths of the Bible. Let the church and the world see we are on your side as you are on ours. In the name of our Lord and Savior Jesus, Amen."

Haller didn't let on that he had just been with Storck and Gehrke. He hid the meeting, not to keep his promise, but to avoid getting ribbed for making a command performance. Also, he didn't want to dwell on his son's getting into trouble for helping him out.

"From what I'm hearing," he said, "Oberhausen doesn't seem particularly worried about the trial. I'll bet they think they have it sewn up. So, what can we do to move the odds in our favor?"

After considerable discussion, the group mapped out the following five strategies:

-Use Haller's social media skills to hammer away at Gehrke's reputation. Post information about him that would make him look suspicious to Lutheran churchgoers, such as his post-seminary education at Harvard, his fascination with jazz and the blues, his unconventional dress and appearance, his love of exotic cuisine. Anything that fell outside the norms of bland Lutheranism was fair game.

-Create a think tank called the Lutheran Institute for Conservative Theology to provide intellectual underpinnings for the upcoming anti-heresy trial and those to follow.

-Establish an elite email list of affluent laypeople likely to oppose Gehrke. Give them talking points to discuss with their pastors and encourage them to threaten withholding their financial support if the trial failed to convict the heretic.

-Seek speaking time at congregations and pastoral gatherings to fan the flames on the idea that Gehrke was not the only heretic within the CLCA. He and his kind had to be stopped now, or the whole church body would be infected with false teaching.

-Choose wisely in selecting their representatives on the panel that would hear the case. According to the CLCA bylaws, both the accused and the accusers had a say in who would be on the panel. The accusers needed to pick the most staunchly conservative people they could find.

"That should keep us busy until the trial begins," Haller said. "Let's appoint people to make each of these things happen. I'll take care of the website, of course. Who volunteers to take on the other jobs?"

Once the duties were assigned, Haller had some parting words.

"One thing I know I can promise you. Most of the pastors, and nearly all of the CLCA lay people, won't stand behind Gehrke and the other heretics. They still believe in the Bible, that Adam and Eve and Noah and Moses were real, that Jesus performed miracles and rose from the dead. When I was at seminary, some of the professors didn't believe these things, but when I called them on it, they didn't pay a price, I did. This time, if we do our jobs well, we can flush out the heretics and reclaim our church."

* * *

Before leaving Des Moines, Haller invited Caleb out for coffee. At Starbucks, he told his son to grab an isolated corner table so they could talk without being overheard. He ordered a black Americano for himself and the caramel macchiato Caleb requested, not quite sure what to make of his son's preference for such a froufrou drink.

"I can't believe the prices they charge," Haller complained as he sat down. "Maybe we should open a coffee shop at the church. If Frohna would support one, I wouldn't have to worry about donations anymore."

Caleb, in clerical collar as always, asked whether he might yet face retaliation for recording the video of Gehrke. His father said if Gehrke and Storck kept their word, and if Caleb lay low, he should be receiving his degree in the spring.

"And as long as you hand over your tuition money, the seminary will be glad to admit you." Haller shrugged. "It seems people your age aren't flooding the seminary with applications. You can help scout the infidels for me, but let your old man actually call them out. No sense getting yourself kicked out of the church too, although I'll never understand why that matters to you. I'm proof that there's life after expulsion.

"Did your mother and I ever tell you why we named you Caleb? In the Bible, when the Israelites reached the promised land with Moses, a lot of them were skeptical that they'd be able to take it from its inhabitants. But Caleb believed. He obeyed God's instructions, he encouraged other people to believe, and God rewarded his faithfulness by giving him special rewards in the promised land. That's what we want for you, Caleb. That you'll be faithful to God and end up with him with special rewards in the promised land of heaven."

Caleb had heard the story a dozen times before, but nevertheless he appreciated it. He thanked his father for coming to Des Moines, especially because it aggravated Haller so much to do so.

"Now I have another favor to ask," Caleb said. "Can you lend me two hundred dollars?"

Haller did a spit take with his coffee.

"Most weeks that's like twenty percent of what gets put into the collection plate at church," he informed his son. "That's a lot of money to me and your mother, and if history is any indication, this could turn out to be a 'loan' that never gets repaid. Why on earth do you need it?"

"For … uh … well, for love," Caleb gushed. "I've asked a girl to dinner, and I want to impress her. Denny's won't cut it with this one. I want this date to be just right. I want to take her to Skip's. I need the money. I promise I'll repay you. I can do odd jobs at the church this summer until we're even."

Haller unloaded a barrage of questions. Where's her hometown? (Chicago) Does she go to chapel? (Sometimes) Does she go to church? (I don't know.) How does she dress? (Jeans and sweatshirts, usually.) What's she getting her degree in? (I don't know.) Oh, and what's her name?

"Detter!" Haller exclaimed. "The Chicago Detters? First, I don't approve. They're too liberal for my blood. Second, she should be taking you to dinner. The Detters are loaded. Everyone in the CLCA knows that. Word is her dad invests in real estate, mainly houses and apartments. No one is sure how the family made their money in the first place—booze, maybe?—and no one cares. You know what they say. Sooner or later, all money becomes respectable. They're welcome in church circles because of their bank account. Their money doesn't impress me. But she agreed to go out with you? That's kind of puzzling. How'd that even happen?"

"Truth is, I don't know. I'm fascinated by her. I guess I caught her in the right mood. I'm not sure she's thrilled about it, but she's going, and I need the money. What do you say?"

Haller shook his head. He said from what he knew about the Detters, Caleb should steer clear. They give their money to some really liberal church causes, like efforts to bring denominations together. They probably back Gehrke and his kind.

"I don't want you going out with her. You get in her orbit, and who knows what will happen to your faith. I can't stop you from your date, but I'm not putting up the money for it. Figure out something else. I'll see you whenever you come home. Easter, I guess."

Caleb grew angry, but he wasn't surprised. It didn't take long to develop Plan B. One call to his mother, and the money was in his bank account within two days. She wasn't sure how she'd handle things with Otto, but maybe what he didn't know wouldn't hurt him.

* * *

The campus chapel bell tolled as Gehrke sat alone in the vestry, seeking a quiet place for contemplating the implications of being tried as a heretic. He wasn't, of course, but who could say how a heresy hearing might go?

Some of the "jury" will call me arrogant. They'll say I've twisted the Word. That I've led people astray. But what is arrogance, if not the refusal to question? What is humility except doing that which God demands? What is cowardice? I'm not giving into cowardice. I'm not going to follow in the steps of Peter when speaking up is needed.

He looked at the cracked plaster on the wall; it spidered out like a wound.

I love this Church. I gave it my youth, my voice, my loyalty. And now I'm to be judged by some who fear the very questions Christ welcomed? Who mistake certainty for faith? Who wield distorted doctrine like it's Gospel truth itself?

They think I want to destroy this church. But I want to save it. I want to strip away the fear, the shame. I want to speak of grace that doesn't come with a ledger. Of love that doesn't require a pedigree. Of a God who walks with the broken, not just the unfailingly obedient.

His hands trembled slightly. Not from fear. From resolve.

If they cast me out, so be it. If they brand me a heretic, let the ink dry. I would rather be condemned for truth than praised for silence.

He stood, straightened his coat, and picked up the Bible.

Let them come. Let them ask. I will answer. And if they refuse to hear, I will speak louder. Not for them, but for the ones still listening.

Getting to Know Ashley

aleb arrived at Ashley's dorm in a button-down, oxford-blue shirt, a black, cable-knit sweater, black cotton pants, black chukka boots, and a black car coat. She greeted him in a beige, beaded, empire-waist cocktail dress and a medium-heeled pump, a 21st-century girl with more than a touch of old Hollywood glamour.

"You are beautiful, and I'm underdressed," he said. Worse, he thought, I'm thoroughly outclassed.

"Don't be ridiculous. We're going to Skip's, right? You're fine. Still a little ministerial, but you're fine. I'm just glad to see you in something besides that stupid collar."

Caleb had often jogged past Skip's, about three miles from Oberhausen, thinking it was the classiest restaurant he had ever seen. He liked the simple, black sign mounted on posts with "Skip's" in gold lettering. Online, pictures of the building—a two-story, upscale, white, wooden house that had been converted into a restaurant—showed dining rooms decked out in intricately carved wood paneling with fresh flowers on each table. Caleb verified that Skip's offered vegetarian and vegan dishes, just in case Ashley preferred them. He also thought he could impress his date with the extensive wine and cocktail menu. Lutherans are many things, but not teetotalers.

When Caleb pulled out his phone to order an Uber, Ashley told him to stop. "I'll drive." He protested he'd rather take care of the entire evening, including the transportation.

"You never know what you're getting with an Uber. Let's take my car." She threw on her coat and rushed out the door, forcing Caleb to follow her to the campus parking garage. He resented having to sit in the passenger seat, but he couldn't help but quiz Ashley about her Firenze Red Jaguar E-Pace hybrid. What year is it? How fast? How long can it go before it switches from electric to gas? What does this do? What does that do? The only question he couldn't bring himself to ask was "how much?"

"Stop with all the questions. I'm actually embarrassed about having it. I mean, it's convenient, it's cool, but I'd be happy with a used VW Bug or a Nissan Sentra. Dad insisted, though. He bought it. He wanted me in a safe car that would get me between Des Moines and Chicago. He went a little overboard, don't you think?"

As they approached the restaurant, Caleb asked Ashley to head to self-parking. If they were going to valet, he should be in the driver's seat, handing the keys to the attendant, taking care of tipping when they retrieved the car.

"Well, first, there's no key for a Jaguar, only a fob. And what, I have to walk two blocks in the freezing cold just to protect your ego? Forget it. Tell you what, though. You can handle the tip."

Inside, Caleb told himself to stop being annoyed and focus on having a good conversation and a pleasant meal. Skip's was noisier than he anticipated. Good restaurants get crowded on a Saturday night. He asked the maître d' if they could have a table in a corner, thinking it might be quieter. The maître d' smiled, recognizing a nervous young suitor, and accommodated his guest's request.

Once a waiter led them to a table, Caleb sat himself, but only after pulling out Ashley's chair for her.

Almost immediately, a staff member approached.

"Good evening. I'm your sommelier."

Caleb gave him a look that signaled "I do not have a clue what on Earth you might be talking about."

"Your wine steward. Would you like to see a wine menu?"

Oh, of course, Caleb said, bluffing his way through his fine-dining naivete. As he studied the wine selections, he tried making a joke for Ashley.

"I guess you can tell, I don't do this kind of thing every day. The staff knows for sure, huh? I guess I come off as kind of a rube. One time, I asked a waiter what the soup du jour was. He said, 'Sir, that's another way of saying soup of the day.'"

Ashley had been agitated around Caleb since their evening began, but now she laughed. A good, hearty laugh. Caleb kept looking at the wine menu, trying to keep cool, but he couldn't help but smile. He kept hemming and hawing over the menu. Red or white? Dry or sweet? France or California?

"You know what, Caleb, I'm really more of a beer girl. How about you just order me a Stella?"

Relieved, he set the wine list aside. "Two Stellas it is."

Caleb informed the sommelier, who curbed his disdain as best he could. As he walked away, the conversation between Ashley and Caleb stalled. Finally, Caleb broke the ice.

"I chose Skip's because it has vegetarian dishes, just in case that might be what you would want."

"No, not my style at all. You know I'm from Chicago, right? The stockyards and all that. I come from a long line of meat eaters. I'm having steak. Ribeye steak, medium rare."

Ashley was by turns getting friendlier.

"You know, just the fact that you thought about what I might want is really sweet! Thank you for putting so much work into this evening. I had no idea what to expect, but this is exceptional! Maybe there really is a heart beating under that doctrinal warrior veneer of yours. You're not exactly the cold fish I feared you might be."

"Doctrinal warrior" wasn't meant as a compliment, but Caleb enjoyed it. He said he felt pretty ordinary, especially after his father clued him in about the Detter family money. But at least he knew his way around the knives and forks of formal dining, thanks to his mother's few etiquette lessons.

"She seems to have done her job well. Your manners are good. A little stiff, maybe, a little by the book, but good. But it's your father who interests me," Ashley said. "When I told my folks I was having dinner with you, my dad flipped out. He calls your dad the Alex Jones of the CLCA. He tried to forbid me from seeing you, but I'm a little old for that. He asked what possible reason I could have for going out with you."

"Honestly, I've been wondering myself, ever since you said yes."

"Me too. The truth is, I was too tired to argue and too tired to say no, and I don't back out once I've made a commitment, even if I've had second thoughts. There are things about you that don't make me happy. You're kind of the campus dork with that collar you wear. You're a little pompous, at least in class. But that stunt you pulled with Dr. Gehrke, that was inexcusable. What was that all about?"

"I've apologized for it. Shouldn't that be the end of it?"

"You apologized with a gun pointed squarely at your head. I don't think that counts. Try again."

Caleb said he was protecting the faith and protecting the church. The Bible is clear about things that Gehrke questions or outright defies. He conceded he shouldn't have made the video, but he still believed Gehrke should be driven out of the CLCA.

"Yeah, I'm not sure the Bible is as clear about a lot of things as you think it is," Ashley said. "It's really not even one book. It's not a concept album, it's a mix tape. It's sixty-six separate books, seventy-three by the Catholics' count. But setting that aside, I've never understood how God can order all sorts of killing in the Old Testament and then do a 'love your neighbor' about-face in the New. It's puzzling. Anyway, I'll take the New any day. And I think one of the clearest things in the New Testament is St. Paul's saying if you don't have love, your words just come off as a clanging cymbal. That's what I hear from your dad, lots of clanging … not an ounce of love. I think you should wise up and let go of the cymbals before it's too late. Your dad too."

This was Ashley Detter, being as direct as he should have expected. Normally, Caleb would write her off as rude, ignorant, or worse, blasphemous. His first instinct was to strike back in defense of himself and his father. But, he realized, he had never wanted anything as much as he wanted to sit across from Ashley at dinner, admiring everything about her, and he wanted to try to make it happen again.

"Look, I'm not real happy with my dad right now, for reasons I don't want to get into. But I support what he's doing with his website. My dad would tell you that standing up for truth is the greatest act of love anyone can perform," he said. "And he really thinks people will be damned if they don't accept the Bible as inspired, inerrant, and infallible. But maybe we can talk about all this another time. If it's okay with you, could we just have a pleasant conversation? This might be the last evening I'll ever have with you, I know. I'm sure I'll look back on it forever. I'd like to create some pleasant memories tonight."

The wait staff delivered their food—a ribeye, baked potato, and sauteed mushrooms for Ashley, and a porterhouse, baked potato, and green beans for Caleb.

"You know what? Let's do have some wine," Ashley suggested.

Caleb had his doubts. "You really think it's okay to mix beer and wine?"

"Well, you know, my dad used to be in the beer business. He has a saying: 'Beer before wine, and you'll feel fine.'"

They each had a glass of house merlot.

As they ate their meals, Ashley steered the conversation toward learning more about Caleb.

"So, do you have a favorite movie? A favorite book? And for Pete's sake, please don't say the Bible."

Caleb thought for just a second. "Favorite movie … *Galaxy Quest.* It goes back a few years, I know, but I love how the crew of a TV show finds the guts to be real heroes when they need to be. Favorite book … let me think. I know. *1776* by David McCullough. He's got great stories about the ordinary people who won freedom from England. Wonderful book. How about you?"

"Favorite movie … Mine goes even further back. It's *Ferris Bueller.* One of the great Chicago movies! And I have to admit I played hooky a time or two in high school. Favorite book … *All the President's Men.* Makes sense, huh? I'm going to be a journalist, and there've been none better than Woodward and Bernstein. And just so you know, I'm a *Galaxy Quest* fan too."

The conversation paused a bit as they ate. Then, Ashley asked:

"What exactly is a Frohna, Missouri, anyway? Is it even on the map?"

Caleb thought about it a bit, then said it's like living in a history museum.

"The town came to life in the 1840s, founded by Lutherans who came from Europe and wanted to live among each other. A lot of the cabins they built still stand today. People tend to eat the crops they grow and the animals they raise. Most of the time, they live their lives within a twenty-mile radius of our little town. Their world isn't expansive, but in crazy, mixed-up times, maybe that's not so bad.

"And really, it's not isolated. TV comes out of Cape Girardeau, and the town has internet service. My family buys the fastest internet available in Frohna so dad can do research and run his website. So, just about anything you can see in Chicago, I can see in Frohna.

"The politics are conservative, the morals are biblical, and the culture is a throwback to an earlier century," Caleb summarized.

"And you're comfortable there?"

"Why wouldn't I be? I grew up there. I'm in a friendly congregation. I can run. I can shoot rabbits. I'm not an urban guy. So, yes. I like the pace, I like the people. I like Frohna. I've been to Chicago. My dad and I went once for a Cardinal-Cub game. It was kind of overwhelming. Way too big for my taste. You must like it, huh?"

Ashley said she grew up in suburban Oak Park, about twenty minutes west of the Chicago Loop. She attended a Lutheran grade school but went to Oak Park-River Forest High School. She played basketball and was on the debate team. She managed the editorial page of the student newspaper, *The Trapeze,* for two years.

Ashley's home was one of twenty-four in Oak Park designed by Frank Lloyd Wright, who built one for himself on Chicago Avenue. Ernest Hemingway grew up in Oak Park, she said, and gangster Sam Giancana lived there for years. "Architects, authors, mobsters. We're into diversity," she joked.

"My mom is more or less a society matron. She belongs to the Junior League and serves on the boards of Lutheran Services of America and our local United Way chapter. The ladies' guild at our congregation, Hope Lutheran, was too slow-paced for her, but she led the planning committee when Hope expanded about a decade ago. It's a rarity in Oak Park—a church of 1,200 members that's actually growing a little.

"My dad's family made a lot of money in brewing. They sold the business a couple of decades ago, and since then, he's been in financial management and real estate. His firms have financed some of the most prestigious modern buildings in Chicago. His passion, though, is creating affordable housing for the poor."

Ashley said she had two brothers, both in high school, and a sister in seventh grade.

"So, what's your plan when we graduate?" Caleb wanted to know.

"Dad invited me to join the family business, but omigod, no! I'm headed to Northwestern University for a master's in journalism. It's a chaotic field these days, and I won't make a fortune, but I'm kind of like Anderson Cooper. I have family money, so I don't have to worry about how much I'll make. I believe there's still a place for speaking truth to power. That's what the best journalism does. That's what I want to do."

"Funny. My dad talks about speaking truth to power all the time. The two of you may have more in common than you think." Caleb knew he'd made a mistake as soon as the words left his mouth.

Ashley grimaced. "I don't think so. I've seen his website. The Holocaust was a hoax? The church is filled with heretics? Dr. Gehrke is a heretic? I have a word for what he's speaking, and it's not 'truth.' It starts with 'b' and ends with 't,' and that's all you need to know."

Caleb wanted to defend his dad, even though he knew some of his website postings were indefensible. Mainly, he didn't agree with his father's Holocaust denials, and he guessed his dad's combative style offended Ashley.

As he was trying to come up with something to say, he saw Ashley's face turn ashen. She was looking behind him toward the bar. A man staggered past him, knelt down next to Ashley, and put a hand on her shoulder. He was tall, well-dressed, dark-haired, and beefy. She shrank down in her chair and turned her head away from him.

"So, Ashley, long time no see," he said, smirking. "Think you can just skate out on me? You can't, you know. You owe me another date. What say we begin it now?"

"I don't owe you a thing. I'd hoped I'd never see you again. Go away. Leave me alone. Just go!"

Caleb took charge. "I don't know who you are, buddy, but you're not welcome here. Ashley's with me. Leave her alone."

"Big man, big man. Why don't you just run along and give me that chair you're sitting in? I'll order a little dessert for Ashley and me. I'll make sure she gets home."

Caleb stood and hovered over the man, who used the table to steady himself as he rose.

"Mike, don't make any trouble here," Ashley managed to say, even as she trembled. "Please just leave."

"I'll leave when and if I'm ready. And I'm not ready." He slurred as he spoke, and then he took a ferocious swing at Caleb and promptly found himself off balance when he missed.

What Mike didn't know was that after Caleb found himself on the wrong end of a wedgie in fifth grade and a toilet swirl in sixth, his father decided to do something about it. Pastor Haller bargained with one of his congregation members, a former college wrestler, to teach self-defense to his son. "Do this, and all the baptisms, weddings, and funerals in your family are on me," he told the man.

Caleb used his attacker's imbalance to quick advantage, slinging him to the ground. Caleb moved away to stay out of reach of the man, who made his way back to his feet. He charged again, but Caleb stepped aside, grabbed hold of one of the man's shoulders, and pushed him into a wall.

The maître d' brought two members of the wait staff over to the scene. They subdued the assailant, keeping him in check until they delivered him to the front of the restaurant, where two patrol officers took charge. The maître d' summoned several bussers to take care of the mess caused by the skirmish. Caleb's plate and wine glass had found their way to the floor during the scuffle.

After apologizing to nearby guests, the maître d' turned his attention to Caleb and Ashley.

"I'm so sorry," he said. "I thought that man looked like trouble as soon as I saw him. He followed you in, and it seemed like he was on a mission. He took some time at the bar to fuel up before he came over your way. Needless to say, your dinner is on Skip's. And order whatever you'd like for dessert. I hope this won't discourage you from patronizing us in the future."

Caleb assured the man he'd be back. No reason not to make a return visit, he thought. I'll just use the money Mom gave me next time.

Ashley saw a side of Caleb she didn't know was there. She disliked his conservative ways, but she enjoyed being admired and appreciated how he had kept her safe. Maybe he was worth getting to know a little better. And maybe, with a little work, she could turn him around.

"Who was that guy?" Caleb asked as they shared a helping of baked Alaska.

"Oh, last semester someone in my dorm set me up with him. His name is Mike McLaughlin. What a bore! A business major at Drake. All he could talk about was how he drove a BMW and how he bought his clothes at Brooks Brothers in Chicago and how he'd be joining Goldman Sachs after he graduated. On and on and on. Like I'd be impressed. He didn't ask me a thing about myself. I ended our date early. I told him I was sick. By which I meant bored stiff. He said we'd have to pick it up again sometime. I said sure, by which I meant 'yeah, right.' I didn't think I'd ever run into him again. I was wrong. Thanks for dealing with him."

Glad to help, Caleb said. Outside, as they waited for the valet to retrieve her car, he brushed his hand against hers, surprised that she actually took hold of it. At Oberhausen, he walked her hand in hand from the parking garage to the dormitory. He turned to face her, nervously contemplating how to end the evening.

"Thanks for coming with me, Ashley," he said. "You can't imagine what it means to me. And yes, this is an evening I'll never forget."

"Me, either," she said. And she kissed him. Nothing dramatic, just a quick kiss on the cheek. But to Caleb, it was everything.

Gehrke's Heresy Hearing

illman Gehrke's heresy hearing began the morning of Monday, March 17, 2025, at the CLCA headquarters in Des Moines, a simple, unadorned, three-story building. "A story for each person in the Godhead, Father, Son, and Holy Spirit," church leaders liked to say. Several pieces of contemporary Christian art hung on the building's walls, including a depiction of a non-Anglo, middle Eastern, very Jewish-looking Jesus. The church was doing what it could to keep up with the times.

The hearing came more quickly than the accusers anticipated, and they couldn't fully implement their plan to influence opinion within the denomination. Haller hammered away at Gehrke on his website, and a handful of sympathetic, well-to-do laypeople had been instructed to inform their pastors they'd be withholding donations if the hearing didn't result in Gehrke's expulsion. The Lutheran Institute for Conservative Theology had been formed but hadn't had a chance to publish any treatises and tracts. Still, the accusers felt good about their progress, and they vowed to continue to build out and strengthen their arsenal of weapons.

The day of the hearing, winter was just beginning to ebb. There wasn't a cloud in the sky, and the sun shone brightly. Gehrke surveyed the street below from the third-floor hearing room.

"Couldn't have picked a better day," he told Storck, who as president of Oberhausen was among a handful of people allowed to observe the proceedings. "When we're done, win or lose, let's head to Mickey's for some corned beef, cabbage, and beer, lots and lots of beer! In case you forgot, it's St. Patrick's Day."

"A good day for driving the snakes away," Storck whispered, looking over at Gehrke's accusers.

Church bylaws spelled out how to constitute the panel of five members who would try the case. Two presidents of the church's geographical districts were to sit on the panel. One "reconciler," a layman trained by the church to help disputing parties find resolution between them, also had to be included. Because heresy was involved, two of the denomination's theologians had to take part. A facilitator—in effect, a parliamentarian—presided over the hearing but had no vote in determining Gehrke's fate. All these individuals were, of course, men.

As the accused, Gehrke had the right to select one of the district presidents. He chose the Reverend James Wittrock of the New England District, who had been a friend since Gehrke's days at Harvard. He also got to pick one of the theologians, and he named the Reverend Dr. William Taglauer of the seminary in Cape Girardeau.

The Reverend David Bohnert, Otto Haller's friend from Paducah who had co-written the heresy charges, represented the accusers. He designated the Reverend Charles Happel of the Indiana District as the district president he wanted. His theologian of choice? The Reverend Dr. Jeremiah Marquardt, the seminary professor who had presided over Otto Haller's installation ceremony twenty-five years earlier.

The reconciler was "chosen by God's hand," in the parlance of the church. The names of all the laymen trained as reconcilers were thrown into a hat, literally, and the secretary of the church body fished one out. The duty fell to Samuel Zesch, who owned a medium-sized manufacturing firm in Rockford, Illinois. Zesch's politics and theology were unknown to all parties in the dispute, but theoretically, those things didn't matter. His job was to try, as best as he could, to help the voting members of the panel reach a fair, well-reasoned decision.

Observers, in addition to Storck, were the Reverend Carl Walters, president of the CLCA, and the Reverend Randall Bertram, president of the seminary in Cape Girardeau.

The facilitator, Jeff Handrich, set the ground rules. Gehrke could take as long as he wished to present an opening statement. The panelists would then have thirty minutes apiece to ask questions. They would appear in alphabetical order, which meant each of the accuser-selected panelists would speak before the Gehrke-selected panelists. Zesch would go last, which seemed to be a fortunate development. Presumably, the lay facilitator would be the least partisan and most objective of the panel members.

The panelists sat at the front of the room at a long table equipped with jacks and plugs to accommodate laptop computers. Zesch and Handrich sat in the middle of the group of six. Gehrke's panelists sat to Handrich's left; the accusers' panelists sat to Zesch's right. Gehrke was instructed to stand in front of them to present. He declined an offer to project any presentation materials he might have. What he had to say could be said without the help of visual aids. He took his time before beginning, standing silently, using his piercing blue eyes to focus for a few seconds on each man he faced before he spoke.

"I've been provided with an accounting of accusations against me," he began, "and the question to be decided is whether I am a heretic. There are things on the list that stick in the craw of my accusers, I understand. Some of them are just not true. None of them rises to the level of heresy.

"Let me say first that I believe, teach, and live my life in accordance with the Lutheran confessions. I am Lutheran to the core. I believe God's law shows us our need for him, and his Gospel, the good news that he loves us and seeks us out, is the salvation we pine for. No one in this room would see that as heresy, right?"

The room was silent.

"It's being alleged that I see other religions as being equal to Christianity. That's not true. I believe Christianity is the clear, true revelation of God and the relationship God wants to have with himself, with humans, and with the world. He's the creator who overflowed with joy as he made us and everything in the universe. He's the redeemer-shepherd who comes after one lost sheep when he has ninety-nine in the fold. He's the sanctifying spirit who works with us hand in hand to improve us, comfort us, strengthen us, and keep us faithful, hopeful, and bound to God. He uses the Law to make us see our need for him and the Gospel to shower his love upon us. No one in the room would see that as heresy, right?"

The room was silent, although Happel and Marquardt thought Gehrke's language was too flowery for their tastes.

"So, I hope we can all agree that I'm thoroughly in the Lutheran tradition. I will tell you I enjoy studying other religions, to explore their wisdom and the question of how they relate to Christianity. I appreciate the spirituality of the Buddhists. I see that Muslims understand the majesty of God. I prefer to build bridges, not walls, to those of other religions, but I never confuse them as being the same as Christianity."

Marquardt erupted.

"You shouldn't even be talking to Buddhists and Muslims, much less seeing any 'wisdom' in them," he objected. Handrich cut him off, reminding him that this was Gehrke's time. Marquardt could speak later.

"Now, moving on," Gehrke said, "several issues have been raised about my teachings. A number of them stem from the question of whether I see scripture as inerrant. Factually, historically, scientifically inerrant.

"I'll answer that question. Understanding scripture is not a simple task. The Bible is not one book but many, with numerous authors who had varying purposes when they wrote. Still, they all worked to convey truths about God and his relationship to creation and humanity. They were not scientists as we think of scientists, or historians as we think of historians, and their writing shouldn't be thought of as conforming to our modern norms of science or history.

"This idea dates back centuries. For example, St. Augustine, who died in the year 430 CE, took the view that, if a literal interpretation contradicts science and reason, the Biblical text should be interpreted metaphorically. While each passage of scripture has a 'literal sense,' this sense does not always mean the scriptures are mere history; at times they are more like an extended metaphor.

"Augustine also believed that God and scripture accommodated themselves to the limited understanding of people at their time in history. How could you allude to quantum mechanics in a world that didn't even know Newton?

"So, when Genesis 1 and the early part of Genesis 2 portray Earth as being created in six days, the chapters were not conveying scientific or historical fact as we think of those things. Instead, their message is God is good, brings order to chaos as the creator, cares personally about all of creation, and has a special relationship with humans, who, by virtue of being made in the image of God, are the crown of creation.

"There is a second creation account in Genesis 2, with a different order of when things appeared. Again, this account was not meant as science or history but rather to convey the idea of a special relationship between God and humans.

"Scripture contains different types of literature, including legends, poetry, wisdom literature, apostolic letters, parables, history, the Gospels, and apocryphal and prophetic literature. I see scripture as revelation, that God is revealed through the writings of people who believed in him. But no, I don't think Earth was created in six days, and it's not heresy to say so.

"Frankly, it's not totally accurate to call the Bible God's word. Jesus is God's word made flesh. He dwelt among us, full of grace and truth. The Bible is a written testimony to how humans have encountered that word. If we fail to make that distinction, the Bible becomes not an aid to worship but an object of worship, and that is idolatry."

Happel and Marquardt nearly shook with anger.

"Now let me address the other accusations.

"It's said that I advocate for the ordination of women, which is true. People who are against ordaining women cite a couple of passages from St. Paul, who might have been addressing only specific situations in a couple of congregations, not meant as rules for all time. Furthermore, you'll see in I Corinthians that there are women prophesying and praying in the church. There are women deacons. Women like Priscilla teach men in the New Testament. Given all this, I believe there's room within the church to ordain women. In fact, I believe it's mandatory that we do so.

"Moving on. It's said that I support homosexuality, although to state it that way seems cold. I support gay people. Bi- and trans people too. I don't believe God turns his back on them, and I don't think we should make them feel guilty for being who they are and loving who they love.

"I don't believe it, but for the sake of argument, let's say that being gay is a sin. If so, why do we single it out among many other chronic 'sins'? Harming your body by smoking, overeating, and failing to exercise are sins. I believe materialism is a sin. But we never condemn smokers, overeaters, couch potatoes, and conspicuous consumers as sinners, and we don't close the church's door to them. So why are so many people hung up on condemning gay people and driving them out of the church? And don't tell me you love the gay sinner but hate the sin. You may believe that, but I guarantee your position still feels like hate to a gay person.

"It's also alleged that I commune with people outside our denomination. In fact, I have done so. My position is simple. If we agree on the creeds of the church, the dogma of the church, we are one. We might disagree on certain doctrines, but we are one on the major teachings. We are both part of the church and the Christian faith. If we're part of the church, I believe, the Lord welcomes us to his table. Who am I to say I won't join a fellow believer in the meal God offers to both of us?"

Now, Happel and Marquardt became visibly upset, glaring at Gehrke and shaking their heads at what they had heard.

Gehrke stopped talking, letting his words sink in. Handrich asked if he was finished.

"No, I have a much bigger point to make. The issues being raised against me have been dissected and discussed for decades within the CLCA. They've been the subjects of symposia and academic journals. This church has never declared an official position on these issues. Those of us who are interested in them have always agreed to disagree when we can't find our way clear to come to a shared position.

"You know why there's not an official position? It's because there is no magisterium in our church, no single authority that says what will and will not be, what can and cannot be taught or believed. It's a matter of due process. If you want to convict me of heresy, this church needs to define exactly what heresy is. Until that happens, I can't be called a heretic.

"I'm not advocating for a magisterium. I'm not advocating for a heresy hunt. I think we're much better off by continuing to discuss contentious issues among us. I hope that will be one outcome of this proceeding, that we continue to talk instead of crying for the heads of people within our denomination."

The questioning by the panel unfolded as anticipated. Wittrock and Taglauer praised Gehrke as a man of faith and an insightful, thoughtful theologian. Happel and Marquardt used their time to skewer the defendant, saying he should be ashamed of himself for leading countless believers down a path to damnation.

"This magisterium mumbo jumbo is just a dodge and a smokescreen," Marquardt said. "It's not hard to spot heresy. If you say the Bible contains errors, that's heresy. End of story. We need to expel Dr. Gehrke from our church. Until we do, we can't proclaim that we teach the Gospel in its pure, unadulterated form. He needs to go, and he needs to go today."

Samuel Zesch, the reconciler, worked up the courage to ask a question of the man accused of heresy.

"Dr. Gehrke, if you had to state your faith in a sentence or two, what would it be?"

The professor thought for a minute, and then he said: "God is perfect love, truth, and beauty. Those things are the essence and hallmarks of salvation, and God shared all of them with us through the birth, death, and resurrection of Jesus Christ. He gives us power to become his children in both this world and the next, and he wants that for all people."

Zesch nodded and smiled.

After the questions stopped, Zesch tried his best to broker a solution that would be acceptable to everyone on the panel, but he couldn't. Before taking a vote, Handrich called for a fifteen-minute break, warning the panel not to discuss the case outside the room.

The voting commenced and took only a couple of minutes. Gehrke's supporters voted to exonerate him, and his accusers voted to expel. Zesch's vote would break the tie.

"I don't agree with everything Dr. Gehrke said today," he said. "But it's obvious to me that he's a man of faith. I know what a serious matter it is to expel someone from an organization. I'm inclined to avoid doing so unless the arguments in favor are airtight. I don't feel they are."

Happel and Marquardt grimaced. Marquardt's face turned bright red.

"I'm no theologian," Zesch continued, "and despite Professor Marquardt's contention that heresy is easy to spot, I'm not so sure. Dr. Gehrke said these issues have been debated among ministers and theologians in the church for years without resolution. Neither Reverend Happel nor Professor Marquardt said he was wrong about that. If people more educated than I can't come to agreement, I'm not ready to expel a respected theologian from the church.

"And I see his point. We haven't defined what heresy is, so how can we declare someone a heretic? Mr. Handrich, I'm casting my vote to exonerate Dr. Gehrke."

Happel slammed his fist on the table in anger. Marquardt glared at Zesch. Handrich urged both men to be gracious, especially to a layman who volunteered his time. Both Happel and Marquardt rose quickly from the table and walked out the door in a huff. As they passed the modern painting of Jesus, Marquardt said to Happel: "That's not my Jesus."

Happel then walked back to the hearing room and stood by the door.

"This isn't over," he bellowed. "We'll get another bite at this apple. Enjoy your time at Oberhausen, Dr. Gehrke. It won't last much longer."

Once Happel left, Gehrke thanked Handrich for running the hearing so smoothly and thanked the remaining panelists for their support. Storck and Gehrke lingered for a bit after everyone left the room.

"Congratulations," Storck said. "Now, let's go scarf down some of that corned beef and cabbage."

"And don't forget beer. Lots of beer."

The Reformation Restoration Alliance

T he news of Gehrke's exoneration spread quickly around the Oberhausen campus, and both students and professors took time to read the hearing transcript released by the church. The outcome could have driven a wedge between Caleb and Ashley, but neither of them was inclined to let it. It was too early to say they were in love. They were infatuated with one another, and the infatuation showed no signs of ending. They regularly ate together in the campus cafeteria and held hands as they walked across campus.

"Caleb must be serious about her," a friend observed. "He hasn't worn his collar in weeks."

Ashley's friends couldn't believe she had taken up with Caleb until they heard the story of the skirmish at Skip's. He has some strange ideas, they thought, but it's always good to have a guy like that around. And if he's in Ashley's orbit, who knows? She might just turn him around.

Over drinks at Twisted Bean Coffee, Ashley tiptoed into talking about the Gehrke verdict with Caleb, gently asking his opinion. It had caused an argument between his dad and him, he said, mainly on the matter of women's ordination.

His father said the language in the Bible was uncompromising. Paul said women shouldn't speak in church. Paul said women shouldn't have authority over men. He's very clear, and that was that.

Caleb said it wasn't so clear to him because women obviously were active in the early church, and not just by cooking meals and keeping house. Paul called Phoebe a deacon of the church in Cenchreae. He praised her as a leader of the congregation. Then there was Priscilla. She taught men about Jesus and appears to have been more of a leader than her husband, Aquila. It made Caleb wonder whether the church had wrongly declared that women cannot be ordained ministers.

"Dad turned really horrible with me," Caleb said. "He asked whether Gehrke and his ilk were wearing me down, blinding me to the simple truths of the Bible. He said if I didn't get myself turned around, I'd find myself in hell. And if I didn't get myself turned around, he and mom wouldn't be coming to graduation, and I wouldn't be welcome at home."

Ashley shook her head and told Caleb she was so sorry to hear it. It got worse, he said.

"He asked whether you were putting ideas in my head. Those Detters back liberal causes, he said. Stick with her and she'll play with your mind, he said. And, never, never let your libido drive your theology, he said. He was brutal."

Ashley told him to get up. She rose, took his hand, and led him outside to bask in a mild, sunny day. There, she saw the start of a tear. She embraced him, held him, and when he finished crying, gave him a long, tender kiss.

"You'll be fine," she told him. "Relax. We'll take a walk. You'll feel better. And about that libido? Let's go see what we might do to coax it along."

* * *

On his website, Otto Haller railed against the outcome of the Gehrke hearing. He posted pictures of Gehrke with a bullseye superimposed over his face. Gehrke cowering before a cross as the fangs of Dracula protruded from his mouth. Gehrke hanging from a gallows. The more graphic it got, the more Caleb hung his head. He feared running into Gehrke on campus. Eventually, he knocked on the professor's office door to have a word with him.

"I want to thank you for giving me a second chance to stay at Oberhausen. I also want you to know, I think my father has no business smearing you. I'm ashamed and embarrassed by what he's doing. I have nothing to do with his actions. I'm sorry I made the video of you."

Gehrke said he appreciated Caleb's visit. Yes, it's unpleasant to be one of his father's targets, but the professor didn't believe Otto Haller could hurt him. Then he changed the subject.

"Are my eyes deceiving me? Are you and Ashley Detter a thing now? I wouldn't have expected that in a million years, but I think it's a good thing. For you, for sure. Probably for her too."

Caleb smiled. He nodded his head.

"My dad's not happy about it. After I told him I thought you had made some good points in supporting women's ordination, he said I was letting my libido drive my theology. Who knows? Maybe I am. I don't think so. I'm beginning to think that many things, scripture included, aren't always what they seem at first glance."

"A respect for scripture demands that you give it more than a glance, right?" Gehrke said. "If you walk out of Oberhausen remembering nothing more than that, I think your time here will have been time well spent."

Gehrke told Caleb he had come to understand that things and ideas fall into three categories. Some are old-fashioned and need to be discarded. Some are modern and serve a good purpose, until they become old-fashioned and need to be discarded. And some are eternal, as solid and trustworthy yesterday as they are today and will be tomorrow. He urged Caleb to dedicate himself to searching for the eternal, the things and ideas that will last until the end of time and beyond.

"I think you'd really enjoy the writings of people like G. K. Chesterton, C. S. Lewis, and J. R. R. Tolkien," Gehrke said. "Most people would never accuse any of them of being liberal, but they're not fundamentalists or biblical literalists. I don't agree with everything they have to say, but I agree with much of it. And I think you'll find plenty to think about as you read them."

People who take the Bible literally, "at first glance," are refusing to apply what scholars have learned about literature and literary criticism, Gehrke told Caleb. If they were practicing medicine, they'd still be using leeches to suck the sickness out of people. Caleb might want to consider at least learning more about how modern scholars approach biblical texts.

"And, Caleb," Gehrke said, "thanks for coming by. I know you're graduating soon, but if you ever want to talk, please get in touch. I think you're a bright young man. I'll always be happy to hear from you."

***

Two weeks after Gehrke's exoneration, Otto Haller organized a Zoom call of all the pastors who filed the heresy charges against Gehrke. Some of the men handled the technology well. Others struggled. After ten minutes of "Can you hear me?" "Can you see me?" "There, I can see you. Oops, now I can't," the meeting finally began.

Haller wanted to do a post-mortem to figure out how such a heretic could possibly have escaped expulsion from the church.

Some laid the miscarriage of justice at the feet of Zesch, an ignorant layman who couldn't understand the issues and was intimidated by Gehrke. Others said Gehrke was such a smooth talker that Zesch couldn't help but be taken in by him. Still others put the blame on a system that included uneducated laymen at all.

Haller offered his perspective: "I'm livid about the whole process. There's no way we could have won, or at least no way to guarantee a victory. I learned years ago the deck in this church is stacked against me. Against us. We have to get the deck stacked in our favor, or we'll never turn this church body around."

Some participants grumbled that most people in the church—ministers and laypeople—didn't care about doctrine, at least not enough to get behind major change. As long as the unofficial Lutheran sacrament, coffee and doughnuts, was available after Sunday worship, people were happy, one pundit said. Lutherans aren't exactly firebrands, he observed. Most of them live by that passage in James: Let every person be quick to hear, slow to speak, slow to anger, for the anger of man does not produce the righteousness of God. Over the generations, Lutherans have had the "slow to anger" gene bred into their DNA.

Haller said it's time to reacquaint the church with the notion of righteous anger. Remember Jesus in the temple chasing out the moneychangers with a whip? We need to be chasing the heretics out of the church, and we need some help to do it. We're going to wage a campaign to fire people up, sic them on the heretics, and get this church body cleaned up.

"We can do this," he said. "Once more people learn how professors and pastors in this church body are questioning the truthfulness of the Bible, they'll get behind us."

The problem, as he saw it, was to achieve a major shift in leadership of the church. In place of the timid crop of caretaker managers at the top, the group needed to install leaders who would enforce pure doctrine and banish the heretics.

The ministers were skeptical it could be done.

It can be done, Haller said. But it will take a lot of long nights and shoe leather to make it happen.

"We need to put the right people in place. By the time the next church convention rolls around, in 2027, I want to see conservatives dominating the delegate pool so we have voting muscle. For every board and commission in the CLCA, there should be at least one conservative on the ballot, more whenever possible. At the convention, sample ballots should be handed out so our hand-picked delegates will know exactly who to vote for. They'll fall in line without ever knowing they're falling in line. With the right combination of pliable laymen, concerned clergy, and nonstop persuasion, we will be victorious."

An Indianapolis pastor said one of his congregation members was a political consultant who had led successful campaigns for several of the most well-known conservatives in America. He might be willing to help. Haller said to talk with the consultant, but be sure he understood this would have to be a labor of love for him unless money turned up unexpectedly.

"I'll work personally on what might be the most difficult task," Haller said. "We need a new president of the CLCA, and Jeremiah Marquardt will be perfect. It might take a while, but I'll talk him into running."

Everyone on the call agreed to make presentations at congregations throughout the country. They all committed to weekly Zoom calls so they wouldn't lose momentum. Haller asked to be introduced to the political consultant as quickly as possible to work out a master game plan.

Then he took the lead in naming the group.

"Gentlemen, from this day forward, we and our sympathizers will be known as the Double R A, the Reformation Restoration Alliance. If he were here, Martin Luther would be begging to sign up."

* * *

Early one Monday morning, Caleb's cell phone awakened him.

"Have you seen what your cretin of a father has done now?" Ashley asked him. "Go look and call me back!"

Caleb went to his bathroom, splashed some water on his face, then made coffee before calling up the latest content on GodsTruthIsMyTruth.com.

"I've warned against the power of heretics to lead our young people to damnation," Haller was saying in a video. "Well, here's the proof. The editor of Oberhausen's student newspaper, *The Spectator,* is overjoyed that her hero, Hillman Gehrke, has been cleared of the heresy charges against him. Just by siding with him, she's advocating for the ordination of women. She's an evolutionist. She's all but saying the Bible is a work of fiction. I posted her editorial on the website. Go read it, then tell me we don't have a problem in this church.

"And to young editor Ashley Detter, I say, change your ways and repent now. If you don't, you'll find yourself in hell. You and your friends too, if they walk down the same path."

Caleb folded shut the screen of his laptop and sat stunned. "No, no, no, no, no," he muttered. Until now, he had avoided having to choose between his girlfriend, the woman he was starting to love, and his father, the man who had to know how awkward this would be for him.

He hesitated to call Ashley, not knowing what to say. His phone chimed, signaling a one-word text: "Well?"

"I've read it," he texted back to Ashley. "Let's talk about this face-to-face. Want to meet for breakfast at Bakers Square?"

"No. I can't eat right now. Just come get me at the dorm."

When he arrived, he discovered they were almost identically dressed—

jeans, dark sweatshirts, and tennis shoes, the main difference being that while Caleb was wearing Reeboks, Ashley had on a pair of Alexander McQueens.

They walked for a while in silence, trying to find a way to launch a conversation.

"I'm coming to think you're a good guy, but I can't do this," she finally said. "How could I possibly get more involved with you? I never want to meet your father, not after an attack like that. How dare he say I'm going to hell! As if he cares anyway. I'm just fodder to him, an amuse-bouche to load into his hate machine and feed to his followers. I've never been angrier in my life. It's not your fault, I know, but I can't deal with him. There's no sense in us going on."

Caleb tried to embrace her, but she stepped back. He grabbed her shoulders, forcing her to look him in the eye.

"My father said the same thing to me, you know. That I'd be going to hell unless I turned myself around. That he and mom wouldn't come to graduation. Truth is, I'm not sure what I believe about so many things right now. Maybe my dad is right in his beliefs. I don't know. But I don't appreciate him treating me like that. And I'm not going to stand for him treating you like that."

"Like I told you, Caleb. He's loveless. A clanging cymbal. I want nothing to do with him. If I were with you, how could I avoid him?"

"One step at a time, okay? I'll call him to see if he'll take the post down."

"And if he won't?"

"If he cares about me, he will."

Caleb made the request. Haller said no. And Caleb realized he had some difficult decisions to make.

"Ashley, I want to be with you. I want to see where we might go. How would you feel if I put off seminary and came to Chicago after graduation?"

"And do what?"

"I've got time to look into that. It doesn't matter to me, really. Just so I make enough to live on. I just want to be close to you."

She kissed him. Her dad might be able to find something for him, she said, but Caleb answered he wanted to find something on his own. She nodded.

"Okay, come along. But keep your head on straight. We're a long way from being a permanent thing, right?"

Caleb nodded in agreement, but he hoped she was wrong.

On graduation day, Martha Haller sat in the audience alone. Otto Haller forbade her to attend, but for once, she defied him. She wasn't about to let her husband's obsession with pure doctrine come between her and her son. After the ceremonies, Ashley's family invited Caleb and Martha to a celebration dinner. They reserved a private, upstairs room at Skip's. Martha thought Ashley was an absolutely lovely young woman, and she came from an absolutely lovely family.

* * *

While Martha attended Caleb's graduation, Haller tended to his pastoring job, knocking gently on the door of a small bungalow. The porch light flickered. Inside, the sound of a television faded as someone shuffled toward the entrance.

"Pastor Haller," said Mrs. Kappel, her voice thin but warm. "I wasn't expecting you."

"I was in the neighborhood," he lied gently. "Thought I'd check in."

She ushered him inside. The living room smelled faintly of lavender and dust. A framed photo of her late husband sat beside a half-knitted scarf.

"I haven't been to church in weeks," she said, lowering herself into the recliner. "The arthritis is worse. And I just... I feel so tired."

Haller nodded. "You're not forgotten, Mrs. Kappel. The Lord sees you. And so do we."

He reached into his coat pocket and pulled out a small jar. "I brought you something. It's a balm Martha used to make. Eucalyptus and clove. Good for sore joints."

She took it with trembling hands. "You remembered."

"I remember a lot," he said. "You taught Sunday school for twenty years. You prayed over more children than I can count. You've earned rest."

She smiled, eyes misting. "I miss the hymns."

Otto stood and walked to the piano in the corner. It was out of tune, but he played anyway—slow, deliberate chords of "Abide With Me." His voice was rough, but steady.

Mrs. Kappel closed her eyes.

When he finished, he sat beside her and opened his Bible. "May I read?"

She nodded.

He chose Isaiah 46:4: *"Even to your old age and gray hairs I am he, I am he who will sustain you."*

They sat in silence for a moment.

"I don't know what I'd do without the church," she whispered.

Haller smiled, but it didn't reach his eyes. "Neither do I."

The next morning, Haller stared through his office window. He walked outside to greet Rachel and Thomas—a bright-eyed, eager, engaged couple. Thomas and his parents had attended Ebenezer for decades, and for the past three months, Rachel had been joining them.

"Pastor," Rachel said, smiling. "We wanted to ask if you'd consider officiating our wedding."

Haller returned the smile, but it was measured. "Of course. I'd be honored—provided we're aligned on a few things."

Thomas glanced at Rachel, then back at Haller. "We're happy to meet any requirements."

The pastor nodded. "Good. I'll need to see your baptism certificates. And I'll ask that you attend six weeks of premarital counseling. We'll cover doctrine, headship, and the sanctity of covenant."

Rachel's smile faltered. "Headship?"

Haller's tone remained gentle. "Biblical headship. The husband as spiritual leader. It's not about control—it's about order. God's design."

Thomas shifted uncomfortably. "We've talked about sharing responsibilities. Rachel's finishing her master's degree."

Haller's expression didn't change. "Education is a blessing. But marriage is a calling. And calling requires submission—to each other, yes, but also to scripture and God's design."

Rachel became quiet. "Would you marry us if we can't agree to that?"

Haller paused. "I would counsel you to wait. To pray. To seek unity in truth. A divided foundation cannot bear the weight of covenant."

They nodded politely, thanked him, and walked away. Haller watched them go, his smile fading.

They'll either bend or break, he thought. *Better they break now than build their marriage on sinking sand.*

Courting Dr. Marquardt

Even though he was in his early fifties, Otto Haller could not bring himself to call the Reverend Dr. Jeremiah Marquardt by his first name. Haller was just twelve years younger than Marquardt, but he could not be anything other than deferential to the man who inspired him at seminary and installed him as a pastor when no one else would.

Marquardt seemed almost majestic, and not just to Haller. Everyone in the Reformation Restoration Alliance agreed. He held the requisite Ph.D. in systematic theology so important for a professor. His was granted by the conservative Southeastern Baptist Theological Seminary, which subscribes to the Chicago Statement on Biblical Inerrancy.

But more important, he had the bearing of a leader. He stood erect, emphasizing his six-foot-plus frame. He had a full head of glorious, salt-and-pepper hair. His face could by turns be beatific if he smiled or intimidating if he scowled.

"Dr. Marquardt, would you have time in the next week to meet with me?" Haller asked over the phone. "I have something important to discuss."

Marquardt thought well of his one-time student. Most CLCA pastors and theologians frowned upon Haller's vitriolic barrage of allegations, rumors, and innuendoes on GodsTruthIsMyTruth.com. Marquardt, however, thought the sleepy CLCA needed shaking up. Haller's methods might be disagreeable, but he was definitely drawing a following, and that was good.

"It was a shame about Gehrke skating away," Marquardt said when they got together in the living room of the professor's home in Cape Girardeau. Haller thought it would be best not to be seen with one another in public.

"I saw it as an open-and-shut case. Years ago, I argued against letting him graduate from seminary. Even then, I felt his views were beyond the pale. When I saw his articles in academic journals, I just shook my head.

"I served on his heresy panel because I was asked, even though I would rather have laid low. But because I was there, I can tell you the things Gehrke said were abominable. Then when it was time to vote, the charges didn't stick, all thanks to some well-meaning, ignorant layman. Well, him and the two panelists hand-picked by Gehrke, who ought to be thrown out of the church along with him. A shame, and I don't say this lightly—it was a damned shame."

Haller knew Marquardt would be sympathetic. They had talked several times over the years about how certain professors were wandering away from CLCA orthodoxy. They both saw a need to confront the problem before it overtook the denomination.

Marquardt, though, had hesitated to be visible on the issue. In the academic world, collegiality often took precedence over truth, and Marquardt wanted to live reasonably peacefully among his fellow professors. Private conversations about disagreements were preferred over public grandstanding, and Marquardt initiated them often. He left it to gunslingers like Haller to call out heresy in public, and he was even more inclined to fade into the woodwork as he approached retirement age.

"I knew you'd feel the way I do about Gehrke," Haller said. "I've put together a group of pastors who want to do something about him and the other heretics, once and for all. The CLCA needs a major overhaul, and we want you to join us to make it happen."

Marquardt shook his head. He was sympathetic, of course, but he was in no position to help. Retirement was two years away. His wife wanted to travel. He wanted to spend time with his grandchildren. He was psyching himself up to be nothing more than a member of a congregation and maybe do some occasional guest preaching. Besides, he hadn't been highly visible in the church in many, many years. No one would care what he had to say about much of anything.

"With great respect, Dr. Marquardt, you sound like Moses resisting God when he was asked to lead the Israelites out of Egypt."

"Just out of curiosity, nothing more, what exactly is it you would have me do?" Marquardt asked.

"We want you to be the next president of the Confessional Lutheran Church in America."

"No!" Marquardt bellowed as he slammed his hand down on the arm of his easy chair.

Haller didn't flinch.

"Hear me out. There is no one better to lead the drive against heresy. You're intelligent, persuasive, vigorous, and you look the part. You are the only one who can take this church body where it needs to be."

Marquardt shook his head and reiterated his plan—retirement, travel, grandchildren, occasional preaching.

"If you put off retirement for just a couple of years, you could make an impact that would last a lifetime," Haller said. "Several lifetimes. Maybe lifetime after lifetime, until the Lord comes again. You're being called to do this, and you need to take our proposition seriously," Haller told him.

Marquardt said he didn't have the first clue about how to run an organization as big as the CLCA. He barely kept his department running when he headed it for a few years.

That's what subordinates are for, Haller said. They take care of the day-to-day nonsense. It would be Marquardt's job to set the right tone for the church and to focus on cleaning out the doctrinal pollution that continues to creep into the denomination.

Marquardt protested he wasn't sure he wanted to cope with the hostility that would come with trying to take on the heretics. The CLCA always has been a placid, don't-rock-the-boat kind of church. Even people who oppose the heretics might still frown on the warfare it could take to clean it out.

"There'll be some resistance, sure, but nothing you can't handle. I'm confident there will be overwhelming support. Look at the response to my website. There's a large, enthusiastic throng of people ready to stand behind you. There'll be many more once they start to realize we have professors and pastors in the church who don't believe the Bible is true. You will be loved by the overwhelming majority of people in the CLCA."

Marquardt said he wouldn't even know how to get on the ballot. Haller answered that the Reformation Restoration Alliance would handle it for him. In fact, they would handle his whole campaign.

"The what?" Marquardt cried. Haller explained about the new group formed to bring doctrinal purity back to the CLCA. The professor from Cape Girardeau seemed surprised to have the group's support and resources behind him. He was pleased, if he could keep them at arm's length. He didn't want to be associated with any ham-handed politicking. He didn't oppose it. He just didn't want to be associated with it.

Marquardt had run out of objections, but he wasn't ready to commit. He said he'd think about it, and he'd have to talk with his wife.

"You say she wants to travel? Tell her that as president of the church body, you'll tour the world inspecting church operations and visiting with other Lutheran dignitaries. As the first lady of the CLCA, she'll be right by your side. You'll do more traveling than you ever dreamed possible, and on the church's dime."

Of course, Marquardt said, there were no guarantees he would win.

"Put your name in the ring, and we'll deliver the presidency to your door," Haller promised.

A week later, Marquardt sent Haller an email: "Two words. I'm in."

Haller let out a shout of joy.

* * *

When he returned to Frohna, Martha was preparing dinner.

Since Caleb's graduation, things had been awkward between the couple. At first, Martha received a barrage of condemnation from Haller, charging her with sinful defiance for not obeying his command to boycott Caleb's Oberhausen ceremonies. He backed off after having to fend for himself for a week of breakfasts, lunches, and dinners. While never apologizing, he proposed just trying to move beyond the tension between them. She agreed to resume her cooking duties, but she made it clear she had little to say to him until he made up with his son and stopped trying to lord over her.

"A little tenderness would be in order," she told him. Haller had no idea how to respond.

At dinner, Haller said a table prayer, helped himself to a helping of pork sausage and baked beans, and enthusiastically shared his news with Martha, who was growing weary of his forays into church politics.

"We've landed the perfect candidate to be the next president of the CLCA! Jeremiah Marquardt!" he told her.

She shrugged her shoulders. With a bite of food still in her mouth, she simply said, "That's nice." Or as the kids say, she thought, "Big whoop."

The Pool Party

When Caleb told his parents he wouldn't be coming home for the summer, and he wouldn't be enrolling in seminary, he expected an avalanche of anger. It never came.

"Now that you've taken up with that Detter girl, you're a lost cause," his father said matter-of-factly. "I don't care what you do. Just don't come running to me if you need bailing out. Make your bed, sleep in it, that's how I feel. And if you're sleeping with her, you'll both end up in hell. If you come to your senses, and I hope you do, we can talk."

Martha, of course, kept in touch with Caleb. At least twice a week, usually more, they talked by phone.

"Explore what you need to explore," she urged. "This is your time. Use it to figure out who you are, who you love, and what you want to do with your life. If I have any regret in life, it's that I committed to too much, too soon. I'll honor those commitments, I suppose, but I've had second thoughts about a few of them." She avoided stating outright to Caleb that her marriage was weighing heavily on her, but he understood.

In Chicago, Caleb quickly had to answer two questions: How would he make money, and where would he live? His pre-seminary curriculum at Oberhausen was demanding, but with an emphasis on courses like Old Testament, New Testament, Hebrew, Greek, and Lutheran doctrine, it didn't provide a strong résumé for seeking real-world employment. He explored several options—retail sales at Target or Walmart; telephone-based customer service; warehouse stock boy; dock worker at a boat yard.

He settled on driving for Uber after learning he could rent a car from the company for $260 a week and still clear about $1,000 a week. The hours would be long, but he'd be his own boss, and he could walk away quickly if it wasn't working out.

Caleb lived with the Detters for a few weeks in their magnificent Frank Lloyd Wright house. He thought about asking to stay with them indefinitely and pay them for room and board. But he wanted to show Ashley he could be his own man and make his way in the world. They weren't anywhere near talking about moving in together, and besides, he thought that would be morally wrong, so he needed a place of his own.

When he started looking through apartment ads, he became discouraged. An unfurnished, one-bedroom apartment in a safe, decent neighborhood would be at least $1,300 a month and probably more. He might be able to afford it, but it would be a stretch. Ashley's father had a proposal.

"Look, Caleb, I'm in the real-estate business," he said. "A lot of people owe me favors. I can get you into a really nice, one-bedroom place for $700 a month. How about letting me help you? Where would you want to live?"

Caleb thought about demurring, wanting to handle things himself. He also feared he would be obligated to Mr. Detter in ways he couldn't conceive. The offer, however, was too good to pass up.

He asked whether he could live near downtown Chicago, close to where Ashley's classes and apartment were going to be. Mr. Detter said he could make something happen on West Elm Street. He did as promised, putting Caleb in a furnished, one-bedroom unit, normally $1,600 a month, for $700.

"One thing you have to do for me, though, Caleb, and I think it will help you with Ashley, too," he said. "By Christmas, I want you to have a plan, a path forward, for your life. I don't know you well, but I know Ashley, and she seems to see something in you. I'm sure you're not meant to be an Uber driver forever, so put some thought into what you really want to do. Going to seminary would be fine, if that's what you choose, but as long as you have this breathing space, think about other things too. I'm eager to see what you come up with."

Andy Detter's words frightened Caleb. He realized he had never given a moment's thought to setting a course for his life. He had simply been channeled into becoming a minister. Only now did he see there were thousands of other paths to explore.

* * *

Not long after returning home, Ashley decided to have a get-together with her friends from high school. They had all just graduated from college. Most of them had landed jobs. Like Ashley, a few were headed for graduate school.

The event, a Saturday afternoon pool party, would be a tame affair at Ashley's parents' home. There would be light to moderate drinking, but drugs would not be present.

"I think it's a good idea for you to meet some new people," Ashley told Caleb. "We'll see each other a lot, of course, but we need a bigger circle of friends. I don't want us to be just an island of two."

Caleb saw her point, even though he'd rather catch bowling balls with his teeth than attend the gathering. As he ventured into Walmart to buy a pair of swim trunks, he resolved to try to be at least cordial to Ashley's friends. He feared they would look down on him as some small-town hick. As things turned out, some did, some didn't, and he got a glimpse of other lives that might be open to him.

As Caleb looked on, a party caterer laid out a spread of hors d'oeuvres. A bartender struck up a quick conversation, boasting he could whip up any mixed drink known to man. It was all Caleb could do not to bolt before the guests arrived. This was going to be a league apart from Frohna's beer and potluck gatherings, and from the keggers he attended once or twice at Oberhausen.

About twenty of Ashley's friends showed up, some coupled, some not. Two of the couples, all male, held hands during much of the party, setting Caleb on edge. He hadn't considered that some of Ashley's friends might be gay. He had made it a practice to avoid the gay students at Oberhausen, believing they had to be decadent and sub-Christian. The Detters, who like him were churchgoers, must have had some different thoughts. If he and Ashley were going to be a couple long-term, he saw, one of them would have to make some adjustments. He suspected it would have to be him but decided he'd think about it another time.

As he filled his plate at the hors d'oeuvre table, an incredible, bikinied body with a face to match worked itself next to him. She introduced herself as Marianna, Ashley's friend since first grade and a recent graduate of the Loyola University nursing program.

"You're different from the other boyfriends she's had," the brunette said. "I can't say I've known her to go for the overly religious type. Not that she's wild. Just intelligent and not much for dogma, as far as I know."

Caleb, who was getting agitated merely by Marianna's presence, mustered the wherewithal to point out he wasn't exactly dumb. Not many people could excel in Greek and Hebrew, and he graduated in the top tenth of his class at Oberhausen.

"Well, opa and oy vey! I don't know, sweet cheeks, I don't see a lot of want ads for Greek speakers, at least not outside Athens. One thing I'll tell you, though. Looking at you in those swim trunks, you've definitely got something going on. Tell you what. If you and Ashley ever split up, give me a call. I'll be glad to sign up for Greek lessons. Or Hebrew lessons. Makes me no never mind."

She held out her hand for Caleb's phone, offering to give him her digits. He declined, looking around to make sure Ashley wasn't watching.

"No, just leave me alone," he growled. "I'm not about to do anything to shake Ashley's trust in me. What kind of friend are you, anyway? Why would you do anything to hurt her?"

"Just a little friendly flirting, preacher boy. Don't get all bent out of shape." Marianna walked off in a huff to slither into the pool.

The cockiest of Ashley's friends turned out to be Tom Beakmeister, a finance major from the University of Chicago. The wavy-haired strawberry blond competed in Greco-Roman wrestling for the university, the 192-pound class.

"So you're Caleb," he said. "Interesting name, like something out of Kentucky or Alabama."

"Out of the Bible, actually," Caleb said.

"Guess I have a biblical name too. Thomas, like Doubting Thomas, right? One thing I don't doubt is you're not going to have a pot to piss in if you don't find yourself some other line of work. Churches are fading fast, and even if you find one to work for, you won't make much anyway. I tell you, pal, you need to be exploring your options."

Caleb said that's exactly what he would do over the next few months.

"Look at me," Tom said. "Fresh out of school, and I've already got a six-figure job lined up with one of the Big Four. We're the same age, my friend. I'm just telling you, you need to be looking around."

Caleb had no idea what the Big Four meant, but he wasn't about to ask.

"I'll figure it out, my friend," Caleb managed to spit out. "One thing I'm sure of, though. Money isn't everything."

"Find me something better, and I'll take a look," Tom said. "I tell you, though. Ashley's accustomed to a certain standard of living. That Jaguar she drives tells the whole story. I doubt whether she'll adjust to anything less than what she has now." Like Marianna before him, Tom wandered over to the pool to take a dip. Mentally, but not physically, Caleb flipped him the bird, or came as close to doing it as an uptight, pre-seminary student could.

He sat down in a chaise lounge, and a fellow named Joel came over, kneeled next to him, and started a conversation. A real conversation. He asked all about Caleb. Where he came from. What his parents did. How he met Ashley. Why he was moving to Chicago. Joel spoke not as an interrogator but simply as someone interested in Caleb as a real person. Caleb relaxed enough with him to level about his own worries and insecurities.

"The truth is," Caleb said, "I'm really adrift right now. I came to Chicago to be near Ashley, of course. But I'm also taking a timeout, trying to figure out my next steps. You know, I thought I was going to be a Lutheran pastor, but now I'm not so sure. I've got questions about what I believe, and I've started to see that ministers can be as ugly and ruthless as anyone. I don't have a clue what I want to do with my life. By the way, what do you do?"

Joel said he had just signed on for an entry-level job at Chicago's PBS station. He'd be writing, producing, and editing promotional pieces and filler material. Often, PBS shows don't run a full hour, and the station needs four or five minutes of material to fill the gap before the next show begins. What he really wanted was to write and produce documentaries, but the PBS gig was a good place to get started.

"Good for you! I'd have no idea how to do something like that. Sounds interesting, though."

Joel graduated from Columbia College in downtown Chicago with a bachelor of fine arts degree in film and television. He'd taken courses in everything from storytelling to directing to film editing.

"If you're ever interested, I could set up some interviews for you at the college," Joel said. "You already have a degree, and who knows? You might have credits that would transfer over. I know the school offers a philosophy and religion minor. You might be able to carve out a career for yourself creating documentaries about religion. Lots of people look down on religion, I know, but you might be able to broaden their understanding.

"Me, I'm open to learning more about it. I wasn't raised religious, but I don't knock it either. Some of the best people I know practice it, people like Ashley. I can't handle the holier-than-thou types, or the jump-and-shout types, but she's not one of them. I'm guessing you're not either."

Actually, I just might be one of the holier-than-thous, Caleb thought. He was beginning to see his father as one of the most judgmental people he knew, and he sensed he was infected with the same virus. Maybe, he thought, it was time to find a cure.

After the guests scattered, Ashley came over to the pool. Caleb was soaking his feet to relax. She sat down next to him and gave him a hug.

"Now, that wasn't so bad, was it?" she asked.

"Better than I expected, although I thought there were a couple of rotten apples in the barrel. That Tom guy had to be one of the most pompous jackasses I've ever met. Marianna's suit was barely there, and she actually came on to me!"

"What can I say? Tom is Tom, and Marianna Pelletier has been a flirt since birth. It's just who they are. Get to know them. You'll see they have their good points and their bad points, just like me, and just like you."

Caleb stopped himself from asking what his bad points were, and he chose not to ask about the gay guys and their handholding. Instead, he said a few good words about Joel.

"He's been a good friend for a long time," Ashley said. "I think you'd be smart to get to know him better."

With that, they kissed one another and headed to their separate bedrooms. Caleb's brain kept trying to make the pieces of his life fit together—his father, his mother, Ashley, Oberhausen, Dr. Gehrke, Marianna, Tom Beakmeister, Joel, the gay guys at the pool, Chicago, Uber. It wasn't in his nature, he knew, but it might be best just to let things play out and sort themselves out. Once he resolved to try, his body found a way to sleep.

Meeting Gearshift

Otto Haller had one objective for the Summer 2027 convention of the CLCA, scheduled for the Iowa Events Center in Des Moines: control. He had thoughts about how to achieve it, but he saw the wisdom of drawing on the experience of political consultant Kurt Richter. His clients called him Gearshift. He could speed up voter support for them, slow down scandals and controversies, and reverse negative poll numbers.

The two made quite a pair when they met for lunch at Café Napoli in St. Louis, one of the city's finest Italian restaurants. Haller's ill-fitting clerical garb, his collar and a black suit from J. C. Penney, threatened to swallow up his gaunt frame. Richter would never be mistaken for someone who missed a meal, and his $500 haircut and midnight blue Ferragamo suit spoke to some handsome paydays, both from political consulting and various real-estate ventures. Still, they hit it off, sharing a mutual interest in seizing and controlling levers of power, either political or ecclesiastical.

Once Haller learned that Richter had been a friend of Rush Limbaugh, he gushed like a fanboy. Haller condemned Limbaugh's cigar-smoking, pill-popping, divorce-'em-when-he-wanted lifestyle. But he identified with Limbaugh's conservative politics and admired his media savvy. He fancied himself to be the Limbaugh of the CLCA, sans the sinfulness.

Richter admitted he wasn't the most faithful churchgoer, but he showed up when he wasn't on the road, at least once a month. Yes, he was Christian. He wasn't raised Lutheran. He joined Concordia Lutheran in Indianapolis because his wife wanted to be part of a church, and he pushed her toward the congregation because of the blandness of the CLCA. He was happy to get involved with Haller's cause, as a favor to his pastor.

"You know who really got me interested in Lutheranism?" he asked Haller. "It wasn't your famous Lutherans, like Martin himself or J. S. Bach. It wasn't Kierkegaard. No, it was Garrison Keillor and all the ways he found to make the religion seem so ordinary.

"In my business, it's best not to affiliate with organizations that are highly political, other than a party, of course. I'd just as soon fly under the radar, and I don't want to give any opponents ammunition to characterize me as some kind of wigged-out nutcase. I don't want to be associated with anyone like a Jerry Falwell Junior or a Franklin Graham. I think it's great that I can't name one famous modern Lutheran. If anyone is looking for a brush to tar me with, it's sure not going to be my religion. Why, Lutherans aren't even on most people's radar!"

Richter said they should begin their partnership with a toast, suggesting they order some wine to kick off their relationship. Haller said he was on a tight budget and would have to pass, but he could toast with a glass of water. Richter told him that would be bad luck, and Haller should order anything he wanted because Richter was picking up the check.

When the waiter came, Richter ordered a Caesar salad and veal piccata. Haller asked for an appetizer of eggplant. He ordered a small filet mignon as his main course along with a side of spinach. Richter instructed the waiter to bring a bottle of the restaurant's best pinot noir.

After he tasted the wine, Richter signaled his approval and offered a toast.

"Here's to the cause of … how do you say it, exactly?"

"The cause of pure doctrine and faithfulness to the Bible," Haller said, and they clinked their glasses together. They drank, and Haller smiled with approval. "Before we go much further, I should tell you we have little to nothing to pay you. I understand your time is valuable. Just having this opportunity to get your advice is highly appreciated. As is the meal!"

Don't worry, Richter said. He was happy to help, and who knows, maybe down the road, there'll be ways for him to benefit. If not, it won't be a problem. Anything for the cause of pure doctrine. He asked for more details about how the CLCA convention works.

In the CLCA, the congregation is supreme, Haller explained. The national church body has only as much power as the congregations allow. He was the pastor of Ebenezer Lutheran in Frohna over the objection of the national church body, he said, because his congregation could call him despite the denomination's opposition.

"We call our CLCA purification group the Reformation Restoration Alliance," Haller said. "We have an agenda, and we want the power to enforce it. We want to seize control of the national church body to fortify pure doctrine and drive out heretics. Legally, of course, by controlling the outcome of the national convention."

The first task would be to control which delegates come to the meeting. Second would be to control which candidates for church offices are nominated and win. Third would be to control which issues come to the floor and how they are framed.

The bylaws require an equal division of delegates between pastors and laymen. Congregations don't send delegates directly. Instead, they are grouped into circuits representing anywhere from seven to twenty congregations. There are 512 circuits in all, so 1,024 delegates. Haller said he would like to have at least 575 of those delegates on the side of pure doctrine and biblical inerrancy, just to make sure his group had a healthy cushion over the fifty percent plus one mark of 513.

Richter took some time before speaking.

"Let me give you my SWOT analysis of where you stand," he finally said.

"SWOT analysis?"

"A review of your strengths, weaknesses, opportunities, and threats. One of your greatest strengths is your website. Congratulations on naming it, by the way. GodsTruthIsMyTruth.com puts you squarely on the side of the divine, and you're a skilled propagandist. Not a popular word, but there's nothing wrong with it. Take away the connotations, and it just means you're good at promoting a cause.

"A second strength is the dedicated corps of people standing behind you. To do what you need to get done, you're going to need a strong ground game, and your people can be your leaders and organizers. You have a head start, so that's good. I imagine the men you've recruited are highly committed.

"Strength Number Three: Most CLCA members are anti-intellectual. I don't mean they're not smart. I just mean they don't trust people who think too much and see life as gray, not black and white. My impression of a lot of CLCA members is they're mainly meat-and-potatoes, oom-pah-pah types. They'll be with you, not with the eggheads.

"Hand in hand with that is your strong subculture. Honestly, it was a little hard for my family and me to settle into your church. To us, so many of your hymns are like funeral dirges, but your people love them, and they bind you all together. And it seems like everybody is related or has CLCA friends of friends of friends throughout the country. There's power in that. To generations of people, the CLCA has been a home, and they're going to oppose anything that threatens their home. What's one of the biggest threats? Heresy, of course."

Haller got antsy wanting to contribute. "Our biggest strength is we have truth on our side, which means we have God on our side. Our enemies deny the truth of the Bible. I don't see how they can win."

Richter nodded but remained noncommittal, encouraging Haller not to let his belief that God was with him make him complacent.

"Now, as to your weaknesses. Your committed workforce seems small, just ten or twelve, right? You need five times that many. You'll have to scale up in a hurry if you're going to be able to do what you want by the summer of 2027. It's not impossible, but you have to know it won't be easy.

"Second, you're lacking in money. You told me so yourself. You don't need to pay me, but you'll have to pay for expenses like travel, printing, postage, meeting halls, and tchotchkes like T-shirts and banners.

"Another weakness. I'm aware of the Gehrke case and how he skated free of expulsion or even any discipline. He had a point. There is no way to say, officially, what is heresy and what's not in the CLCA. His case made that clear, so that will have to be addressed.

"Then there's the matter of the existing national leadership in the CLCA. They don't seem concerned about issues like heresy and pure doctrine, and they won't rally behind you."

Haller interjected a comment. "They're from the old school. They like sending the tough issues to conferences and journals. It's all very polite. But politeness won't win the heresy war. I'm trying to light a fire under people with the website, and I'm making progress, but my tactics aren't popular with a lot of church bureaucrats and old timers."

Richter said they'd have to be pushed out of the way if Haller and company were going to succeed. Haller nodded.

"Now for the opportunities. As a nation, we're undergoing some major changes in the economy, in technology, and in morals and values. People fear change, and they look for stability wherever they can find it.

"The truth is, most people don't really want freedom. They don't want to have to take responsibility for the choices they make. They want someone to tell them what to believe and what to do. That's an opportunity for you. You and your group . . . what's it called? The Reformation Restoration Alliance? . . . you can be the people in the CLCA standing against change and serving as a beacon for pure doctrine rooted in the Bible. People will follow you. They want what you're offering because it represents security and authority.

"A second opportunity is to breed a little distrust at the congregation level, just to get people personally involved in fighting heresy. Offer a twenty-question document so people can put their pastors to the test. Does he believe Adam and Eve were real? Does he think Jonah really spent three days in the belly of a big fish? Does he think Jesus was born of a virgin? I can't imagine any pastor worth keeping around would object, can you? This will get everybody thinking and talking about heresy and what a threat it is to the church.

"A third opportunity, I think, is for your group to become the source of easy-to-grasp religious education. I've looked at what's being produced by the CLCA publishing house these days. It's a little dry, and it's written at the high-school level. People don't want to have to work too much to learn about God. Talk at the fourth-grade level, and they'll be on your side. Less of Martin Luther's catechism, more of Dr. Seuss's *Green Eggs and Ham*.

"This won't cost much. Just use your website and others to host online lessons and provide pdfs that congregations can print out. You might even be able to get some Oberhausen students to do the artwork and design for you for free. Let them call it an internship. You can become the go-to source for educating the laity, and you can control doctrine anyway you want."

Richter said the biggest threat he saw was the inevitable backlash that will be caused by a heresy hunt. Inside the church, all the people who prefer politeness and moderation will denounce Haller's efforts, especially as they gain real traction. The polite crowd will put up a semblance of a fight, as best they can. External media coverage will paint the effort as intellectually barren, narrow-minded, and mean-spirited, devoid of brotherly love.

"So be it," Haller said. "I've been called intellectually barren, narrow-minded, and mean-spirited all my life. The loveless ones are those leading people to hell by getting them off the path of pure doctrine. I'll take a few punches if I can turn people back to the truth of the Bible."

Richter asked for a rundown on the current president of the CLCA, the Reverend Carl Walters. Haller called him a peacekeeper, the kind of man who wanted a lake smooth as glass on the surface, even as the waters roiled below. He had been in office for twelve years. No one had really challenged him, but the Double R A had a perfect candidate in Jeremiah Marquardt.

Have you ever really dug into Walters's background? Richter asked. Does he have any secrets, any hidden skeletons to exploit?

The man seemed both honorable and honest, Haller said, although there were rumors of a son who had trouble with drugs and alcohol.

"Those rumors could be worth repeating," Richter noted. "How can a man run a church body if he can't even keep his own household in order, right?"

Haller winced, recalling his own difficulties with his wife and son. Still, he saw the value of questioning Walters's skills as a father. He resolved not to call out Walters's problems—which may or may not exist—unless necessary to push his cause over the top.

The two men traded cellphone numbers, and Richter shared some final thoughts: "Peter Drucker has always been one of my favorite management consultants. The best Drucker quote? 'Plans are only good intentions unless they immediately deteriorate into hard work.' I can't emphasize enough that if you're going to achieve your objectives, words and propaganda will help, but what you really need is a strong ground game. You need to do everything you can to get at least 513 conservative delegates elected before the opening gavel of the convention. Do the hard work to get that done, and you control the fate of the CLCA for generations to come."

Haller had one last thing on his mind. "Mr. Richter, I have a personal question, if it's all right. Do you, personally, believe the Bible is inspired, inerrant, and infallible?"

"Uh … sure. Sure I do," the man known as Gearshift responded. The minister chose to take Richter's word at face value.

Haller couldn't finish his meal and asked for a doggie bag. He took it to Martha as a kind of peace offering. She told him he could eat it for lunch another day.

Marquardt on the Road

On the next Zoom call after Haller's meeting with Richter, he called the Reformation Restoration Alliance to order.

"Let's pray. Dear Lord, make us instruments of your truth. Give us the power to drive your enemies out of the church. Give us the strength to get the job done. In Jesus's name, Amen."

It's time, he said, for the Double R A to shift into high gear. The national church convention was two years away, but the war would be won months before then, when the circuits met to elect convention delegates.

The core group had ten members, but it needed at least fifty, and each of them had to take responsibility for ten to eleven circuits. In a perfect world, the group would pick every pastoral and lay delegate from every district, but that probably would be impossible.

"Here's the deal," Haller said. "We need a minimum of 513 delegates who will back us, our candidates, and our issues. I want a cushion, though, so let's aim for 576, which means we'll have to corral candidates, one pastor and one layman, from 288 circuits. That's our mission.

"And another thing: We need more hands on deck. Each of you has to find five others to join us, and you have to find them by this time next week."

At this point, one of the Double R A members, Robert Rehwaldt of Lindsborg, Kansas, expressed hesitation about the group. He didn't like the power politics the group wanted to pursue. We can voice our concerns, he said, but we should let the Holy Spirit move freely among the church body. It feels wrong to do any politicking beyond what God can do for himself.

"No!" Haller screamed. Then, more calmly: "There's nothing wrong with us giving the Holy Spirit a helping hand. As far as I'm concerned, he'll be working through us. You need to see it this way: We'll be the tools that let the Holy Spirit achieve what he wants to achieve. If you're not comfortable with that, tell me now. If you don't want to be remembered as one of the leaders that saved this church, tell me now. You can't be lukewarm about this. Are you in, or are you out?"

Rehwaldt announced he would be stepping down from the group, effective immediately. Haller told him to leave the Zoom call. There would be consequences if he revealed to anyone what the group was trying to do.

"Does anyone else want out?" Haller asked when Rehwaldt left. Everyone shook their heads. Everyone remained quiet.

"Fine. Now, each of us has to find six members to join us. Get it done.

"Next issue. We need money. Between now and the circuit meetings, we'll have to do a lot of traveling to organize our ground forces. I also want to arrange a speaking tour for Jeremiah Marquardt. He needs to hit all the major Lutheran population centers so people can see how good he is. We don't want it to seem as though he's campaigning for the presidency. Instead, he'll say he's presenting a vision for the CLCA of the future, and he'll be a champion for its Bible-based roots and beliefs. He'll deny he's running for the presidency but keep open the door by saying if he's nominated, and if he feels the call of the Spirit, he will not oppose being placed on the ballot.

"But back to my main point: we need money, and I don't mean bake sale money. We need somewhere in the neighborhood of $1 million. So how do we get it?"

Someone volunteered the idea of getting 1,000 people to donate $1,000 apiece. Haller said an effort like that would take too long and be too labor intensive. The group would probably have to approach 5,000 to 10,000 people to find 1,000 willing to donate.

Another person proposed sponsoring a 50/50 online lottery. Preposterous, Haller said. Now you're talking about raising two million to get the million.

"Look, the easiest way to raise a million is to get one person to write you a check for a million," said Luke Geisler, a pastor from Camanche, Iowa. "Or to get two people to write checks for $500,000. We all think we don't travel in circles like that, but maybe we do. I want each of you to think about the wealthiest family in each of your congregations. Now, does anyone think they have a member or two or three who would write checks like that? We'd have to hurry up and establish a nonprofit organization so they could get the tax deduction, but does anyone have any candidates?"

No one came to mind for $1 million, but one of the Minnesota pastors had a member who might be able to swing a half million. He and his family owned a copper fabrication plant in Arizona. His grandfather and father had been Lutheran ministers. He had followed the Gehrke case and complained openly about the outcome. He just might be willing to join the battle on the side of the Reformation Restoration Alliance, soon to be a 501(c)3 nonprofit organization. He promised to approach his member as soon as he got off the Zoom call.

Potentially, that left $500,000 to be raised. Seven other ministers thought they might have members who could donate $100,000 apiece. They promised to get on the case immediately, and Haller adjourned the call.

Eventually, six of the seven rich Lutherans agreed to kick in $100,000. The copper fabrication magnate put a condition on his donation. He would make it, he said, if a special chair of Old Testament studies at Martin Luther Seminary could be named after his father. It would be the Daniel Berringer Chair for Old Testament Studies.

"If we win," he was told, "it will be done. And we promise, that's not a big if." Soon, $500,000 in copper money found its way to the Reformation Restoration Alliance, sweetening the group's war chest to $1.1 million.

* * *

Jeremiah Marquardt resisted being on an extensive speaking tour, but he agreed to a pilot program of appearances in Indianapolis, St. Louis, Des Moines, and Phoenix. The Double R A did a splendid job of turning out crowds. At the event in Indianapolis, Eric "Gearshift" Richter passed along an idea. To warm up the crowds in other cities, they should hire Jim Steiger, a personable, retired TV personality who just happened to be Lutheran.

"I've used him at political events," Richter said. "He'll create a whole new level of enthusiasm at your gatherings. People will go crazy."

In each city, the group found a sympathetic congregation to host the events. They publicized Marquardt's appearances on social media and provided bulletin inserts to congregations willing to use them. The theme of the evening? "Defending Truth in the CLCA."

Attendees gathered in church sanctuaries, thus appropriating the presence of the Almighty Himself. When possible, most of the lights were dimmed, keeping the attendees in the dark and focused on Marquardt, who was bathed in light as he positioned himself near the altar.

Steiger opened the program by leading the crowd in the hymn "Onward, Christian Soldiers." He asked people where they were from, how long they had been part of the church, what their faith meant to them. He revealed that he, long ago, had been a graduate of Oberhausen University, and he credited the school for strengthening his faith, which kept him on the straight and narrow in the often-immoral field of show business.

He offered a brief bio of the speaker of the evening, calling him a defender of the faith and a champion of the word.

"Before Dr. Marquardt comes forward, let's show him where we stand!" For five minutes, sometimes more, he led the crowd in cheers written by the Double R A.

"The Bible is our compass, the Bible is our light, the Bible is our fortress, the Bible is our might!"

"The Bible is our comfort, the Bible is our guide, the Bible is our refuge, the Bible never lied!"

By the time Marquardt appeared, dressed simply in a navy-blue suit and a red necktie, normally docile Lutherans had been whipped into a frenzy, and they liked the feeling. It took the speaker a couple of minutes to calm everyone down.

"Pray with me, won't you?" he started each speech, bowing his head and lifting his palms up toward heaven. "Lord, we live in difficult times. Christians are attacked, the Bible is attacked, the values and morals you've taught us are attacked. Help each of us see we have to step up. We have to be strong. We have to be warriors for the Bible. We have to fight false doctrine wherever it emerges. Please help us do so. Amen."

He built his speech like a funnel. At the top, he railed on about how the world was straying from God. Abortion, homosexuality, transsexuality, promiscuity. People were accepting all these deviations without batting an eye, he said. The reason? No one listens to the Bible anymore. We're a society unmoored from our biblical anchor.

Eventually, he followed the funnel down to the crowd's own church body, the Confessional Lutheran Church in America.

"Most of our pastors and professors are fine, upstanding people, true to the faith and true to the word. But we have doubters and false teachers among us, people who don't believe the Bible is infallible. People who would have you risk your salvation by encouraging you to believe the universe is billions of years old, that Adam and Eve weren't real, that Jesus wasn't born of a virgin. It's a small infection now, but it must be destroyed.

"I have colleagues who espouse false doctrine, who fail to teach the truth. They need to be chastised. They need to be called to repentance. They need to be expelled from the church if they won't change. Unfortunately, the church doesn't seem to have the stomach to call them to task.

"You all remember the case of Hillman Gehrke. Now, I taught Gehrke in seminary. I could see then he might be headed down a treacherous path. And so he was.

"When it came time for his heresy hearing, I sat on the panel. I voted to remove him from his position and from the church. But we couldn't get it done. Some of the panelists supported him. One, I maintain, didn't really understand the issues. We can fix that in 2027. Together, we must ensure that we have Bible-believing delegates attending the convention. We must ensure that we have strong, faithful candidates running for church posts. We must establish a body, once and for all, that can declare what will be and what won't be taught in our church.

"All of you here tonight can help. If you're with me, run for a church board or commission! Encourage others to run! Put on the armor of God and join the fight! Make it happen, and we'll have the strongest church in the world!"

When he finished, the crowd erupted in cheers. Then, he invited questions.

"Dr. Marquardt, just how pervasive is heresy in the CLCA?"

"No one knows for sure. I'd say there are at least eight heretics at my seminary, maybe four or five others at Oberhausen. What's really unclear is how many there are among the pastors of the church. You can help us smoke them all out.

"Download the questionnaire from GodsTruthIsMyTruth.com. The one called "The Test for Truth." You'll have twenty questions you can ask your pastor to see exactly where he stands. If he fails, or if he balks at answering the questions, just let Otto Haller know. We'll add his name to the list of people to be investigated."

"What kinds of offices will be on the ballot at the national convention?"

"Delegates will be electing candidates for every board and commission of the church. Anything from finance to pension administration, from the board of regents for Oberhausen and the seminary to the boards for national and international missions. Anything from the commission on constitutional matters to the commission on doctrinal review. If you run, you can help set the direction of the CLCA for decades to come."

"How did heresy come to gain a foothold in the church?"

"I have to hand it to Hillman Gehrke. He pointed out the problem for us. There is a commission on doctrinal review, but it's weak, and it hasn't really established a clearcut understanding of what will be and won't be tolerated in the CLCA. That's another thing we can fix at the national convention. There's a group, recently formed, called the Lutheran Institute for Conservative Theology. Every one of its members is a God-fearing, Bible-believing pastor or professor of the CLCA. I could see formalizing them so they can be what Gehrke called a magisterium, a body that rules on what will and won't be tolerated in the church. Okay, one last question, please, and then I have to go."

"Dr. Marquardt, are you willing to run for the presidency of the CLCA?"

The professor paused for quite some time, appearing to give deep thought to the question. Finally, he told his lie:

"You know, I'm not far from retirement, and my wife is looking forward to the day we can enjoy time together and travel. I'm here tonight to present a vision of the future for the CLCA, and I'll always be a champion for Bible-based beliefs. I don't want to run for president. But I've prayed about it, and I'm being led to say that, if I feel the call of the Spirit, and if I'm nominated, I will not oppose being placed on the ballot. If God were to lead the delegates to vote for me, then yes, I will serve. Thank you all for coming tonight, and God bless you!"

He walked off to thunderous applause, and Jim Steiger reappeared.

"Volunteers are coming out among you to distribute two cards. The first is yours to keep. It gives you some important dates leading up to the convention, and it reminds you to go to GodsTruthIsMyTruth.com to download the questionnaire you can use with your pastor.

"Please return the second card to give us your name, email address, and phone number. If you're interested, put checks by any board or commission you might wish to run for. We want to do what we can to make sure qualified candidates get on the ballot. If you pass our screening process, we'll help you run. Again, thanks so much for coming. And one more time, before you go, join me in the cheers:

"The Bible is our compass, the Bible is our light, the Bible is our fortress, the Bible is our might!

"The Bible is our comfort, the Bible is our guide, the Bible is our refuge, the Bible never lied!"

* * *

After his last speaking engagement in Phoenix, as he sat at Sky Harbor Airport, Marquardt pulled his cell phone from his pocket and called Haller.

"I didn't want to do these engagements. I didn't want to load my schedule up with traveling," the seminary professor said. "But praise be, these rallies are so powerful, so invigorating, and I can't get enough of them! Let's do more. I'll go wherever you want."

Of course, Haller said. You're doing the work of the Lord. And, he thought, like all of us, your ego loves to be fed.

Caleb Meets Chicago

After settling into his apartment, Caleb began his life as an Uber driver. He tried most weekdays to be on the streets by 6 a.m. and off by 5 p.m. During the fall and winter, he learned, some of the best money to be made came when the Bears were in town. A lot of people preferred Ubering to the games over hassling with parking, and Uber rates were among the highest before and after a game. He decided to work those Sundays, which ruled out church attendance and time with Ashley. On those weekends, on Saturdays, he turned off the Uber app and made plans with his girlfriend. Sometimes they attended Saturday evening services at Hope Lutheran in Oak Park, Ashley's home congregation. Then they'd head to Rush Street for live music and a good meal. Maybe someday, he thought, he should see if Rush Street was anything like Memphis's Beale Street.

Most days, he planned his evenings around Ashley, who quickly became swamped with her academic requirements. If she could see him, he was available. They would have dinner together, maybe see a movie, and then head to her apartment for libido lessons. It turned out Ashley knew more than he did—he didn't ask how—and she was patient as he struggled with his conscience over giving up his virginity. As he gained more experience, he became less conflicted over the issue. Still, he hesitated.

"I really want to do this," he said. "I've always believed, though, that you should be, if not legally married, then totally committed to one another."

To which Ashley replied, "Mister, I can promise you this. If you'd asked me a year ago, I would never have believed I would say this, but I love you. I'm not going anywhere. I am with you, yesterday, today, and until the day I die." And I with you, Caleb said.

And so, despite his churchly morality, despite his parochial upbringing in tiny Frohna, Missouri, despite being his father's son, he found it surprisingly easy to say goodbye to his innocence. Recalling his mother's words helped: "Explore what you need to explore." He definitely needed to explore this, he decided, and it opened a whole new world of passion and intimacy for both of them. Even without a marriage license, their sex life wasn't "sinful," he believed. It was simply lovely. Frightening sometimes, a little intimidating, but lovely. The best day of his life was when Ashley said: "Damn, mister, I do believe you've earned a master's degree in bedroom technique."

If Ashley was occupied, Caleb used his evenings for self-guided theology study. At Oberhausen, he'd been exposed to a steady diet of Lutheran thought. In Chicago, he delved into Augustine, Aquinas, Milton, Niebuhr, Marcus Borg, and N. T. Wright, among others. He came to see all of them as deeply Christian. Few of them subscribed to the notion of biblical inerrancy as held to in the CLCA.

Caleb also hung out on occasion with Joel Hardaway, the Columbia College graduate he met at Ashley's pool party. Usually, they would have dinner together and watch a vintage movie like *Casablanca, Dr. Strangelove, Silence of the Lambs, Rear Window,* or *Singin' in the Rain.*

"Once in a while, you just have to laugh," Joel said of the musical. "And the other thing about *Singin' in the Rain* . . . it's a real celebration of humanity. Have you ever seen anything as incredible as Donald O'Connor's pratfalling through "Make 'Em Laugh" or Gene Kelly's splashing through all those puddles? I know you're the theology guy, Caleb, but those performances are about as close to heaven on earth as we'll ever witness."

Caleb found it hard to disagree.

Ashley had adjustments of her own to make. Northwestern's Medill School of Journalism required her to declare a specialization for her master's degree. She considered politics, policy, and foreign affairs, but that would have forced her to spend most of her time in Washington. She looked at business, economics, and money, because she had grown up in the world of business. But she decided on social justice, because she wanted to help call out issues of classism, racism, and income inequality.

"Those issues will always be with us," she told Caleb. "And there are plenty of stories to cover right here in Chicago. Just look at what's happened since the city dismantled public-housing complexes in the early 2000s. So many people who were displaced still haven't figured out how to rebuild their lives. I love this city, but it's got a lot of problems. If I specialize in reporting on social justice, I can spend my entire life here."

Having to make his way in the city, Caleb's appreciation for the importance of money grew quickly. In Frohna, he realized, money wasn't as necessary because people could, in large measure, live off the land. They ate the crops they grew and the animals they raised. Housing wasn't an issue for most of them because their homes had been in their families for generations. Yes, they needed money, but it was easier for them to adjust to going without when necessary. That would be impossible in any urban setting. He could easily make a career in the city doing anything from ministry to career counseling to helping people manage their money. Or maybe the Detter family would teach him how to make money in real estate.

The excitement of Chicago was getting into his blood. And despite multiple warnings that driving for Uber would grind him down, he loved it. He could immerse himself in downtown Chicago's magnificent architecture. He could explore the textures of city and suburban neighborhoods. He could take a break whenever he needed. But most of all, he could engage with his passengers. Some were local, many were not. Some lived in places as exotic as Paris, Tokyo, Johannesburg, and Canberra. Many made a living in occupations he never dreamed existed. Most practiced religions far different from his, or not at all.

Before they stepped into Caleb's rented Toyota Corolla, they knew a little about him from the picture and profile that popped up on their phone as they waited for their ride. "Your driver is Caleb," it said. "He's from Missouri. He might be going to seminary, or he might not." Almost always, people had something to say to him.

"Praise the Lord! You need to get yourself to seminary right now. There's nothing more important than saving souls for Jesus!"

"Seminary, huh? I was raised with all that religious jibber-jabber. It nearly drove me to suicide. The best day of my life was the day I walked away from the church. You should do the same. Only downside is my family disowned me, but what are you gonna do?"

"So, what do you think about Jews? I'm Jewish. One of my best friends was Christian, until he got serious about it and told me I'd be damned to hell if I didn't believe accept Jesus as my Lord and Savior. What kind of God would that be, anyway? I'll just stick with my own religion, thank you."

"I like what Gandhi said. 'I like your Christ. I do not like your Christians. Your Christians are so unlike your Christ.'" Caleb knew Gandhi might not have said this, but he stayed silent, and he was starting to understand the sentiment. He sensed that contradicting his customers could end badly.

"John Lennon had it right, man. Instant karma's gonna get you. What goes around comes around, right? Just be good to folks, that's all you can do."

"You know what I think? Eat, drink, and be merry, for tomorrow we die. You can take that to the bank, preacher boy."

"If you decide to become a minister, do it for the right reasons. It's not about showing off on Sunday with your sermons to feed that 'look at me' mentality preachers have. It's about helping people make sense of their lives, and especially the tragedies of their lives. Me, I've lost a sister and a nephew to suicide. I wish I could figure out what that's all about. I just can't." Caleb realized he had nothing to say, at least in the moment, other than expressing his sorrow for the man's loss. Maybe that's all that was needed.

"I hear that minister gig comes with some good perks. You can make a lot of money officiating at baptisms, weddings, and funerals. Don't ever feel bad about making a little extra money. God knows you'll need it."

"Let me ask you this. If your God is so good, why is there suffering in the world? Never made sense to me. Does it to you?"

As a pre-seminary student, Caleb would have leapt at the chance to pursue verbal jousting with his passengers in the name of educating them, maybe even "saving" them. As an Uber driver, he learned to listen, to empathize, and to practice simple kindness. I might never become a minister, he thought, but maybe I'm becoming a better person.

* * *

In early November, Caleb realized that Christmas would arrive soon, and he had to make good on his promise to Ashley's father to have a life plan put together. He decided to tap into Ashley's dad's wisdom, and to flatter him, by seeking advice on how to make such a plan.

Mr. Detter suggested they meet for lunch at Crushed by Giants, a small, downtown brewpub sitting above the AMC Theatre on Michigan Avenue. Caleb, bundled up to protect himself from the early winter winds that nipped at him, waited outside until Ashley's father appeared.

"A Reuben!" Mr. Detter exclaimed when Caleb ordered. "My favorite sandwich. I'll have one too. And Caleb, if you're into IPAs, this is the place to be. It makes me yearn to get back into the beer business."

"Mr. Detter, thanks for meeting with me. And such a cool restaurant too!"

"I think it's time you stopped calling me Mr. Detter. I'd really prefer you to call me Andy. No sense being so formal."

"I'll try, but it'll be a little awkward for me … uh … Andy. Anyway, I've been thinking about your request, to put together a life plan for myself. I've got some thoughts, but it would help me to know whether you did this when you were my age and how you went about it."

To be honest, Andy said, he never really had to. He thought he would end up in the brewing business, but his parents sold it, so that didn't work out. To get ready to run the business, he earned a degree in finance from the University of Chicago, which is all about figuring out which of a number of possible investments has the potential to work out best. It wasn't difficult to make the leap into real estate development.

He told Caleb he learned that much of what successful people do with their time—with their lives—is tied to what they value. If their work isn't advancing their values, it's not satisfying, and it's probably not sustainable. He advised Caleb to spend a great deal of time figuring out what he valued, then figuring out his strengths, and only then surveying what kinds of careers he might wish to pursue. If he made all those things mesh together, he probably would have a good career and a good life.

Andy said he enjoyed the money he made through real estate, and he was happy to be able to provide well for his family. His real satisfaction, though, came from providing affordable housing for the poor.

His vision was to create public-private partnerships in the Chicago area to build simple, affordable, stylish, easy-to-maintain homes for people of limited means. He worked with the Frank Lloyd Wright Foundation to obtain plans for some of the architect's Usonian homes, which the architect built for people of modest means. Andy enjoyed building similar homes in and near Chicago, often with donated materials and volunteer labor. Local, state, and federal officials helped select residents for the homes.

He admitted he could make only a small dent in the overall problem of poverty and homelessness. Still, he said, there's nothing like the satisfaction of helping people get into a home they can manage that gives them security and a place to raise a family.

"My rock-bottom value is giving to people so they have a chance to make better lives for themselves," Andy said. "I know you're a man of faith, Caleb. I'm not as learned as you are on the fine points of theology, but I know Matthew 25 pretty well. It's all about feeding people, and clothing people, and giving people a place to stay when they need it. That's what I try to do with my life."

They finished their lunch, and Caleb thanked Andy for his insights. He thought about how Andy used his life, and how his father used his, spending time running people's reputations into the ground. He might not know what he wanted to do with his life, but he knew what he didn't want.

As the cold Chicago wind greeted them outside the restaurant, Andy shook Caleb's hand.

"I really had my doubts when Ashley first told me about you," he said. "I've spent more time than I should on your dad's website. I worried you would be like him, especially when Ashley told me you made the recording of Hillman Gehrke. But I can see you've been changing and growing. Ashley sees something good in you. I do too. You keep growing, keep taking care of my daughter, and I'll keep helping you."

For the first time, Caleb felt totally at home in the Windy City.

Frustration

In early 2027, Robert Storck and Hillman Gehrke asked for an appointment with Carl Walters, president of the CLCA. His administrative assistant said he was just about to leave town to visit with fellow church body presidents in Hamburg. He'd be back in two weeks, and he could meet with them then.

"No, this can't wait," Storck told her. "The future of the CLCA is in jeopardy. We need to talk with him now. Just give us half an hour. He needs to be thinking about this as he's traveling. Please fit us in."

Storck and Walters had been classmates in seminary. They played basketball together on the school team. Walters led in points scored, Storck in assists. Walters had more fan appeal, but he knew he was nothing without Storck. The two men rose to top positions in the CLCA, and they cultivated a lifelong friendship that allowed Storck to be candid with the president of his church body.

Walters was preoccupied as Storck and Gehrke entered his office, signing papers, taking last-minute phone calls, placing folders in his briefcase as he packed for his trip. He sat behind an antique walnut, leather-top executive desk that reflected the character of the CLCA—sturdy, solid, quietly understated. The walls held pictures of Walters posing with Desmond Tutu, the Archbishop of Canterbury, George W. Bush, Barack Obama, and other dignitaries. He was comfortable traveling in such circles, and he enjoyed it.

"Sit down but be quick, gentlemen. I don't have much time."

"You don't know how true that is," Storck said. "Let me get to the point.

There are people gunning for your job and our church. They're determined and well organized. They've made up a fancy name for themselves, the Reformation Restoration Alliance. If they take control, the CLCA will have a heresy hunt on its hands that will tear the church apart."

Walters said he was well aware of Otto Haller, the Missouri malcontent, but he was just that, a mini-sized malcontent, with lots of flash but no discernable firepower.

"Carl, you're wrong. You're underestimating him. He's put together a band of real zealots. They're power hungry, and somehow, they have a pot of money. They're a threat, and you need to take them seriously."

He won't succeed, Walters said. The CLCA won't fall prey to that kind of nonsense. Our people run from controversy. They're all about potluck suppers, not political infighting.

"I'm just not worried about Haller and his kind."

Gehrke said he never worried about Haller either, until he found himself on the wrong end of a heresy hearing he barely escaped. Haller ginned it up out of nowhere.

"He published the so-called 'evidence,' got his cronies to file charges, and had a hand in picking the two panelists who voted against me. Jeremiah Marquardt was one of them, as you know, and he's traveling around the country campaigning for your job. He says it's about articulating a vision for the church, but believe me, he's campaigning. Do you remember who installed Haller at his congregation when no one else would? Marquardt! No, Haller's building a machine, and it's more powerful by the day. These people are laser-focused, and they're relentless. They need to be denounced. They need to be stopped."

The last thing Walters wanted to do was acknowledge the existence of Haller and his rat pack. Why dignify them by recognizing them? he asked.

"Why not fight back?" Gehrke said. "You might think the good people of the CLCA wouldn't get behind a heresy hunt. But I attended Marquardt's campaign rally here in Des Moines. I'm telling you, President Walters, the good people are malleable, and let's face it, most of them were raised believing the Bible is inspired, inerrant, and infallible, to use Haller's catchphrase. We need to educate them, we need to go on the offensive, and we need to show people just how destructive this so-called Reformation Restoration Alliance will be."

Walters said he couldn't devote another minute to thinking about this, and he didn't want to. He told Storck and Gehrke to meet with the church's vice president of public relations. Maybe he would have some ideas.

* * *

Harold Kreiss, the well-spoken, well-groomed PR executive, had been recruited to the church's headquarters after a successful career at a Fortune 50 pretzel and potato chip manufacturer. His father and mother had been CLCA missionaries in Papua New Guinea. He gave up stock options and a high-six-figure income because he wanted to do something more fulfilling than keeping the world safe for salty snacks.

Kreiss greeted the two men warmly as they entered his office. He heard them out. After they told their story, he said he was sorry, but the church had to stay neutral in these kinds of controversies. It couldn't appear to be taking sides with one group over another, but he thought Storck and Gehrke were worried for nothing. Attacks against church organizations usually died out quickly, especially in 21st-century America, where most stories drop in and out of the news cycle faster than Usain Bolt could run the hundred-meter dash.

"We're not talking about what happens in the media," Storck said. "This is about smear campaigns and power politics, and the battles are being fought on the ground, in classrooms and church pews. You don't get it. What I'm hearing is that, except for sending out an occasional news release and running some dead-end accounts on social media, you're useless. Thanks for nothing."

Like the well-trained PR man he was, Kreiss carried on, unfazed. "I'm really sorry you all feel that way, but I hope you have a nice day." He walked them to his office door, offering them some cookies as they left.

"Well, that was pointless," Storck said.

"Yeah, I heard he used to be really good. I think he has something in common with Usain Bolt. Neither of them is as fast as they used to be."

* * *

Gehrke tried for the next few months to mount a counteroffensive to the Double R A. He asked Oberhausen to let him write about Haller in the university publication. Not happening, he was told. He asked fellow professors to be part of a speakers bureau. Too busy, they said. He called congregations to see whether they would host rallies to counter Marquardt's appearances. Too divisive, they feared. He asked media outlets in key CLCA markets to cover the story of the band of insurgents in the church. Too esoteric, they responded.

People just didn't believe Haller and company could damage the church. Most people were convinced they would fade as quickly as they had emerged.

Gehrke's friends who pastored congregations assured him their members wouldn't fall prey to the Reformation Restoration Alliance. Many members understood the complexities of biblical interpretation, and they weren't likely to rally behind Haller.

"Many don't," Gehrke would respond. "Look, Haller doesn't need to convince the whole church he's right. He only needs to mobilize half the delegates to the national convention. Half plus one. He needs to put candidates on the ballot who agree with him. He and his cronies are making it happen, even as we speak. They're riling up people to attend the circuit meetings. They're going to get their delegates elected. Do the math. I assure you, Haller has, and the numbers are adding up in his favor."

Meanwhile, Marquardt kept making appearances throughout the nation alongside his cheerleader, Jim Steiger. Wherever they went, they handed out "I I I" lapel pins and bumper stickers that said: Proud Member of the "I I I" Brigade. Which, of course, stood for "inspired, inerrant, and infallible." Before long, an assortment of Triple I merchandise—caps, mugs, T-shirts, even golf balls—was available for purchase at GodsTruthIsMyTruth.com.

During one rally, an audience member raised his hand, forming his thumb and pointer finger in the shape of the "okay" sign. This left the middle finger, ring finger, and pinky pointing upward like three I's. The gesture caught on among supporters of the anti-heresy crowd, who called it the Triple I Salute. They used it to show solidarity whenever they got together. Whether they knew the supporters of white power used a similar gesture wasn't clear. Nor was it clear whether they would have cared.

The Hallers Fall Apart

Otto Haller increasingly lived in his office, cranking out content for GodsTruthIsMyTruth.com. He became more aggressive in identifying heretics in the church, adding each week to his published list as congregation members administered, or attempted to administer, his twenty-question questionnaire to their pastors.

One of the pastors who balked at submitting to the questionnaire found his name on the list. He wrote to Haller in protest:

"Many things you and your followers call heresy are really secondary and tertiary issues. Someone might be considered to hold a wrong position on one or more of these issues. But calling someone a heretic isn't the same as arguing they are wrong. Calling someone a heretic means they've departed so far from Christianity that they can no longer be considered a follower of Christ. This is serious business. You and your followers need to examine your motives and your accusations. You have no right to empower untrained church members as heretic hunters, especially with the faulty tool you place in their hands. You owe an apology to the church and the many people you're libeling.

"If you have evidence I'm a heretic, take it to my district president and file formal charges against me. Otherwise, back down."

Haller published the letter and offered his response: "This gentleman refused to submit to the questionnaire. We cannot vouch for his faithfulness to God and the Bible. If he were faithful, he would have nothing to hide. And of course, he feels confident urging us to file charges with his district president, New England's James Wittrock. You'll recall that Wittrock served on the heresy panel that tried Hillman Gehrke. Wittrock voted to clear Gehrke of all charges. There's no doubt that he, too, is a heretic."

As the national convention came closer, Haller devoted most of his time to propaganda and politics. His congregants received the bare minimum of his attention, a sermon on Sunday and, if needed, hospital visits during the week. Most people in Frohna went to Cape Girardeau for hospitalization. When Haller made his visits, he also called on Marquardt, strategizing their heretic hunt over a beer or two and receiving updates on how the Triple I rallies were going.

"Lifelong CLCA members are telling me they had no idea how serious a problem heresy has become in the church. I think we're onto something powerful here," Marquardt said as he and Haller watched a Cardinal spring training game on a muted TV in Marquardt's living room. "We should think about turning these events into weekend seminars. We could give in-depth training in how to spot a heretic and how to drive him out of a congregation, a seminary, or a university. The church procedures for trying heresy can be long and cumbersome. It might be easier to chase heretics out just by making life in a congregation uncomfortable for them.

"And the thing is, what's a pastor going to do? Sue? Good luck with that. The courts don't like to get involved in church matters."

Haller smiled. He liked how Marquardt's thinking was progressing. He and the Double R A had picked the right man for the job. The professor was becoming a politician.

"Of course," Haller said, "if we win at convention, we can find ways to streamline the procedures."

* * *

Even in the early days of their marriage, Otto and Martha Haller had not been close. Otto's ministry kept him active in the lives of his congregants. When he wasn't visiting their homes, he was having breakfast or lunch with them at Virgie's Restaurant. The couple had dinner together after a nightly devotion. They might watch TV in the evenings or just read quietly. He immersed himself in theology journals while she preferred a wide range of novels, anything from Steinbeck to Twain to an occasional romance novel. Once Caleb was old enough, the three of them sometimes played board games together or rented a movie from the Redbox down the road at Hiram's Convenience Mart. They rarely went out together, either as a couple or a family.

Martha's father, Ed Schroeder, had been a pastor, so she had a good idea what she was signing up for when she married Otto. Still, there were marked differences between her father and her husband. Her dad was friendly, and he enjoyed conversation. He indulged in tennis and golf, even though he was terrible. "I don't really play golf," he would say. "I play at golf."

Martha both loved and enjoyed her father, who continued to be active in retirement. He joined the family for holidays in Frohna, or they drove to Cape Girardeau to be with him many weekends. At least Martha and Caleb did. Otto often protested he had too many duties and responsibilities to take even a short break from Frohna.

Since their argument over Caleb's graduation, Otto and Martha's relationship had become strictly transactional. As she promised, Martha prepared meals. She cleaned the house as well, more for her comfort than her husband's. Their conversations touched only on tasks that had to be completed or information that had to be passed on.

"You need to call the insurance company about how much they raised our premiums this quarter."

"Next time you go to Cape Girardeau, please bring back the order I placed at Home Depot."

"Mrs. Damm asked if you could make it to bridge club next week."

Dinner conversation was nearly nonexistent. Once they sat down, Otto said grace. He tried to strike up a conversation about sports, the news of the day, or his burgeoning campaign to control the CLCA, but Martha had nothing to say. As she had told him, "a little tenderness would be in order," but Otto couldn't crack the code and couldn't deliver, and Martha had no interest in conversing with her husband.

She needed more to fill her days and her heart. She wasn't one to sit all day, eat chocolates, and watch *Live with Kelly and Mark,* so she set about figuring out how to find more satisfaction in her life. Eventually, she devised a plan and announced it one evening at dinner.

She had fixed a meal of roast beef, mashed potatoes, and green beans. Otto sat down, wearing his clerical collar as he always did, and told her the food looked and smelled delicious. He was wired and a bit jittery from all the coffee he drank each day to keep him energetic enough to create and post his anti-heretic screeds.

As they approached the end of the meal, Martha told Otto she had something to say.

"I need more in my life, Otto, and I'm going to make a change. I've always wanted to go to college, and I'm told it's not too late. So, beginning with the summer session, I'm going to start taking courses at Southeast Missouri State. I've signed up for their writing degree."

Otto sat silent for a few seconds, then scoffed. "What makes you think you can write? You're forty-five years old, and you haven't sat in a classroom since high school. Now you're going to be a big-time writer? What would you do with a degree anyway? You're being ridiculous."

Who's to say what I'd do with a degree? Martha countered. Who knows? Maybe I'll teach. Maybe I'll sell articles. Maybe I'll just enjoy the accomplishment of earning a degree. Who knows?

"But I'll tell you what makes me think I can write," she said. "I've already submitted writing samples, and the department head was encouraging. She said my writing displayed a sensitivity and maturity that couldn't be matched by a younger student. She said I'd be welcome in the program."

When did Martha have time to write any samples? Otto demanded.

"Come on," she said. "While you're holed up in your office, it takes me about an hour to do the day's chores. I got tired of sitting around reading, watching TV, maybe taking a walk past the same old houses and stores. I've had plenty of time to write. You've walked right by me as I was writing and didn't even take time to notice."

Otto protested that she couldn't be driving forty minutes and back to Cape Girardeau every day because they had only one car, and he might need it.

Not a problem, she said. Her father hardly ever used his car, and he was willing to let her have it as long as she helped him run errands while she was in Cape.

"Well, we can't afford to send you to college. Besides, I need you around here. You're vital to me. I need you to support me and the congregation. And I'm knee-deep in my website and trying to get Jeremiah Marquardt elected as CLCA president."

She would take care of her duties, and money wouldn't be a problem, she said. In-state tuition isn't much, and the department head said she would help find scholarships for Martha. What's more, Otto's church politics were none of her concern, and she didn't support them anyway. So far, all they had done was alienate their son and turn Otto into a maniac. He had always been a little strange, she said, but he had become downright warped by his stupid "pure doctrine" crusade, and she wanted nothing to do with it.

He got up, came over to her side of the dinner table, grabbed her wrists, and squeezed them so hard she screamed.

"You did this without even talking with me? I'm your husband! I get to say whether you go to college or not! I won't allow it!"

She stood up, broke his hold, stepped back, and slapped the side of his face. He came toward her, but she kicked his shin, stopping him in his tracks.

"You have no right to stop me," she screamed. "I'm going to college!"

She ran out the front door and headed to Hiram's Convenience Store, figuring that even if Otto caught up to her, he wouldn't want to cause a public scene. He never came.

Once inside the store, she called her father and asked him to come get her and let her stay at his home in Cape Girardeau. He asked what was happening. She said she'd explain once they got together.

* * *

Haller spent the next couple of weeks avoiding the obvious, that his family had fallen apart. He buried himself in his work and devised a cover story for why Martha had left town. If someone asked where she was, he'd say she had to go to Cape Girardeau to help her father. He'd gotten word that she was there from some of the seminary faculty members.

He convinced himself that his wife and his son were responsible for the debacle. If only Caleb would honor him, as the Bible commanded. If only Martha would submit herself to him, as the Bible commanded. If only they would acquiesce, everything could return to normal, as God intended.

Mostly, though, he tried to divert his attention from his family problems, and mainly, he succeeded. There were, after all, heretics to expose, conventions to orchestrate, and propaganda to be posted. How could he ignore God's call to be a voice fighting for truth?

As days turned into weeks, as he sat at his computer screen, he started hearing those small, quiet house noises that usually go unnoticed when people are living together. He learned to ignore them. One day, he thought he heard creaking from the front door, but he dismissed it as a product of his imagination. Until someone flung his office door open.

Caleb had driven six-and-a-half hours to give Haller a message. He stood in the doorway, staring at Haller, not saying a word.

"Caleb," Haller said. "What are you doing here? Why didn't you tell me you were coming?"

"Where's my mother?" the young man asked, continuing to stare, frowning, drawing himself up to his full height.

"She's not here."

"And why not?"

Haller didn't answer right away.

"Why not?" Caleb demanded.

"She's got it into her head that she's a college student now. She's staying in Cape with her dad. I'm sure she's fine."

"Well, I'm not so sure!"

Caleb charged his father, came around to the back of his desk, forced him to his feet, manhandled him, and pinned him against a wall.

"I heard what you did to my mother! If you ever lay a hand on her again, you'll answer to me. We're both tired of you and your sanctimonious, holier-than-thou attitude."

Haller's shallow breathing made it difficult for him to talk. Caleb told him not to bother.

"There's nothing you can say to make this better," he said. "I know my mother. I'm guessing she'll come back here. Eventually. I think she'd be crazy to do so. And if she comes back, you keep your hands off her. I wish you weren't my father. I wish you weren't her husband. I promise you, if I ever hear of you abusing her again, it'll be the last time. Is that clear?"

Haller couldn't speak. He let out a quiet whimper. With his eyes squeezed shut, he nodded rapidly.

With that, Caleb said nothing more. He released Haller, left the house, and made the trip back to Chicago.

Haller was of a mind to disown his son and divorce his wife, but how could he? What would the town say? What would his fellow pastors say? He decided just to pray to God that Caleb and Martha would come to their senses and give him the respect he deserved.

***

The guest room at Ed Schroeder's home smelled faintly of cedar and old hymnals. Martha sat by the window, watching the wind stir the branches of the oak tree in the yard. Her father's house was quiet—too quiet. The kind of quiet that makes memories louder.

She pulled a quilt tighter around her shoulders and stared at the journal in her lap. She hadn't written in days. The words wouldn't come. Or maybe they were there, but she was afraid of what they'd say.

What am I doing here?

She had asked herself that question every morning since arriving. Her father had welcomed her with warmth and grace, but she could see the worry in his eyes. He didn't ask about Otto. He didn't ask about Caleb. He just made coffee and offered silence.

I used to think marriage was a kind of sanctuary. A place where you were safe, known, loved. But with Otto, it felt like a courtroom, and he was the judge. Every word was evidence. Every silence was guilt. I kept trying to defend myself, even when I didn't know what I was accused of, even when I didn't know how.

She looked down at her hands. They were trembling.

I thought I was weak for leaving. But maybe staying was the weakness. Maybe silence was the sin.

She stood and walked to the mirror. Her reflection looked older than she remembered. Not tired—just weathered. Like someone who had walked through a storm and was still drying off.

I'm not the woman Otto married. I'm not the woman he wanted me to be. I'm not the woman who stayed quiet to keep the peace. I'm someone else now. Someone who asks questions. Someone who writes. Someone who wants to be heard.

She touched the glass, as if to steady the image.

I don't know what comes next. I don't know if I'll ever feel whole. But I know this: I'm not going back. I'm not shrinking. I'm not apologizing for wanting more.

She turned away from the mirror and picked up her pen.

Let's see what happens when I write the truth.

Wedding Plans

s Hillman Gehrke began thinking more strategically about how to counter the Reformation Restoration Alliance, he concluded the fight would come down to geography and demographics. His research indicated it would be an uphill battle. Independent researchers already had determined that CLCA members were reliably conservative, with about sixty percent of them usually voting Republican. This didn't necessarily mean they would be on Team Triple I. It meant, however, that they would be uncomfortable with change. Even if they didn't buy the argument that the church was filled with heretics, they could be susceptible to the notion that Gehrke and others like him were trying to change too much, too fast within the CLCA.

If he was going to find support, Gehrke had to mine key states, such as New York, California, Minnesota, Oregon, and Washington—politically blue states—and major metropolitan areas in other states, like Atlanta, New Orleans, Houston, Dallas, Chicago, St. Louis, Phoenix, and Las Vegas. Focusing on states like Alabama and Mississippi would be a waste of time.

He also had to find allies within demographic groups. He looked for areas and congregations with sizable populations of younger, college-educated, reasonably affluent members. Quickly, he gave up hope of finding a markedly young subset of the CLCA. Churches simply weren't attracting many young people. Still, especially in urban areas, a number of congregations skewed toward college-educated, affluent members. They became a priority on the hunch that they would be less likely to support a fundamentalist view of the Bible and the Christian faith.

Gehrke had gone to seminary and stayed friends with many of the pastors who might help his cause. He also had taught and come to the aid of many younger pastors who could be counted on to help. He used his relationships with those men to enlist their support.

The Oberhausen professor recruited a cadre of students sympathetic to the goal of stopping an all-out CLCA heretic hunt. He asked some to go through the CLCA roster of ministers to gather phone numbers and email addresses of those likely to be opposed to Haller and the Double R A. Others volunteered to write email copy to be sent to the pastors and to develop CLCATrueDisciples.com, a Johnny-come-lately website to counter GodsTruthIsMyTruth.com. Another group volunteered to plug email addresses into MailChimp and cell phone numbers into EZTexting. Others signed up to call pastors to determine where their congregations stood and how they intended to vote at the circuit meetings, where delegates would be elected to the national convention.

After several frustrating weeks, the group found a small number of professors at Oberhausen and at Martin Luther Seminary willing to make personal appearances at congregations if their expenses were covered. These men traveled as their schedules allowed to key locations, not to change the minds of fundamentalists but to rally the support and commitment of those who believed in the cause of stopping the heretic hunters.

One of the congregations open to hosting a True Disciples rally was Hope Lutheran in Oak Park, Illinois. An Oberhausen Old Testament professor volunteered to go, but Gehrke snatched the venue for himself, explaining he was friends with the pastor and a few members, including some former students he wanted to check on.

After his presentation, two of Hope's young adults, Caleb and Ashley, waited until Gehrke's well-wishers scattered, then walked to the front of the sanctuary to give him a hug. He suggested heading over to Petersen's Ice Cream, his treat.

The shop had been founded in 1919 by a Dane, Hans Petersen, who prided himself on making the finest ice cream in the state. His ancestors kept the tradition alive. Petersen's products had won blue ribbons at the Illinois State

Fair an amazing nine times. Many a romance had started over a dish of Petersen's cinnamon ice cream.

The three of them chose to walk, taking time to notice how stately the oaks were, even though they were several months away from sprouting their leaves. Ashley walked between the two men, her mentor on her left, her lover on her right.

Once they arrived and settled in with generous scoops of peppermint, pistachio, and rocky road, Gehrke asked how his two former students were doing. Ashley said she would be graduating with her master's soon and had an interview lined up with the *Chicago Tribune*. One of her professors was tight with the managing editor, and Ashley felt her chances of getting on were good.

"How about you, Caleb? What's going on with you?"

Caleb talked about how Andy Detter had led him to develop a life plan so he could think constructively about a future for himself. He saw the merit in defining his values and skills and finding a meaningful career that would bring them together.

"So, have you picked one?"

"Power broker!" Caleb laughed. "Seriously, I'm leaving my collar behind. I've decided to get a master's degree in nonprofit management from DePaul University. My hope is to find ways to scale up the work Ashley's dad does to provide housing for poor people. There's lots of opportunity there, and I think I can get it done."

"Wonderful!" Gehrke exclaimed. "But isn't Habitat for Humanity already doing that?"

Caleb had a different model in mind. He wanted to create an organization that would provide jobs as well as housing for poor people, paying them to help build their own houses and training them for careers in the building trades. Part of the challenge would be to obtain government funding and foundation grants in support of the plan. Government relations and grant solicitation would be among the skills he would learn at DePaul.

"Well, that's certainly a plan! Hope it all works out. So, what's happening with the two of you? It looks like you're together. Is that a permanent thing?"

Ashley said that's why they were so happy when they learned their former professor would be making the trip to Chicago.

"We have something to ask you," she said. "About a month ago, Caleb and I spent a beautiful, romantic weekend in Lake Geneva, and guess what? We got engaged! And we can think of no one we'd rather have perform the wedding than you. Will you do it?"

Gehrke smiled but hesitated.

"You have a pastor in the family. Seems to me he ought to be officiating at the wedding of his son. I'm not comfortable getting between all of you. I'm sure he wouldn't welcome me."

Caleb explained that he and his father were estranged and weren't talking. The two wanted nothing to do with each other. The last time Caleb saw him was to warn him against ever laying hands on his mother again. Besides, his father didn't approve of Ashley and the Detter family. No, his father wouldn't be performing the ceremony.

Gehrke said major family events sometimes have a way of healing family wounds. An invitation to officiate at your wedding might be just the thing to make Otto Haller see what he'll be missing if the rift between father and son isn't repaired.

Ashley spoke up. "That man posted an article condemning me for defending you, Dr. Gehrke, and claiming I would find myself in hell someday. And you want me, you want us, to allow him to marry us? Even if Caleb wanted it, I don't! I've never met the man. I don't intend to."

"Obviously, he's caused me some major grief too. But even so, he is Caleb's father, and I think you'd be missing a major opportunity to make a fresh start with him. I'll tell you what. I want you to ask him to perform the ceremony. I understand he'll probably say no, but I want you to extend the invitation. If he declines, I'll be glad to do it."

The young couple both frowned but said they would think about it.

They wanted to have the wedding as soon as possible, Ashley said. They were thinking in just a few months. June, to be exact. June 2027. The church was available either June 12 or June 26.

"Man, that's just a couple of months before the CLCA convention. I'm already knee deep in trying to stave off your dad and his heretic-hunting friends, and it'll be even more frantic then. But yes, I'll work it out if your father tells you he won't do it."

Caleb had one other piece of news to share. The circuit Hope Lutheran belonged to was finding it difficult to get volunteers to be the lay delegate to the convention. Late August was vacation time for a lot of families, and most people couldn't get enthused about spending the waning days of summer in Des Moines.

"Long story short, our pastor nominated me. Right now, I'm the only layman on the ballot. The vote will be in two weeks. You're probably looking at one of the youngest delegates to the convention, and I'm in your corner."

"Good news for me, good news for the church! I'm guessing your father doesn't know, right? If you call him, you might as well go for a twofer and tell him about the wedding and the convention. You certainly have a knack for intergenerational warfare."

* * *

"What do you want?" Otto Haller barked into his phone. It was the first time father and son had spoken since Caleb's brief, explosive visit to Frohna.

Caleb told his father about his upcoming wedding. His mother knew, of course, but she and Haller still weren't speaking.

"I wanted to see whether we might start to rebuild our relationship. Ashley and I have talked, and we'd like to invite you to officiate at our wedding."

Haller said nothing.

"What do you say, Dad? Will you do it?"

"No. You marry her, you join that family, and you're dead to me. Do it, and I never want to see you again."

Caleb said the wedding would take place in June, and he would see his father in August.

"I've been elected as a delegate to the CLCA convention. You can count me as a firm 'no' on anything you and your Reformation Restoration Alliance bring to the floor. I'll do my best to keep your poison out of the church."

Haller disconnected from the call. Their conversation was over.

* * *

After the call, Caleb cried just a bit, then composed himself and went to find Ashley. She was curled up on a couch with a copy of her favorite novel, *The Great Gatsby*. She looked up and immediately sensed his sadness.

"You okay?" she asked.

"I'm fine, I guess, for a guy who just got disowned by his father," he said. "Not where I ever thought I'd be, but it's okay. I'm worried, but not about that. I think I need to talk."

She set the book aside. "Sit down."

He did, but not beside her. He sat on the edge of the coffee table, facing her, elbows on knees, hands clasped.

"I've been thinking about Dad. About everything I used to believe. About what I said to people. What I said to Dr. Gehrke and so many others. How I judged them—their faith, their lives…"

Ashley nodded slowly. "Your dad raised you that way. It was your world."

"I know. But I wasn't just passive. I was active. I defended him. I repeated his words. I thought I was protecting the church, but I was just protecting his ego. And mine."

Ashley reached out for his hand and held it lovingly. "You were trying to be faithful. That's no sin."

"I was trying to be right," Caleb said. "And I think I forgot how to be kind."

Ashley didn't respond right away. She let the silence settle.

"I remember," she said finally, "when we were dating, you told me that truth mattered more than feelings. I didn't know how to respond to that. I thought maybe you were just being philosophical. But now I think you really believed it."

"I did," Caleb said. "And I was wrong. Truth without love isn't truth. It's just a weapon."

Ashley's eyes welled up. "You've changed, Caleb. I see it. You listen now. You ask questions. You don't judge. You're softer. In the best way."

"I just wish I could undo the damage. To you. To the people I hurt."

"You can't undo it," Ashley told her future husband. "But you can live differently. You already are."

He shook his head.

"I'm not."

"You are," she whispered. "And that's just one of the many reasons I've come to love you, mister."

They sat like that for a long time, the city quiet around them.

A Couple's Impasse

Otto Haller hadn't spoken to his wife in two months. He had called his father-in-law's house several times, but no one answered. Each time he drove to Cape Girardeau for a hospital visit, he stopped by the home and knocked on the door, but it never opened. Finally, he wrote a letter, not to his wife but to his father-in-law.

"Dear Ed, I'm writing to you pastor to pastor, asking you to talk with Martha for me. I can't imagine you support her in leaving me. It's not God-pleasing, after all, for her to dishonor me and our marriage by living under your roof. She took a vow to honor and obey me, and she's in violation. I expect you to chastise her and remind her of her obligations to me.

"As a fellow pastor, you can appreciate the tremendous embarrassment this situation is causing me. People in Frohna are starting to talk. If this goes on much longer, it's going to cripple my ability to minister to my congregation. Please tell her to come back to me. Tell her I'll find a way to live with her going to college."

Martha's father took his time in responding. Just as Haller concluded he would never hear from his father-in-law, he received a letter.

"Otto, I've made it a point never to meddle in Martha's marriage, and I'm not going to do so now. I'll give you some advice, however. It sounds to me as though you've fallen into a common American trap, wanting to enforce your rights while ignoring your responsibilities.

"You expect 'obedience' from my daughter, and yes, I allowed the word to stand in your wedding vows when I officiated, even though most couples were striking it even back then. I told you if you wanted the word in the vows, and Martha agreed, you would need to approach the 'obedience' provision with the purest of intentions. You should try to evoke obedience with a loving heart and only on things that deeply matter, I said. And you should seriously consider Martha's opinion on contentious issues that come between you. You're supposed to be a husband, after all, not a drill sergeant or a dictator. I found it interesting that, in your letter, you never once said anything approaching a simple 'I love her.' I'm not sure you have it in you to know what that means.

"I had real misgivings about Martha's marriage to you, but I decided it wasn't my place to tell her so. It sickened me then that you were attacking seminary professors, and it sickens me now. On your website, you say that God's truth is your truth, but I see no evidence of that. God's truth, above all, is that we should love him and love one another with patience and kindness. I'm not seeing you do that with your fellow ministers, with the church I love, the grandson I love, or the daughter I love. And honestly, after you attacked her, I would fear for her if she were once again under your roof. I'm an old man, but if I were younger, I would have done exactly what Caleb did to you. Yes, he told us about it. I'm proud of him.

"If you want Martha back, the first thing you need to do is tell her you love her, apologize to her, ask her for forgiveness, and commit to counseling. Marriage counseling, yes, but also personal counseling to work out the demons that haunt you. You'll have to decide what's more important to you, your wife and son or this campaign you've mounted to clean the CLCA of alleged 'heretics.' Each day you drive the campaign, you also pollute your heart with hatred.

"If and only if you will disengage from your heretic hunt, call my home. If we see your name displayed on caller ID, we'll see that as your signal that you're willing to turn your life around, and Martha will answer."

Haller sat at his desk, angered and rebuffed by the letter. The national CLCA convention was just eight weeks away, and he couldn't abandon the Reformation Restoration Alliance now. The alliance needed him. The call to Martha would just have to wait. He could always say he repented later, when it was more convenient.

* * *

The Double R A steering committee convened in Des Moines in early June for one last face-to-face meeting before the national church convention in August. Haller invited Jeremiah Marquardt to attend, but the presidential candidate declined, insisting on keeping his distance from overt ecclesiastical politicking.

"Remember, it's the spirit of the Lord that will put me in office," Marquardt said with a wink, "not the manipulations of collared folk." Despite its echoes of racism, he had always found it funny to call ministers "collared folk."

Haller also invited political consultant Kurt Richter—Gearshift—to provide counsel if necessary. After a brief introduction, Richter expressed support for the group, then moved to the back of the room to avoid taking the spotlight from Haller.

The group commenced to assess where their campaign stood in the final weeks. If they could think of any weaknesses, now was the time to shore them up.

On the plus side, they figured they could count on the firm support of about 550 delegates, more than enough to feel comfortable. All of them had engaged in speaking appearances at various congregations, and they had recruited others to do so. Laymen were more educated than ever about the growing threat of heresy. When they went to their circuits to elect convention delegates, they made sure to elect people who wanted to snuff out heresy before it became widespread within the church. The group hadn't made many inroads in the liberal pockets of the East Coast or the West Coast, but that was to be expected. The convention looked to be in the bag.

The group agreed they had a powerful presidential candidate in Jeremiah Marquardt. Articulate, polished, neighborly, but tough when necessary. He'd be able to root out heretics while imaking the rest of the church think he was doing it compassionately and with love.

"And if it's a magisterium Gehrke and his kind want, we'll give him one," someone said. "We've crafted a resolution to convert the Lutheran Institute for Conservative Theology into the CLCA Theological Magisterium. We'll have heresy specifically, thoroughly defined just a couple of months after the convention adjourns. Gehrke and his fellow travelers will be gone within six months."

"So, there's nothing to worry about? Things rarely go as smoothly as you're telling me they will," Haller said. "Dig a little deeper. What could go wrong?"

The group guessed that the heretic lovers coming to the convention would mount protests, and they would be articulate. They probably would argue that everything is moving much too quickly and without enough deliberation. They could sway some support their way, but it was doubtful they would win over enough delegates to be victorious.

Haller asked the group what else they worried about. No one spoke up. After a long, awkward silence, David Bohnert, Haller's friend from Paducah, slowly raised his hand.

"Well, Otto, uh . . . this isn't easy to say, but we've been talking among ourselves. The thing is, we think it would be best if you stayed away from Des Moines during the convention."

Haller said he knew he couldn't attend as anything but an observer. He wasn't on the CLCA clergy roster, but that didn't mean he couldn't come and watch the proceedings, like any interested party. He already had tried to get press credentials by virtue of his website, but that wasn't going to happen. The mighty church public relations officials couldn't stop him from sitting in the gallery like anyone else, though, could they?

"You're right," Bohnert said, "and we can't stop you either. But there are two good reasons for you not to come. Three, really. First, you're a lightning rod. You and your website kindle a lot of emotion from our enemies, and even some of our supporters think your language often crosses the line. Second, we're not sure you can keep your temper in check if you get involved in an argument, and we don't like the prospect of having some video of you screaming at a delegate going viral."

Haller was seething. He stared Bohnert down. "What's your third reason?" he snarled.

"This is really hard to say, Otto, but there are a lot of rumors about all the strife in your family. Martha's not living with you, Caleb hasn't followed through on his plans to go to seminary, and he's cozy with the heretic-loving Detters. It looks like your family life is falling apart, and that's never a good look for a pastor. If you come to the convention, you're going to be the target of endless rumors. Some of them will be voiced anyway, but with you there, they'll be nonstop. It won't be helpful, for you or for us."

Haller bellowed that he was surrounded by ingrates. He singlehandedly smoked out heresy in the church. He recruited the next president of the CLCA. He organized opposition to the church into a powerful political force. And this was the thanks he got?

"My family life is nobody's business. I am coming to Des Moines. The church can't stop me, and you can't stop me. If you shun me, there's nothing I can do about that. But when the convention is over, when the victory has been won, when a new regime is in place, I'll publish my analysis of how everything was accomplished. And you, gentlemen, will not fare well."

With that, he stormed out of the room. Richter followed him and asked him to wait up.

"You know, Otto, they may have a point. You've done great work, and I'm sure they appreciate it. But tactically, it might be smart for you to stay home and watch the livestream."

Haller scoffed. With advice like that, he said, Richter's counsel was no longer needed. Haller alone had gotten the group where it was, and Des Moines would be the Super Bowl of the heresy hunt. He would be there.

Back in the meeting room, the remaining members of the Reformation Restoration Alliance shook their heads, shook hands, and then headed home. Many of them preached that weekend on the epistle lesson prescribed by the church, Galatians 5:14-15: "For the entire law is fulfilled in keeping this one command: Love your neighbor as yourself. If you bite and devour each other, watch out or you will be destroyed by each other."

A couple of days later, Haller called Marquardt, asking him to help persuade the group that Haller should be welcomed by them at the convention. Marquardt said he didn't think it would be proper for him to get involved.

"After all I've done to get you nominated, you can't do this simple thing for me? I'm really disappointed, Dr. Marquardt."

Hillman Meets Martha

I pronounce you spouses for life. Now, please begin your adventure of marriage with a kiss."

The wedding of Caleb Haller and Ashley Detter took place, as planned, at 5 p.m. on June 12, 2027, at Hope Lutheran Church, Oak Park, Illinois. The couple's wedding announcement in the *Chicago Tribune* noted that Ashley would be joining the newspaper as soon as she and Caleb returned from their honeymoon in Aruba. Caleb, the article noted, would begin studying for his master's degree at DePaul.

Aruba, and a three-bedroom condo in Lincoln Park, were presents from Ashley's parents. Caleb's new life was feeling a bit otherworldly to him, but he was adjusting well.

He had become friendly with Ashley's friends, even the two gay couples he spotted at Ashley's pool party. He smiled and nodded to them when he saw them in their pews at the wedding.

The couple agreed that Ashley would keep her last name. Even though she loved his son, she couldn't imagine carrying the name of Otto Haller, the man who had declared her to be bound for hell.

Ashley selected Marianna Pelletier as her maid of honor, and Caleb approved. He'd learned to look past Marianna's flirtatious ways to see her as a good-hearted person and, not incidentally, a top-notch pediatric nurse. She enjoyed trying to make him blush whenever she could.

Caleb asked Joel Hardaway to be his best man. Joel had become Caleb's closest friend in Chicago. They had started a book club together, and they had great conversations about politics, literature, and movies. They both loved baseball and could spend countless hours squabbling over the relative merits of Joel's team, the Cubs, and Caleb's beloved Cardinals.

The couple selected a traditional wedding text, I Corinthians 13:4-7. "Love is patient, love is kind. It does not envy, it does not boast, it is not proud. It does not dishonor others, it is not self-seeking, it is not easily angered, it keeps no record of wrongs. Love does not delight in evil but rejoices with the truth. It always protects, always trusts, always hopes, always perseveres."

When they chose the text, Ashley smiled.

"What are you smiling about?" Caleb asked. "I mean, I know it's a great text. But why are you smiling so much?"

"Well, if you read just a few verses above, there's the text we talked about the first night we dated. You know, the one about your dad."

"My dad?"

"Yeah. Paul's warning that without love, pious words are nothing more than clanging cymbals. Too bad your dad can't figure that out."

The day of the wedding, Hillman Gehrke said he was flabbergasted to be officiating.

"Ashley's wedding, sure, no surprise for me there. But Caleb's! Who would have thought? We didn't exactly mesh well during most of Caleb's time at Oberhausen. It's no secret, I'm sure, that Caleb played a role in setting me up for a heresy trial. Frankly, I was of a mind to throttle him for a long while! He said it would be okay to talk about it today.

"It seems impossible for that divide to have been bridged, and yet it was. Each of us had to work on the strife and resentment in our hearts. But we overcame our struggles, and Caleb is far different from the student I first encountered at Oberhausen. I'm enormously happy to be standing here today. I know he will be good for Ashley, and Ashley will be good for him."

At the end of the service, the couple, dressed in a black tuxedo and a stunning, white wedding gown, walked to the narthex of the church to greet guests before heading to the reception. They made their way to the accompaniment of Beethoven's Ode to Joy, selected by Ashley. His bride, Caleb kept learning to his never-ending surprise, was a progressive but also a traditional young woman.

* * *

The reception took place in the backyard of the Detters' Frank Lloyd Wright house, which was open for anyone who wanted a tour. Tradition continued to rule, with the throwing of the garter to the single men, the throwing of the bouquet to the single women, the newlyweds' first dance as spouses, the dance between the bride and her father, and the dance between the groom and his mother.

Otto Haller stayed holed up in Frohna, but Martha and her father made the trip from Cape Girardeau to Oak Park. She wasn't about to miss her son's wedding. Like most mothers, she cried tears of joy at the ceremony.

She and her father sat alone at the reception until they were joined by the wedding officiant himself, Hillman Gehrke. Ed Schroeder and Hillman remembered each other from Hillman's days at seminary, when he sometimes worshiped at Ed's church. Hillman also had caught Martha's eye, but she had never spoken to him, thinking he was out of her league.

"It's such a pleasure to see the two of you," Gehrke said, "and on such a joyous occasion. I'm only sorry that Otto couldn't find it in his heart to perform the ceremony. Maybe someday, he'll come around."

Martha looked down and slowly shook her head.

"Oh, I'm sorry. It was inappropriate of me to stir that pot. Please forgive me," Gehrke said. Martha graciously told him it wasn't a problem at all. It's always better to acknowledge reality than to run from it.

The three of them spent time catching up with one another's lives. Ed Schroeder talked about how impressed he was with Gehrke's career. He tried to get his hands on every scholarly article Gehrke published, and he almost always agreed with Gehrke's conclusions.

"Enough about me," Gehrke said. "Martha, what's going on in your life?"

She avoided talking directly about her husband.

"Well, now that Caleb's grown, I'm exploring some new possibilities. I'm in college! I'm enrolled in the writing program at Southeast Missouri State."

"I'd love to hear more about that," Gehrke said, but before Martha could elaborate, a waiter came by the table to offer drinks and hors d'oeuvres.

Once he left, Martha downplayed her academic pursuits.

"I'm sitting here in the same city that Ernest Hemingway and Carl Sandburg called home," she said. "It's starting to seem a little silly to think I could accomplish much of substance studying and writing in little old Cape Girardeau, the birthplace of, God forbid, Rush Limbaugh."

"Don't sell yourself short. I'm thinking of one writer who was born in St. Louis, just up the river from you. Maya Angelou. After her parents divorced, she lived in Arkansas with her grandmother. She did okay for herself. Or how about Mark Twain? Grew up in Hannibal. It didn't matter where they came from. It mattered that they lived life, thought about it, and wrote about it in ways that people could connect with."

"Well, that's the thing. They lived life. I've spent almost my entire life within a hundred miles of Cape. There's not a lot to draw on."

"What about Emily Dickinson? She was reclusive, rarely left Amherst. But she's recognized as one of America's greatest poets. She lived life in a different way, in her heart, in her mind, in her soul. Geography didn't limit her ability to think, feel, and write."

"Well, I don't think I'll ever be an Angelou, or a Twain, or a Dickinson."

"And I'll never be Martin Luther or Soren Kierkegaard or Paul Tillich. But we can both contribute to this world, to the people around us and maybe a few beyond, and that's no small thing."

Martha's father had been sitting quietly, listening to the conversation.

"I have to tell you, as far as I'm concerned, you've both done something that matters to me. Martha, you gave me a grandson I'm proud of, and Hillman, you helped get him off that obsession with 'pure doctrine' that his dad got all tangled up in. Caleb will have a much better life because of you."

The three sat quietly for a brief time, then the band struck up the Etta James classic, "At Last." Gehrke, almost sheepishly, said to Martha: "Would you like to dance?"

She demurred, protesting that, except for the night's mother/groom dance, she hadn't danced in many years and had forgotten how.

"Then we're on equal footing." Gehrke smiled. "A lame joke, I know. But seriously, I haven't danced since my wife died more than twenty years ago.

How about we start dancing again, together?"

Martha's father encouraged her.

"Come on, the song is half over. It's now or never," Gehrke said, a bit more insistent. "Well, at least till the next song, when I'll ask you again."

Martha looked down, unsure of herself. Still, she rose from the table, her heart beating like a schoolgirl's, and allowed Gehrke to take her hand and lead her to the dance floor. The two fit together well, as if they were meant for the moment. Martha teared up just a bit.

"Nothing's wrong," she told Gehrke when he asked. "It's just I haven't felt this appreciated in many years."

"You're a woman of many talents, I can tell. You deserve to be appreciated."

They danced to the next three songs, growing more comfortable with each other, and then decided to leave together for a late dinner. As they said goodbye to the newly wedded couple, Ashley and Caleb both smiled. Ashley wagged her finger at them and jokingly warned, "Now you kids keep out of trouble, and don't stay out too late!"

* * *

A light, lazy breeze moved through the streets of Oak Park. It gusted occasionally, once with just enough power to push Martha into Gehrke. As they walked, Gehrke took Martha in, noticing the smell of her perfume, her simple but stylish attire, her striking green eyes, and her long, shiny golden hair fluttering in the breeze.

"How come I never paid any attention to this woman back in my seminary days?" he wondered to himself.

They arrived at the Carleton Hotel, where they both were staying. They decided to eat at La Notte, the Italian restaurant just off the hotel lobby. Gehrke ordered a bottle of chianti, and both he and Martha ordered a Caesar salad and lasagna.

As they took part in the ritual of breaking bread and dipping pieces in olive oil and balsamic vinegar, the two chatted for a while about how beautiful the wedding was and what an interesting couple Caleb and Ashley made.

"So help me, I never in a million years would have pictured the two of them together," Gehrke said. "I mean, they came at life so differently. The Ashley I know is always on the search for something new and different. Curiosity might kill a cat, but it keeps Ashley alive. But Caleb? I didn't think he'd want to know anything outside the pages of the Old and New Testament and his own narrow way of reading the Bible. I know he's really smart, though, and I think Ashley has helped expand his world. I can only imagine what all he was exposed to driving Uber for hour after hour. What a pleasant surprise to see the two of them end up with each other!"

Martha smiled, then took a sip of her chianti. "I know he really regrets recording you in class. He's told me so."

Then she looked directly at Gehrke. "So, what makes you think I wouldn't share that same narrow way of reading the Bible? After all, I am married to Otto Haller, the most literal of literalists."

"Maybe so, but you're also the daughter of Ed Schroeder, and I know enough about Ed to know he doesn't operate that way. I'm guessing he had a strong influence on you before you and Otto ever got together."

Gehrke was right, she said. She wasn't fanatical about the Bible, and she knew enough not to think of it as "inspired, inerrant, and infallible," as her husband proclaimed. She believed whatever science discovered about humanity's origins and the secrets of the universe made God more glorious, not less.

"So, Martha, I don't mean to make you uncomfortable, but I knew Otto back in seminary. I can't fathom how someone like him could end up with someone like you. I mean, jeez! Lucky for him, but for you? Not so much, I'd say. If you don't mind my asking, how did you get together?"

Martha rested her chin on her hand and gently shook her head, thinking about how to tell the story. Finally, she proceeded.

"So, like you, Otto occasionally worshiped at Dad's church during his seminary days. He was already strongly conservative by then and kind of kept to himself. I guess you know that since you were in school with him.

"When he filed charges against the sem profs, my dad and I both thought he was crazy. After he graduated, we learned he'd been hired as a pastor in

Frohna, but we didn't pay any attention to him. He was just forty minutes up the road, but he might as well have been in New York, for all we cared.

"You know he grew up in Queens, right? So much for only liberals coming out of New York. His father grew up not far from Cape Girardeau, but the church sent him to a congregation in Queens after he graduated. Otto told me his dad made sure his family didn't mingle with the Catholics, Jews, Muslims, Buddhists, or even other Protestants in the neighborhood. That's one way to stay 'pure' in mind, body, and spirit, I suppose.

"He told me his father believed competition formed strong men, and he kept Otto and his brothers in constant battle with one another. The best way to gain their father's favor was to demonstrate their love for his conservative, dogmatic Lutheranism. And that's how he became who he became, just a boy who hungered for his father's love and found a way to try to win it."

Gehrke shook his head. "I knew he was from New York, and it never made sense to me that he was as conservative as he was. What you're telling me explains a lot."

Martha continued.

"Honestly, I never gave him another thought, but then one day, a couple of years after he began working in Frohna, he showed up at my dad's congregation. I was still helping out there. It's why I didn't go to college. My mother had died of breast cancer when I was in high school, and I knew my dad needed me.

"Out of the blue, Otto asked if I would go out on a date with him. He said we'd probably have a lot in common since we were both pastors' kids. It was odd, but I had nothing going on in Cape, so I accepted. Free dinner and a movie, I thought. We went to see *Newsies*.

"Anyway, it went well enough. He was . . . I wouldn't say charming, but he was polite and fairly attentive. He asked me out again, and I accepted. Then, well, you know. One date led to another. We fell into being an item, and then we fell into being engaged, then we fell into being married. I guess I just sort of let it happen. My dad didn't say much, but I'm pretty sure he wasn't happy about it. And for me, one of the pluses of marrying Otto was I'd still be living near my father.

"During our engagement, Otto said he thought I'd be a perfect pastor's wife. I'd certainly learned what that might entail, watching my mother and then helping out my dad. And so I was . . . 'perfect' . . . for many years. Dutiful, cordial to our congregants, and uncomplaining about his obsession with so-called 'pure doctrine.'

"I adjusted to being married to Otto, but I can't say I was ever head over heels in love. For most of our marriage, it hasn't been hard to ignore his excesses. But the past few years, now that he's a social-media celebrity of sorts, it's gotten out of hand. I just don't share his thirst for retribution against what he calls 'heretics.' Honestly, I don't think God gets very upset about the things Otto says he does. My guess is he's a lot more concerned about the things Jesus talked about. Feeding people, quenching their thirst, clothing them, loving them."

Gehrke smiled.

"I'm thinking Otto underestimates you, especially your curiosity and your intellect. You might not have attended college . . . until now . . . but I can tell you've always been committed to educating yourself and expanding yourself and your horizons."

He raised his glass of chianti.

"A toast to you, Martha Schroeder Haller. To one fascinating creature! I am so happy to be able to get to know you."

She smiled, even as a single tear rolled down her cheek. They clinked their glasses together.

Their food arrived. As they ate, they kept the conversation light. To complete the meal, they asked for decaf coffee and split an order of tiramisu.

Martha wasn't ready for the evening to end.

"All right, so, you've learned more about me tonight, more than most people know. Now tell me more about you."

Gehrke sighed, looked at his watch, and shook his head.

"I'm not dodging your question, but all of a sudden I feel really tired. How about we continue this soon. Really soon!"

He settled the bill and then walked Martha to her room. Neither of them knew exactly how to end the evening. Without either of them leading or following, they fell into an embrace and held it for a good long time. Eventually, Martha pulled away, said "Goodnight, Hillman," and sent him on his way. Once she closed her door, he turned back to look, wondering what exactly might be happening between them.

Breakfast at Yolk

At 6:30 the next morning, Gehrke called the valet to bring his car around and then dialed Martha's room.

"I hope I didn't wake you."

"No, I'm an early riser. Always have been."

"I thought maybe we could have breakfast together. Not here, though. Still too many wedding guests. If they see us together . . . well, you know, people talk."

Martha texted her dad to tell him she was going out for breakfast. She met Gehrke in the lobby, and the two of them headed to Yolk on North Avenue, a spot just far enough to put them outside the orbit of Caleb and Ashley's wedding guests. The two companions slid into a cozy booth overlooking the street. It normally overflowed with traffic, but not this early on a sleepy Sunday morning.

"It's kind of odd not being in church on a Sunday," Martha said. Gehrke said he thought God would understand.

He ordered the dish of the month, prickly pear and lemon poppyseed pancakes. Martha decided on a simple plate of bacon and scrambled eggs. The waiter also brought a carafe of coffee.

"You don't think I'm letting you off the hook, do you?" Martha said.

"What do you mean?"

"I want to hear all about your life. We're not leaving until I do." She smiled, but she wasn't joking.

"Yes, well, okay," Gehrke said. "I'm happy with my life. I've made my share of mistakes, but, you know, there's no point in dwelling on them.

"So, where to start . . . I was an only child. I grew up in Wausau, Wisconsin. Our claim to fame was the Wausau insurance company. That and a large paper mill.

"It was lily white except for the Hmong refugees that came to the area after the Vietnam War. I became fascinated with them, and my parents encouraged my friendships with them. Even among the practicing Christians, I learned, some of the Hmong held onto their cultural traditions, like ancestor worship.

"Conservative Christians would damn them to hell, I guess, but I didn't see it as all that different from people who went to a grave site to talk things over with their dead relatives."

Martha nodded in agreement. "I do that with my mother. I ask her for advice whenever I visit her grave. I've never thought I was doing anything wrong."

"I don't either," Gehrke said. "I certainly didn't see it as a reason not to socialize or worship with the Hmong who joined our congregation. There's a difference between misbelief and unbelief, I figure, and misbelief is forgivable. Besides, someday we'll probably learn we all had our fair share of misbeliefs. For all I know, unbelief might be forgivable too, especially if you've not even heard of Christianity. I think the only unforgivable sin is aggressively shutting love out of your life. Uber-narcissism, I call it.

"Anyway, my friendships with the Hmong made me start to think about becoming a minister. They also made me want to explore life outside the world of the CLCA.

"I graduated with a history degree from the University of Wisconsin and decided to attend the seminary in Cape Girardeau. One problem, though. I needed money, so I worked two years as a long-distance truck driver."

"You're kidding!" Martha said. "I can't imagine you doing that."

"Probably one of the best things that ever happened to me. I got to see just about the whole country. I loved disc-jockeying for myself, playing everything from Bach to Beethoven to Sinatra to Presley to Depeche Mode to Nirvana.

"On Sunday mornings, I'd worship when I could at one of the Transport for Christ trucker ministries scattered throughout the country. They're good people, but you know, not exactly by-the-book Lutherans. It would be good for more Lutherans to worship outside their own little sphere once in a while. I thought being with the truckers was better than sitting alone in a cab listening to some narcissistic radio preacher who thought "Je-E-sus" was a three-syllable word.

"I met all sorts of people on the road. I got to be known as a guy who could talk sense into travelers on the verge of brawling in a diner. People knew I'd fork over a few bucks for supper if they were down on their luck.

"Occasionally I'd let it drop that I was seminary-bound. I didn't talk about it much, you know, on the notion that there's something to the old saw: Preach the Gospel at all times, and if necessary, use words. But once people knew, you'd be surprised how often they would open up. Family problems, money problems, health problems, I heard them all.

"Usually, I didn't have solutions. People just seemed to want somebody to listen without being judged. I'd tell them to hang in there, that we're all in this together, and somehow, there'd be a solution for them. I wouldn't promise miracles, only support. I have to tell you, that two years on the road did way more to turn me into a theologian than the years I spent knocking around seminaries and universities."

"Okay, that's all interesting. But come on. I want to hear about the mistakes. A man like you . . . what kinds of 'mistakes' could you possibly have made? Not paying your phone bill on time? Jay-walking?"

Gehrke hesitated for a bit. Then he focused on Martha's face. He wanted to see her reaction as he said: "How would you feel about . . . drug abuse?"

Her jaw dropped open. "What? No! No, I don't believe it."

It can be hard to stay alert when you're driving a truck for hours on end, Gehrke said. Taking a little speed makes it much, much easier. It was easy to come by on the road.

"And for me, well, it was sort of like how you explained getting involved with Otto. I fell into taking a little, then I fell into taking more, and then I fell into being married to it. I was pretty strung out, so much so that I spent a month in rehab before entering the seminary. And now, you're the third person to know. My mom and dad were the other two. It was a real gut punch for them, but they stayed by me while I got clean. Their support really meant a lot to me."

Martha looked puzzled. "But weren't you regularly tested?"

"Sort of. Remember, I only drove for two years, and I was only tested twice. You get a little advance notice. For fifty bucks, a guy helped me out. He gave me a little of his urine tied inside a condom. I taped it to my thigh and used his instead of mine. Easy! I mean, I could have been in deep trouble if I'd been caught. But I wasn't.

"Ingenious, huh? But yeah, I know. Dishonest too. I did it, though. I needed to keep making the money for seminary. It made me wonder whether I was really worthy of going to the sem. But, and I'm not proud of this, my attitude was do it now, and square it with your conscience later."

Martha sat quietly, and finally said: "Well. I'm shocked. But there's no reason to worry, right? I mean, that's decades in the past."

Gehrke assured her she was right. He took a sip of coffee. Then, he choked up a bit before going on. Quietly, he said drug addiction hadn't been his worst mistake.

"That would be Laura. Oh, I shouldn't say it that way. She wasn't a mistake at all. We had three wonderful years together. Four if you count the year before we married.

"She came from Maine, and she was gorgeous. We met when I was doing my doctoral work at Harvard and she was studying for an MFA in performing arts. She was just a wonderful actor and singer . . . you should have seen her in *The Sound of Music* . . . and she loosened me up quite a bit. To the extent people think of me as a good lecturer, well, I credit her. She showed me how to turn a lecture into a performance, and I strive for that every time I teach.

"The mistake I made was in not insisting that she see a doctor sooner than she did. She complained about back pain and pelvic discomfort for quite a while. Every time I urged her to see a doctor, she put me off. Said she was too busy with rehearsals and classes. When I finally got her to make the appointment, it was too late . . . stage four ovarian cancer.

"It had spread so far and so aggressively that there wasn't anything to be done other than make her comfortable and make sure she knew she was loved. I took a semester off at Harvard, and we moved to Maine so she could be close to her family. When we went back, her parents were distant with me. I'm not sure why. I've always guessed they needed someone to blame, and they might have blamed me."

Martha reached over the table to take Gehrke's hand in both of hers.

"And it sounds like you blame yourself."

"I don't dwell on it. But yeah, it's hard not to. I know it's not rational. I know a lot played into what happened. But I can't shake the notion that I could have done more."

Martha chuckled, which both puzzled and annoyed Gehrke.

"You think this is funny?"

"I'm sorry. It's just that you reminded me of one of my dad's favorite sayings. We need to get past the 'woulda, coulda, shouldas' in our lives. I don't mean to be unsympathetic, and I'm not. But you know you loved her. You know you would have done anything for her. It's tragic how things turned out, I know. Anyone who dies leaves a hole in our hearts that can't really be filled, and that will always be true for you with Laura. I just hope you can find a way to get rid of the guilt you carry. I really think you need to forgive yourself."

Gehrke sat considering Martha's words for a while. Then slowly, he smiled.

"Other people have told me that, of course, in one way or another. But somehow, coming for you, I'm finding more comfort than I have before."

Martha was still holding his hand in hers. She squeezed it for a bit and then let go.

"Glad to be of service," she said. Then she looked at her watch.

"We need to be getting back. I've got to pack before Dad and I hit the road."

Gehrke paid the bill. When they returned to the hotel, they exchanged phone numbers in the lobby.

Martha asked a question she hadn't expected to voice.

"Hillman, what are we doing? I'm a married woman, you know."

"Yes, and I'm a married woman's friend. I can't see anything wrong with that. Let's just leave it there for now. Okay?"

Okay, Martha said.

After a final hug, Gehrke promised he would call. Soon. Eventually, his promise grew to include both "soon" and "often."

The Last Shall Be First?

Hillman Gehrke and Caleb Haller walked together into the Iowa Events Center, collapsing the umbrellas that had shielded them from the torrential rains of August in Des Moines. Both were serving as delegates to the forty-ninth convention of the Confessional Lutheran Church in America.

After checking their umbrellas, they walked the center's hallways. Over decades of service, Gehrke had made a great many friends in the CLCA, and he wanted to introduce Caleb to them as an up-and-coming young churchman. He found friends, but not as many as he expected. The topic of Caleb's father inevitably came up, but Gehrke's friends made him feel welcome as they learned about Caleb's journey away from the "inspired, inerrant, infallible" obsessions of his father.

As the two of them passed delegates and observers, Gehrke and Caleb noticed that many of them sported Triple I lapel pins. The pin wearers seemed confident, almost gleeful, as they flashed the Triple I hand gesture to one another. Among that crowd, most of those who recognized Gehrke looked away from him. Some actually sneered.

They entered the convention's exhibit hall, which was populated with booths from Christian book publishers, colleges and universities, and mission outreach organizations. As they looked around, Gehrke and Caleb couldn't believe their eyes. There, near the back of the hall, was a booth for the Reformation Restoration Alliance.

Gehrke immediately accosted the CLCA PR man, Harold Kreiss, when he entered the hall.

"I thought you said the church had to maintain neutrality over these unfounded allegations of heresy," Gehrke said, nearly screaming.

Kreiss said the church *was* neutral. When Gehrke pointed to the booth of the Double R A, Kreiss said any opponents of the group would have been welcome to buy booth space as well.

"I don't see any opponents," Gehrke said.

That was because none of them asked to buy. They certainly would have been given space if they had come forward, but of course, now it was too late. Every space had been sold.

Gehrke immediately recognized the tactical error. The CLCA True Disciples had worked the church as well as they could, but the group never thought that politicking would continue at the convention itself.

Even so, Gehrke started to lambaste Kreiss, but he was interrupted by a commotion and a buzz in the hall. Near one of the entrances, a crowd swarmed. Hands popped up over delegates' heads, all forming the Triple I Salute. As they neared the horde, Gehrke and Caleb's suspicions were confirmed. Otto Haller had drawn a crowd, shaking hands, signing a few autographs, and posing for selfies with his admirers.

On his website, Haller had encouraged people to look for him at the convention. Even though he wasn't on the CLCA clergy roster, he was coming as an observer. He would welcome seeing a friendly face, and he would be happy to discuss the issues with anyone who wished to do so.

Now, it appeared, his following was both large and enthusiastic. Not even he had suspected just how big an impact he had had on the church that had spurned him for decades.

Neither Gehrke nor Caleb wished to interact with him. They quietly exited the exhibit hall.

* * *

CLCA President Carl Walters, standing behind a lectern and wearing his clerical collar, faced the mass of delegates, who had taken their places on padded folding chairs arranged to face the podium. He opened the convention with prayer, thanking God for all the blessings that had come to the denomination and asking for peace and harmony to reign during all deliberations.

During his State of the Church address, he offered his usual "church by the numbers" report. The congregation count had increased only slightly, but even a slight increase was a blessing when many people were souring on church life. Donations were holding steady. Overseas missions were making converts every month. Oberhausen University enrollment had grown about two percent a year for the past decade.

He cited two areas of concern. U.S. membership was falling, and enrollment at Martin Luther Seminary had been declining at about three percent a year. And even though Oberhausen enrollment was growing, fewer students were interested in church careers. Long term, the denomination needed to take steps to ensure there would be enough pastors and workers to sustain the work and mission of the church.

"As always, though, we believe the Lord will provide, and the best is yet to come," Walters said. "Now, my current term as president of the CLCA has come to an end, but I stand before you willing to continue serving. I am honored to have been nominated once again. To oversee the election, I turn the gavel over to our church facilitator, Jeff Handrich."

Walters's remarks received polite, tepid applause. Handrich took his place behind the lectern. He banged the gavel and declared the election of president to be underway. He referred the delegates to their convention workbooks, which contained biographies of the two nominees, the Reverend Carl Walters, the incumbent, and the Reverend Dr. Jeremiah Marquardt, professor of systematic theology at Martin Luther Seminary. Both men were given an opportunity to speak.

Walters kept his remarks brief, indicating that he already had spoken at length. He said he believed the denomination had done well under his stewardship, remaining healthy despite cultural headwinds faced by churches in general. He had a passion for his work, he said, and believed there was more to be done. He would be grateful for the opportunity to continue in office.

Marquardt took more time and told the group the church needed new leadership.

"I respect President Walters and the work he has done," Marquardt began. "But it has become increasingly clear that the CLCA is infected with a bad spirit. We have professors and pastors among us who no longer believe the Bible is inspired, inerrant, and infallible."

A sizable portion of the delegates erupted into boos and raised their hands above their heads, making the Triple I Salute. Handrich called the assembly back to order.

Marquardt continued.

"We need to restore ourselves as originalists, adhering not only to scripture but also to the Lutheran Confessions. And remember, Luther preached that the Bible could not contradict itself and was truthful in all it affirmed—in matters historical, geographical, scientific, and spiritual.

"Luther also said, 'It is impossible that scripture should contradict itself; it only appears so to senseless and obstinate hypocrites.' It saddens me to say we have such hypocrites in our church, and we will continue to slide downward into irrelevance and oblivion until we rid ourselves of them."

Handrich opened the floor to comments and questions. A sea of hands shot up. Eventually, after a number of affirmations of Marquardt's remarks, Handrich recognized Gehrke.

"My name is Hillman Gehrke."

The convention went silent. Then a chorus of boos arose. Handrich banged his gavel, called for quiet, and eventually, order was restored.

"As some of you know . . . many of you, it seems . . . not long ago, I was the subject of a heresy hearing in this very city. Dr. Marquardt, in fact, sat on the panel that heard the allegations against me. I was exonerated, and for that I'm thankful. I'm not here to relive my case, but I have a message for you, and I ask you to listen carefully.

"This drive to eradicate so-called 'heretics' from our church does not come from charitable hearts. Nothing so divisive can come from God. Our church has a long history of addressing our differences with discussion and dialogue. Until recently, we have not used the tactics of innuendo, smear campaigns, and power politics to try to drive people out of the church and deprive them of their livelihood.

"Students of history are aware of Senator Joe McCarthy in the 1950s and his allegations of communist infiltration into the government. He eventually was stopped, but only after courageous Americans like Joseph Welch and Senator Margaret Chase Smith stood up to his bullying and his bull. It's time to stop the McCarthys in our midst. For this reason, I stand against Dr. Marquardt and urge you to vote for President Walters."

The delegates erupted. Many raised their hands once again in the Triple I Salute. Another contingent broke into a chorus of "The Church's One Foundation Is Jesus Christ Her Lord," an anthem of sorts for those who saw Christ, not the Bible, as the complete, authoritative Word of God. A teardrop fell from Gehrke's eye as the emotion of the moment touched his heart.

Handrich eventually regained control of the assembly, stating that if there were nominations from the floor, now was the time for them to be heard.

A burly, middle-aged gentleman raised his calloused, working-man's hand.

"My name is Brent Buchholz, and I represent the Mid-South Circuit. My congregation is Living Word Lutheran Church in Little Rock. I rise today to make the convention aware that we have a true churchman among us. He alone alerted us to the problem of heretics in the church. He has been slighted. He has been persecuted. Yet he has remained faithful to the Bible. He, and maybe he alone, has the strength and the perseverance to lead us to a mountaintop of purity. He can make us the beacon of truth within all of Christianity. I wish to applaud his work and to place his name in nomination for the presidency of the CLCA. I nominate the Reverend Otto Haller for president of the Confessional Lutheran Church in America."

Again, the room erupted with both cheers and boos. The Triple I Salute shot above the crowd. Haller, sitting in the observers gallery, did not rise. He was as shocked and surprised as anyone that his name had been placed in nomination. Eventually, a slight smile played across his face.

Once things quieted down, Handrich indicated the motion was out of order for one simple reason: A candidate must be on the clergy roster of the CLCA, and Reverend Haller was not.

Brent Buchholz raised his hand again. "I move that this assembly add the Reverend Otto Haller to the clergy roster of the CLCA."

Handrich ruled the motion out of order because it did not follow the existing procedures for qualifying a candidate for the roster. Mr. Haller had been denied admission to the roster when he graduated from the seminary, and the matter had never been revisited.

Buchholz raised his hand: "I move to overrule the chair's ruling."

The motion to overrule required only a simple majority, Handrich knew, but he warned the delegates that adding Haller to the clergy roster would violate the bylaws of the church.

"Then I move to change the bylaws to allow the convention to add Reverend Haller to the clergy roster," Buchholz said.

Handrich said it was only proper that actual language be presented to the delegates so they knew exactly what they were voting on. That wasn't possible at this time, he said.

"Then," Buchholz said, "let's postpone voting for president until 11:30 a.m. tomorrow. The language will be presented first thing in the morning. I move that the first order of business tomorrow should be to vote on the language amending bylaws so Reverend Haller can be added to the roster."

Handrich could think of no procedural reason to stop the motion. It was seconded and passed by a vote of 520 to 489—some delegates had left the floor for one reason or another—and the meeting adjourned for the day.

* * *

The story quickly went national. Network and cable newscasts described the convention as "chaotic" and "in disarray." Religion writers said the church body had displayed a major split between fundamentalists who saw the Bible as infallible and progressives who believed Bible scholars, and laypeople, must acknowledge the findings of modern science and use the tools of literary criticism.

Delegates saw the stories on their smartphones. While they were interested, they needed to concentrate on how they would maneuver through the next day's proceedings. Regardless of where they stood on the candidates and issues, they spent considerable time watching Haller's musings about what had happened on GodsTruthIsMyTruth.com. He wasted no time in returning to his hotel room to record a video.

"What I saw today is a church body that wants to stand up for the truth of the Bible. If the delegates weren't supporting the Bible, the motion to postpone voting for president would have been voted down.

"If you're watching this, I'm sure you're wondering about whether I am truly interested in becoming the president of the CLCA. Regular followers of this website know I've long expressed my support for Dr. Marquardt as the next president. Never in my wildest dreams did I think I would be in the running for the presidency. And maybe I won't be. That all depends on what happens tomorrow.

"My initial inclination was to put a stop to all this. I'm just a lowly country pastor toiling away in rural Missouri. I know nothing about running a large organization. But you know, neither does Dr. Marquardt, and as I've thought and prayed about this, I'm coming to believe the Holy Spirit might be calling me to the position. And so, I've decided to let these wildly improbable developments play out. If things unfold in such a way that I would be elected, then yes, I will serve. It would be my duty, and it would be an honor. Pray for me, please, and pray that the delegates do the work of the Lord. If you elect me, I promise you the church will be cleansed of heretics and impure doctrine once and for all." With that he signed off.

He kept another thought to himself. It would serve Marquardt and the Reformation Restoration Alliance right to see him elected. They walked away from him after all he had done for them. Besides, God was with him, right? Wasn't it Jesus who said, "The last will be first, and the first will be last"? It looked as though the promise might come true.

* * *

Gehrke and Oberhausen's president, Robert Storck, invited Carl Walters to dinner. The group asked Caleb to join them. He might have intimate information about his father that could be useful, they thought.

Over a meal of burgers, fries, and beer, Storck began the conversation.

"Not to say I told you so, Carl, but I told you so. Now we're at the eleventh hour. To be all Catholic about it, it's time for a 'Hail, Mary.' So, do you have any thoughts?"

Walters said he still couldn't believe the delegates would pick Haller or even Marquardt over him. He, after all, had kept the church on a steady course for a dozen years. Besides, he traveled in the same circles as the late Desmond Tutu and the Archbishop of Canterbury. He had valuable connections. Why wouldn't any right-thinking church member want to keep those relationships in place? How could anybody dream of throwing him out of office?

"President Walters, I'm afraid you're really out of touch with your membership," Gehrke said. "I doubt many CLCA members even know who Desmond Tutu and the Archbishop of Canterbury are. I doubt they care. What they care about is stability and order. And I know you believe you've given them both, and so do I. But they're hearing the church is falling apart and is infested with false teachers.

"Say what you will about the other side. They've scared the daylights out of many of our members, and they're relentless. I've tried to launch a counterattack, but I've had limited success. The sad truth is, if you pit reason against fear, fear wins, at least in the short term.

"Right now, all I can think of is for you to fight fear with fear. Tell delegates the CLCA will become a laughingstock if we vote in a man the church refused to ordain when he graduated. Tell them a major institution like the CLCA will fall apart if we hand it over to a man who's done nothing more than run a website and be pastor to a two-hundred-member congregation. Tell them witch hunts—warlock hunts, I guess—have never ended well, and they won't end well in 21st-century America either. Fear is powerful. It may be the only option you have."

The group asked Caleb whether he had any thoughts about his father. Only that he's a petty man, Caleb said, and he would never doubt his ability to head up the CLCA. Also, his circle of friends is small, and if Marquardt and his friends in the Reformation Restoration Alliance have abandoned him, it's even smaller. If he's elected, he'll look to appoint loyal people to important posts. Not necessarily smart. Not necessarily experienced. Not necessarily competent. Just loyal.

Walters decided to lead the group in prayer before they disbanded. He asked God to protect the church tomorrow. He asked that the delegates be led to a God-pleasing decision. And he pledged that he and the friends gathered here would be faithful to God regardless of the outcome of tomorrow's vote.

* * *

Who is Brent Buchholz? That was the question on the minds of Jeremiah Marquardt and the Reformation Restoration Alliance as they met. They tapped their friends in Little Rock, but they had little information about Buchholz. He was a layman, just a pipefitter who made a good living and took care of his family. His uncle had been a CLCA minister, but beyond that, his family had no known involvement in the church.

They reached Buchholz in his hotel room and asked what his interest was in nominating Otto Haller. Nothing special, he said. He followed Haller and his website and just thought he was a good man and a prophet. If the church needed shaking up, Haller was the guy to make it happen. And the church apparently needed shaking up, he said.

They suggested as diplomatically as they could that Haller wasn't the right man for the presidency. He knew nothing about running a large organization, and if Buchholz knew him better, he would see that Haller was too much of a hothead to be effective as a church leader.

They also tried playing a card they hadn't tried before.

"Otto Haller has some major family issues," Marquardt told Buchholz. "We have not wanted to embarrass him, but you should know he is estranged from his wife and son. He can't keep his family together. What kind of leader can't run his own family? We can't have a man like that at the top of the Confessional Lutheran Church in America."

Buchholz said his best friend was divorced through no fault of his own, and maybe Haller wasn't the cause of his family problems. Besides, God often chose flawed people as leaders. David committed adultery and killed a man. Abraham slept with Hagar, who was not his wife. Solomon had a thousand wives and concubines. Maybe it's time to stop expecting perfection from church leaders.

Please, for the sake of the church, they said to Buchholz, stop trying to get Haller elected.

"I didn't have a lot invested in this before," he told the group, "but now, there's nothing you can say or do that would make me give up. Tomorrow, I'm going to give a holler for Haller. I'll bring that slogan to the convention hall. And you should know, gentlemen, I may be just a pipefitter, but I'm also a union leader, and I know parliamentary procedure inside and out, probably better than Handrich. I'll play by the rules, and I will get this done. Now, leave me alone." With that, he disconnected.

* * *

The next morning, Buchholz and several friends stood at the entrances to the convention hall. They gave delegates language written by Buchholz to change bylaws so that Haller could be added to the clergy roster. When Handrich gaveled the convention to order, Buchholz moved that his language be adopted. The motion received a second, and debate opened.

One of the youngest delegates stepped to one of the microphones placed around the hall. In the observers gallery, Otto Haller appeared impassive, but inside, his heart sank.

"My name is Caleb Haller," he said. "My father is Otto Haller. Many of you appear determined to place him on the clergy roster of the CLCA. If this were two or three years ago, I would be voting for this motion. Seeing him on the roster is something I wanted for most of my life. But no more.

"I've come to see my father, not as a pastor, not as a spiritual leader, but as a bitter man with a black heart. He fights for so-called 'pure doctrine,' but he hits below the belt. I have come to know some of the men he condemns, including Hillman Gehrke. I can't honestly say I know every jot and tittle of

Dr. Gehrke's beliefs and doctrines. But I know he's a believer in Christ and an ethical, caring man. He reached out to help me even after I harmed him. Still, my father tried to get him expelled from the church."

A chant came up from part of the crowd. "Gehrke is a heretic! Gehrke is a heretic! Gehrke is a heretic!" Handrich banged his gavel repeatedly, and eventually the chant died down.

Caleb teared up as he continued. "I've seen my father harm my mother. He has disowned me. He has shown us no remorse. We're a family in name only. Believe me, you don't want to claim this man as a pastor in this church body." He sat down.

The murmur among the crowd indicated some people sympathized with Caleb, but more were willing to overlook any family problems Haller might have. After all, people rationalized, who doesn't have them? And how serious could they be?

The next speaker identified himself as a layman from Minnesota. He stood with Otto Haller, he said. He wasn't interested in Haller's family problems, and the assembly had no idea who was to blame, if in fact they existed.

"I'm here to holler for Haller!" he exclaimed. "You all should do the same. Holler for Haller! Holler for Haller! Holler for Haller!" Brent Buchholz had taught a few cronies the chant, and now it rose from the crowd.

Again, Handrich had to bang the gavel until order was restored.

Carl Walters asked to address the gathering. Nothing good will come from a vitriolic heresy hunt throughout the church, he warned. What's more, the CLCA will become a worldwide laughingstock if delegates elect a man whose biggest achievement in life is running a hateful website filled with lies and disinformation. Walters argued that he had administered the denomination with a steady hand.

"I have had built bridges to others throughout Christendom, and I've expanded the mission work of the church," he said. "Re-elect me, and I will continue to do the work of the Lord."

Another gentleman, this one from Ohio, called the question, which cut off all discussion. When the votes were tallied, the bylaws were changed, and the way was cleared to place Haller on the roster. The assembly quickly did so by a vote of 550 to 474. This was the margin the Reformation Restoration Alliance predicted they had built for their cause. Their verified delegates supported Haller. It remained to be seen whether they would back Marquardt when they voted for president.

Buchholz moved to add Haller to the list of candidates for president, and the resolution carried. Handrich reluctantly ruled that, like Walters and Marquardt, Haller would be given time to address the convention.

The pastor from Frohna, Missouri, had never stood before such a large crowd. He climbed the stairs to the podium, dressed as always in his black suit and clerical collar, and he took time to marvel at the Jumbotron that displayed his image.

He enjoyed seeing the adulation that flowed from his supporters, but even more, he reveled in the disdain emanating from his detractors. Running a website had its ego satisfactions, but seeing the faces of people as they reacted to him brought a whole other level of gratification. He realized he wanted the presidency more than he had ever wanted anything. Before speaking, he made some quick political calculations. Then he opened his mouth and heard his voice amplified through the convention center sound system more powerfully than he had ever experienced.

"First," he began, "it brings joy to my heart to see my son, Caleb, here. I want to tell him and my wife, Martha, that I love them despite their turning their backs on me. I want to heal the rifts between us, and I believe we can when they yield to the word of God. I am ready to resume my place at the head of our family, and I pray they are ready to resume their places as well."

Haller's supporters thought this sounded contrite and conciliatory. Caleb had another word for it—calculating.

"I'm honored by being placed, after all these years, on the clergy roster of the Confessional Lutheran Church in America. Even during my seminary days, I saw that heresy was making inroads into our church. When I tried to fight it, church leaders shunned me and banished me. Today, that has changed!"

A roar of approval emerged alongside a chorus of jeers.

"Now, if you elect me to the presidency, we will restore the CLCA to purity. We will make the CLCA pure again! As Dr. Gehrke once suggested, we will properly define what is and isn't heresy. Where the church has made partnerships with impure denominations and organizations, we will terminate them. And I guarantee you, we will grow as a church. Many people out there are looking for a church with the purity we will create. People will flock to us as they discover we have what they seek.

"I need to say a word of thanks to the congregation that has supported me for many years, Ebenezer Lutheran Church in Frohna. I love the members there, and I'm grateful to them for giving me a place to stand. If I'm elected, I will make sure the congregation is served by a doctrinally pure pastor. Of course, all our congregations will be served by such pastors once you elect me as the leader of this mighty church body.

"I've let it be known previously that I supported Dr. Marquardt for the presidency. He has been a guiding force in my life, and I know if you elect him, he will serve the church well. He is, however, not far from his retirement years. I'm a dozen years his junior. I promise you I will fill the post of president for many years, or as long as you'll have me, if you honor me by choosing me for the job.

"I ask you today to vote not only for me but also for all the candidates who have been vetted by the Reformation Restoration Alliance, a group I am proud to have founded. A sample ballot indicating Bible-believing candidates has been distributed. Vote for them, and we'll be in good hands. Finally, I ask you to vote to establish the CLCA Theological Magisterium. We will at last have the mechanism we need for formally defining pure doctrine and errant heresy.

"Thank you again for nominating me. If elected, I promise I will follow through to make this church a mighty fortress of purity."

After the cheers subsided, a delegate moved that nominations be closed, and the motion was seconded and carried. The bylaws required that the winning candidate needed a majority of those who voted, or 513. After the first round, Haller had 475, Marquardt 400, and Walters 149. The sitting president of the CLCA, shocked and chagrined, had been deposed.

In the runoff, Haller defeated his mentor and former professor, Jeremiah

Marquardt, by a vote of 526 to 349. In protest, the 149 delegates who voted for Walters, including Caleb and Gehrke, chose not to vote. Overnight, an erstwhile pariah had become a church president. The CLCA, once a sea of tranquility within Christendom, had been roiled by a freakish rogue wave powered by equal measures of fear, anger, pride, and vengeance.

Handrich handed the gavel to Haller, who believed God had chosen him to be his warrior for pure doctrine and the Bible in this time and place. Haller blessed the delegates with the sign of the cross then hailed them with the Triple I Salute. Many cheered. Many others, those dismayed by what had happened, flowed into the aisles toward the exits. They joined once again in a verse of "The Church's One Foundation."

As the convention unfolded, the Reformation Restoration Alliance achieved everything it wished. Its candidates won every position of power. The CLCA Theological Magisterium became a reality. Otto Haller had all the tools he needed to enforce doctrinal purity in the church he now led.

II

Part Two

*It is said that power corrupts, but actually
it's more true that power attracts the corruptible.*
-David Brin

Haller's Agenda

After concluding that Martha would not be reconciling with him anytime soon, Otto Haller rented a furnished, two-bedroom apartment within walking distance of CLCA headquarters. The $2,300-a-month rental payment had been unthinkable to him only a month before, but his new salary—$270,000 a year—made it more than manageable.

From his tenth-story unit, he could see the Iowa Events Center, where his people rose up to elevate him to the church presidency. And why not? he thought. He hadn't looked to be elected, but clearly, he was being called to do the Lord's work. He would get on with the business of house cleaning—church cleaning—just as soon as circumstances allowed.

He shipped his volumes of heretic-hunting materials to a storage facility in Des Moines. He wanted them nearby as he started to exercise true power over heretics either alleged or confirmed.

To keep GodsTruthIsMyTruth.com online, he saw to it that Ebenezer Lutheran Church called a young pastor with the skills needed to maintain the website. Haller's plan was to use the site for content too fiery for normal church communication channels.

The congregation agreed to pay the man for his pastoral duties, and Haller appropriated CLCA money to compensate him for time spent on the website. He directed the accountants to transmit the money from his presidential discretionary fund, which Walters had used for traveling when he needed to be present at convocations and disaster response efforts worldwide. No sense dipping into his presidential salary to pay for his website, he thought, even though he was making nine times more than he made in Frohna.

Several congregations invited him to worship with them as he took up residence in Des Moines. A tithe from $270,000 was worth courting, after all. Haller settled on Gethsemane Lutheran Church. He was acquainted with the pastor, Herb Sellmeyer, from his seminary days. Sellmeyer was a Bible believer, Haller knew. He had no taste for the rough-and-tumble of church warfare, but he would make his pulpit available if Haller had anything he wanted to say.

The recently elected president knew he had burned a few bridges with his colleagues at the Reformation Restoration Alliance. They had ruffled his feathers by telling him not to attend the convention, but he calculated they could be valuable foot soldiers. To repair the relationship, he asked them to become an informal cabinet of advisors. Most of them, not used to having influence in the national church body, gladly accepted.

Haller's top priority was the investigation of Oberhausen University and Martin Luther Seminary to determine exactly what was being taught at the schools. On the second day of his presidency—"after learning where the bathroom was," he joked—he commanded Robert Storck, president of Oberhausen, and Randall Bertram, president of Martin Luther Seminary, to forward all the syllabi of theology and Bible classes being taught at their institutions. Additionally, he told Storck to send syllabi of all Oberhausen history, science, sociology, psychology, and political science classes. Within twenty-four hours, Storck called Bertram. Together, they placed a call to Haller's administrative assistant, Betty Neeb, to demand a meeting.

When she went to inform him of the request, Haller was enjoying the view from his third-floor corner office, downing a cup of coffee and reviewing a profile of himself in the most recent issue of *Christianity Today*. The headline: "Upstart Rebel Country Pastor Rides Heresy Hunt to the Presidency of the CLCA." He held out his hand to keep her in check until he finished the article.

"They said it was urgent, eh. Tell you what, Betty. Tell them I'm swamped, and pencil them in for . . . I don't know . . . two weeks from today. And tell them I want my syllabi by the end of the week." The syllabi never arrived.

Storck met Bertram at Des Moines International Airport on the morning of October 7. Before heading to Haller's office, the two of them took time at

Starbucks to calm down and plot out their game plan.

"This place started a real thing in the fall, huh?" Bertram said as they grabbed a table. "Pumpkin spice this, pumpkin spice that. I swear, I saw pumpkin spice Spam at the grocery store the other day. It's like a monster gone berserk."

The two commiserated that they had their own monster to tame. Storck said he was hearing that many people voted for Haller because they thought it would be good to shake things up in a rather placid church body. They hadn't factored in that he might end up pulling the whole church down.

"If he and his storm troopers start meddling in what we teach, he'll have a rebellion on his hands," Bertram said. "My faculty members aren't going to hand over their syllabi without a fight, and I don't blame them. In fact, I won't even relay the demand for them to do so. Haller has to be stopped, and he has to be given a lesson on the limits of power and the respect owed the workers who serve this church. If they were heretics, you and I would never have let them join our faculties in the first place, right?"

Storck and Bertram made a pact before finishing their coffee. No syllabus would make its way from their campuses into the hands of Haller and his Theological Magisterium.

As they exited the elevator to walk toward Haller's office, Storck noticed a certain piece of art had been changed. The modern Jesus in the hallway had been replaced by Warner Sallman's blond-haired, blue-eyed *Head of Christ,* Haller's favorite painting.

Both men stood about half a head taller than Haller as they walked into his office, and their frames were more substantial than the running devotee from Frohna. Haller showed no signs of intimidation as he offered his hand to each man. Still, he chose to sit behind his desk rather than inviting the men to join him at his cluster of couches and easy chairs. The desk established a barrier that Haller wanted to keep in place, and he wanted there to be no doubt about who held the power in this collection of clergymen.

"So, gentlemen, I trust your academic year has gotten off to a good start. You two control the underpinnings of our church. You shape our leaders. You teach them what to think and how to think. There's nothing more important for the ongoing health of the church, and it's my responsibility to know what you're teaching. That's why I asked for your syllabi. My questions to you are simple. Where are they? Why don't I have them? When will I get them?"

The men entered a staring contest with Haller. They were not quick to answer. Finally, Storck responded.

"Randall and I both have worked to foster a spirit of trust with our faculties, and we have assured them their abilities are treasured and their academic freedom is always safeguarded. If we tell them we're going to be a conduit to send their syllabi to you, that we're going to let church headquarters control what they teach, we'll destroy that trust. They haven't forgotten the ordeal Hillman Gehrke had to suffer. We're not about to let them think they're being set up for more of the same."

Haller responded that Gehrke still hadn't received what was coming to him, but he would in time. Then he calmly explained that if faculty members were teaching in accordance with pure doctrine and the Bible, they had nothing to fear. As president of the church, he had an obligation to verify the content of the courses being taught under his authority.

"The church put us in charge of doing just that," Bertram protested, "and our institutions have the respect of higher education executives throughout the country. There's no reason to call the quality and the content of our courses into question."

Storck backed up Bertram, and then he asked why Haller's request was so wide-ranging. Why did he want syllabi from history, science, sociology, psychology, and political science classes as well as theology classes?

"God's word needs to dictate content in all those fields," Haller said. "I want to see what's being taught about the historical reality of the Exodus, about the age of the universe, about Adam and Eve and the lie of evolution, about racism and classism, about human sexuality, about the superiority of capitalism. If Oberhausen is handling those subjects and similar subjects in accordance with the word of God, the university will have nothing to fear."

"As Randall said, the church put us in charge of overseeing what is taught at our schools, not you, not your Theological Magisterium," Storck said.

"We're accountable to our boards of regents for doing so. I'm not willing to hand over that responsibility to you."

A wry smile came over Haller's face.

"That's perfect," he said. "Have you met with your newly elected boards of regents? I think you might find they will have no problem with the request I've made. It's all right, gentlemen. I'll take these matters up with them. You can go now."

Within a month, Haller had the syllabi he sought courtesy of the regents elected at the CLCA convention. The regents asked for the resignations of Storck and Bertram, who were offered generous separation packages in exchange for their silence on the matters that had transpired. Neither man was in position financially to refuse the offer. With them moved aside, Haller began to engineer things so men more to his liking presided over two of the CLCA's major assets.

Haller sent a revised version of his twenty-question questionnaire to each faculty member at the schools, asking for their name, educational background, and years served in the CLCA. He included this linchpin question:

"What is your stance on the irrefutable idea that the Bible is inspired, inerrant, and infallible?"

More than ninety percent of the questionnaires came back with exactly the same response:

"That certainly is an idea."

"Rampant collusion!" Haller fumed. "We'll be doing something about that, and it won't be long."

When they heard about the questionnaire, the Higher Learning Commission and the Association of Theological Schools, the organizations responsible for accrediting Oberhausen and the seminary, reacted strongly. They announced they were suspending the accreditation of the schools pending a thorough investigation of the incidents within the CLCA.

Professors and students at both schools carried on but feared their careers and employment prospects would be jeopardized if accreditation were rescinded. They protested. Most of them began searching for more conventional schools to pursue their careers and their degrees.

Haller ordered his PR man, Harold Kreiss, into his office.

"I want you to issue a news release. Say the CLCA isn't worried about losing accreditation at our schools if it means we're being faithful to the word of God."

"But … but … President Haller, accreditation is a big deal," Kreiss tried to argue. "No one wants to teach at or graduate from a school that isn't accredited."

"Look, Harold. It's not a problem. We can always find some outfit to accredit our schools. Now, go write that release and get it distributed."

* * *

President Haller enjoyed his new title. He chose to believe he had a mandate to enforce doctrinal purity in the CLCA. The pre-convention politicking pursued by the Reformation Restoration Alliance, however, had produced a collection of delegates not representative of the entire church. The mandate Haller claimed to have was an illusion, maybe a delusion.

As a result, within six months after Haller assumed office, nearly 750 of the CLCA's 6,000 congregations initiated actions to withdraw from the church body. Among them were some of the denomination's largest congregations, which consistently delivered substantial chunks of the CLCA yearly budget.

Initially, Haller tried to appeal to loyalty to convince congregations to stay with the national church body. He placed phone calls to pastors like John Entsminger, leader of the 3,000-member Messiah Lutheran Church in Cleveland. The congregation had found a way to thrive as a kind of hybrid Lutheran church with some nondenominational touches. It used video heavily in worship services and on its website. Its sanctuary was dominated by two huge video screens. But true to its Lutheran heritage, it boasted the largest pipe organ in a five-state area.

"Pastor Entsminger, I'm disappointed to hear your congregation is thinking of leaving the CLCA," he began. "What's prompting your decision?"

"We're not thinking of leaving. We've left. And what's prompting our decision? That's easy. You and your brownshirt vigilantes are destroying the church. We want no part of the new-look CLCA."

"So, you're telling me you're willing to fall in with the heretics, that you don't believe in the truth of the Bible anymore?"

"I'm telling you my congregation and I are sickened by the ill winds you've brought into the church. We're not willing to put one red penny behind your administration, and we're not willing to be affiliated with the hate factory you're creating."

"Where's your loyalty?" Haller asked? "Messiah Lutheran is a founding member of the CLCA. It's been with the church for more than a hundred fifty years. You can't walk away now."

"As I just told you, we already have, and we're not coming back. My members and I are of one mind. First, we question the notion that the CLCA was ever doctrinally impure. Second, if the imposition of your idea of 'doctrinal purity' means the destruction of love, civility, and kindness, we want no part of it."

Then obviously, Haller responded, all of Messiah Lutheran's members and its pastor rejected the word of God, and he had pity on their souls. Entsminger offered no response. He simply disconnected from the call.

After failing to persuade unfaithful congregations to remain in the CLCA, Haller turned to filing lawsuits. But in the model constitution and bylaws written for congregations by the CLCA, procedures for leaving the denomination were clearly laid out. As long as congregations followed them, and they did, there was nothing Haller could do to stop them. Pastors of seceding congregations even had the right to take their pensions with them.

Haller provided a list of all the defecting congregations to GodTruthIsMy Truth.com, which updated and published it as needed. The list accomplished nothing, however, beyond satisfying Haller's penchant for revenge.

The coffers of the denomination took a major hit. Haller and the CLCA's board of directors had to come to grips with rapidly declining revenue. The denomination's national publication, *Lutheran Voice,* published an article cataloging how congregations benefited by being part of the CLCA.

John Mueller, the church's vice president of finance, made the case. "Most important, of course, are the faithful, trained clergymen and church workers available to you," he wrote. "Beyond that are Sunday school books, hymnals, communion ware and supplies, top-quality vestments for your pastors, and financing for your building projects at attractive rates.

"You get to expand your ministry's reach through the church's overseas missionaries. Because of the economies of scale, you get all these things and more, cost-effectively. It's vital that the church body prosper so it can continue to serve you in these ways."

Mueller then revealed what he really wanted to ask.

"We're not discouraged by the recent loss of a handful of CLCA congregations," he wrote, "but we need our remaining congregations to step up. We're asking that congregations submit not ten percent but rather eighteen percent of the offerings they collect to support us at the national level. Taking this step will be both satisfying and God-pleasing."

Mueller sent a formal letter to each congregation specifying exactly how much more money the congregation was expected to forward. Church treasurers throughout the country gave a collective groan. Most of their congregations operated week to week, just hoping there would be enough money in the collection plate to keep the bill collectors at bay. One by one, they responded with variations on a common theme: "Fat chance."

* * *

Kurt "Gearshift" Richter, the political consultant from Indianapolis, saw his cherished CLCA blandness evaporating right before his eyes. He was an astute observer of national politics, but church politics confounded him. He never anticipated Haller's ascent to the presidency, but then again, who would have?

Richter saw most church issues as a tempest in a teapot with little impact outside denominational boundaries. He knew Haller was a zealot—a wacky one at that—but the havoc he could wreak, and the negative headlines that came in his wake, took Richter by surprise.

The truth was, Richter got involved with Haller and his cause as a favor to his pastor, doubting that Haller would succeed, even with his guidance. Richter wasn't really invested in the Triple I's of "inspired, inerrant, infallible." He was more in the "whatever floats your boat" camp. Not cynical, exactly. More "live and let live." Whatever was going on between people and their God was their business, not his, he figured.

His guiding light on religion and the afterlife was Laura Nyro's "And When I Die": "I can swear there ain't no heaven, but I pray there ain't no hell." If he was wrong, he figured, well, God loves a great negotiator. Just ask Abraham. Richter believed in his negotiation skills. He thought he probably could talk God into giving him a piece of prime real estate inside the pearly gates.

He took pride in his reputation as a savvy political consultant, but he made a lot more money in real estate. He and his partners at Richter and Rolfe Real Estate Strategies LLC specialized in buying up distressed properties, improving them, and selling them or bringing in new tenants with ideas for profitable businesses.

After thinking about what was happening in the CLCA in the aftermath of Haller's election, Richter convened a conference call with his nationwide network of partners, who knew the ins-and-outs of real estate in medium to large markets. To prepare for the call, he asked his colleagues to send him a back-of-the-envelope calculation of the worth of CLCA congregational real estate in each of their markets. Be conservative, he said.

"Ladies and gentlemen," he began the call, "I've consolidated your estimates. Collectively, CLCA properties in our markets are worth about three billion dollars, and that's only the congregational real estate. It doesn't include district offices, the national headquarters, Oberhausen University, and Martin Luther Seminary."

That's a good chunk of change, someone on the call said. But so what? It's not like the group was going into the church business.

Richter said he wasn't sure exactly where his thinking might lead. But right now, the CLCA was awash in chaos.

"And as we all know, chaos breeds opportunity. Let's keep our eyes on the situation. And if you're not Lutheran, maybe it's time you think about joining a CLCA congregation. As you're shopping around, don't worry about the theology. Just look for a congregation that meets the acid test of real estate: location, location, location."

Courting Dr. Marquardt, Again

aller's rise to the top of the CLCA strained his relationship with Jeremiah Marquardt. For nearly two years, Marquardt believed he would become the church body's president. He convinced his wife they would travel the world at the expense of the church.

He had enjoyed the adulation he experienced on his speaking tour, which was financed by Haller's Reformation Restoration Alliance. He had supported Haller's rabble-rousing, thinking the church needed cleansing. Never, however, had he thought of Haller as presidential material.

It was humiliating for him, an accomplished scholar, to lose the CLCA presidency to a rural pastor whose claim to fame was running an inflammatory website. After an obligatory handshake to congratulate Haller—"something for the cameras"—and a public prayer asking God to bless the new president, Marquardt vowed never to speak to his turncoat of a former student again. Back in Cape Girardeau, the seminary professor took to calling his new church president "Judas" to trusted colleagues.

Then, one morning, about six months after the church convention, Haller showed up at Marquardt's office, a windowless cracker box of a room and a stark contrast to Haller's presidential accommodations in Des Moines. An invitation to sit and get comfortable was not offered.

"Dr. Marquardt," he said, still deferential to his former professor, "I hope you know I never sought the presidency. This Brent Buchholz who nominated me? I have no idea who he is. I would have voted for you, if only I had had a vote. I felt I had to accept after the way things unfolded."

Marquardt glared at his former student. He reminded Haller that "the way things unfolded" included a convention speech in which Haller implied Marquardt was just about ready to be put in a box and lowered into his grave. The younger man apologized, wishing he could take those words back. He just got caught up in the moment and didn't think through everything he was saying. Marquardt reminded him that a requirement for seeking forgiveness is repentance, which Haller seemed to be lacking.

Silence engulfed the two men, and only Haller could end it.

"Maybe this will convince you of my contrition," he said. "I've come to ask you to assume the presidency of Oberhausen University. The church needs you to whip that faculty into shape. We need a true believer who will be a purifying fire to the school. We need someone with the academic credentials to command respect. We need you."

The professor turned his chair so Haller could see only the back of his head. Slowly, he turned around again, glowering at the man who had taken the job he wanted.

"Not interested."

Marquardt should think seriously about the offer, Haller said.

"The presidency of Oberhausen pays four times what a seminary professor makes in Cape Girardeau. The president's office is luxurious, and the presidential home is palatial. If it's travel your wife wants, the two of you could go anywhere—Europe, Asia, Africa, Australia, South America—in the name of visiting and collaborating with other university presidents. And maybe the best benefit of all: there would be a second chance at taking down Hillman Gehrke and others of his ilk at Oberhausen."

Marquardt kept silent, but Haller senses his resistance was thawing.

"I'm still inclined not to accept, but I suppose it's only right that I talk this over with my wife."

Haller told him to take all the time he needed, within reason, of course. An answer in the next couple of weeks would be fine.

* * *

Before leaving Cape Girardeau, Haller, dressed as always in his collar, made one more stop to a wood-frame house on a tree-lined street. After climbing the rickety stairs to a porch in need of painting, he knocked on the front door. No one answered, so he moved to a window to peer into the house.

He saw his estranged wife sitting on a couch. She was reading, but what it was he couldn't tell. He tapped on the window. She looked up but failed to acknowledge him. He kept tapping. She retreated to her bedroom.

Eventually, Ed Schroeder opened the door and stood by it, blocking entrance to the house.

"Go away, Otto. Martha doesn't want to talk with you."

Haller walked back to the door and stood toe to toe with his father-in-law.

"I'm her husband. She has to."

No, she doesn't, Schroeder said. He held back Haller as he tried to muscle his way into the house.

"You might as well hear it from me," Schroeder said. "Come next week, you'll be receiving notice that Martha is initiating divorce proceedings. She's willing to keep it quiet. She certainly has no desire to embarrass you, Mr. Church Body President. But she definitely has no desire to stay with you either. So, please just leave."

Haller became enraged, and he slung his father-in-law aside to search the house for Martha. He failed to notice the two Cape Girardeau police officers who had pulled up in response to the 911 call Martha had made. One of them ran inside the house while the other helped Ed Schroeder to his feet. When Haller saw the officer, he froze.

"Friend, you're not exactly doing your collar proud, are you?" the officer said. "Why don't you come outside and tell me what's going on."

Haller followed the officer but said he'd rather not talk about the incident, and he'd rather not give his name.

"What a surprise! Most people would rather not, my friend. Pastor Schroeder, can you tell me what's going on here?" The officer had been a member of Schroeder's congregation and had known him for years.

"I could, Rick, but if it's all the same to you, I think it would be best for everyone if we just forget about it and send this man on his way. I don't think he'll be causing any more trouble. He doesn't live around here. I think he can figure out he'll be best off just leaving us alone."

The policeman said he was obligated to file a report about the incident and would need the intruder's name and address, which Haller grudgingly furnished. The report would be part of the public record, the policeman explained, but it could be squirreled away if Haller promised never to act up anywhere in Cape Girardeau, ever again, which he did.

The two officers stayed on Schroeder's porch until the man in the collar pointed his rental car toward St. Louis to catch a plane to Des Moines. Only after the officers left did Martha emerge from her room. She sat next to her father on the living-room couch, weeping silently as he comforted her.

On the way back to the station, the two officers stayed silent for a while. Finally, one said: "You know who that was, don't you?"

"I do. I imagine there's quite a story to be told there."

The report was squirreled away, as discussed, but the officers promised each other they'd keep track of it, just in case.

* * *

Fear stalked Haller for days after he returned to Des Moines. He might be able to explain away any divorce proceedings against him. After all, it wasn't his fault that his wife had turned into a feminist. But if word leaked out that the police had been called on him, he didn't think he could live it down.

He tried as best as he could to separate his personal woes from his presidential duties. Eventually, he breathed more easily as neither story surfaced.

The call from Jeremiah Marquardt came exactly two weeks after Haller had visited him.

"I'll accept the offer," he told Haller. "But this doesn't mean you and I are reconciled. I'll work with you to cleanse the university, but our relationship will be strictly business. I'll feign a friendship with you, when necessary. I'll be cordial, when necessary. But I'll never trust you again, and I'll never be your friend."

Haller thanked Marquardt for taking the position. He said he regretted the

160

rift in their relationship. He'd try to make amends so that maybe, someday, the relationship between Marquardt and him could be restored.

He then urged Marquardt to make the reinstatement of accreditation at Oberhausen one of his first priorities. Marquardt said he'd been thinking about how to address the issue.

After he disconnected the call, Haller thought to himself: So, Marquardt's coming to Oberhausen. No surprise there. Mrs. Marquardt just couldn't walk away from that beautiful house and her newfound travel budget. Every man has his price. Every woman, too.

Fired

Jeremiah Marquardt assumed the presidency of Oberhausen University in May 2028, the end of the school year. He used the summer to adjust to Des Moines and make plans for the school he now led.

The last week in October, as the days shortened in their march toward winter, Hillman Gehrke saw a meeting notice pop up on his computer. Marquardt was commanding Gehrke to come to his office at 8:30 a.m. the next morning. Immediately, Gehrke reached out to Martha Haller in Cape Girardeau.

Since meeting at Caleb and Ashley's wedding, the two had stayed in touch via Facetime, often visiting with each other far into the night. Martha would tell Gehrke about her classes and the latest story she was working on. She talked about how her fellow students, decades younger, graciously helped her learn to navigate Canvas, the web-based learning management system used by colleges and universities nationwide. After attending a play on campus, she would share every detail with Gehrke.

When Haller invaded her father's home, Martha turned to Gehrke for comfort. Once she initiated divorce proceedings against Haller, Gehrke was among the first to know.

"You're both in the same city now," she said. "He probably doesn't know we know each other, but in case he does, you should be careful. He could be vicious if he thinks we're an item."

"Which I hope we are!" Gehrke said. "Look, if it's the same Otto Haller I knew during my seminary days, I'm not worried. He's a runner, not a fighter. It doesn't take much bravery to take pot shots at people on a snarky website.

He's really just a little coward. I could hold my own against him, if it ever came to that."

"I have no doubt that's true. And when I say vicious, I'm not necessarily thinking he'd want a fistfight. But he's a petty man, and he wields power over you in ways he never did before. Just be on your guard. I wouldn't be surprised if he's recruiting Marquardt to do his dirty work. And Marquardt might want another go-around at convicting you as a heretic."

"It's possible. There's no provision for avoiding double jeopardy in church law. But I have tenure, so I'll be able to play that card if he comes after me," Gehrke said. "He can try to make my life miserable, I suppose, but he'll find me to be a tenacious opponent. Things will work out, regardless. I'm anxious right now, but I'm not overly worried."

Martha told him to call as soon as his meeting with Marquardt ended. She would be praying for him, she said.

"I think I'm falling in love with you," she told him.

"I know I'm falling in love with you," he responded.

* * *

The next morning, Gehrke woke up early to put in some time at the gym before heading to Marquardt's office. He rarely wore his collar, but Marquardt always did, and Gehrke thought it would be wise to "collar up." It was the proper attire for clergy combat.

He showed up promptly at 8:30. Marquardt and a representative from the university's human resources department greeted him. It went unsaid that the HR rep was there to witness what was about to transpire, and if necessary, to testify about it later.

Marquardt offered him a seat, a cup of coffee, and a Danish. Gehrke accepted them all with a calmness he hadn't been sure he could muster. He had prevailed over Marquardt during their last encounter, the heresy hearing. Marquardt had more direct power over him now, but Gehrke felt neither intimidated, nor inferior, nor subservient to his new boss.

Oddly, Marquardt complimented Gehrke on his many years of service to Oberhausen and the CLCA. He was aware of how popular the theology professor had been with students and how widely published he had been in some of the nation's most prestigious journals. He knew the professor was a dynamic, compelling speaker. The HR representative nodded along as the president spoke.

"We have our differences over doctrine and the Bible," Marquardt said. "I'm sure you know I still consider you to be a heretic, as does Reverend Haller, our church body president." Gehrke thought he detected just a touch of condescension as Marquardt uttered Haller's name.

The new president of Oberhausen continued.

"But I haven't asked you here today to talk about doctrine. Instead, I want to go over the terms of your dismissal from the university."

Gehrke couldn't believe what he was hearing. Outright dismissal without a hearing was impossible, he thought. Tenure, after all, has its privileges, and among them were the right to a hearing, the right to examine evidence and respond to accusations, and the right to have advisory counsel. He raised all these points with Marquardt and the HR rep, demanding vociferously that his rights be observed.

"But Dr. Gehrke, we're not having this conversation because heresy charges against you are being resurrected. It's just a simple matter of economics. As you've probably heard, the church is dealing with some financial strains, and it looks as though the stresses will continue for some time to come."

Gehrke said of course he had heard, and it was to be expected. You can't try to engineer a putsch in a largely volunteer, not-for-profit organization without experiencing substantial opposition. It was no wonder CLCA support was evaporating.

Marquardt ignored his comments and proceeded with his spiel.

"I've been told by the accountants that we have to make adjustments, and I've decided to eliminate your department. We're keeping the Bible department, but we're eliminating the theology department, so you and your fellow theology professors are all being downsized. And as you know, in the event of a downsizing, both tenured and untenured faculty can be let go.

You'll keep your status as a clergyman in the CLCA. Clergyman emeritus, actually, because we can't allow you to serve anywhere with your heretical views. You'll receive a generous severance package. You won't lose your pension. You just aren't going to be a professor at Oberhausen anymore."

The HR rep handed a packet of documents to Gehrke, who said he wouldn't say another word until a lawyer reviewed the terms in the documents. Certainly, he wasn't signing anything.

"When are you going to announce this to the university, and what are you going to do about the students currently majoring in theology?" he asked.

"We'll make the announcement this afternoon. As far as the students, we won't be accepting any more theology majors. For those already in the program, we'll have adjunct faculty members teach the courses so the students can complete their studies."

"But they didn't come here to study with adjunct professors. You won't be delivering the education they were promised. They're already livid about the university's accreditation being suspended."

"Well, I guess they'll have to decide what they want to do. If they're smart, they'll stick it out to finish their degrees. And it won't be long before the accreditation issues are resolved."

"How are you going to pull that off?"

"I'm not at liberty to discuss that, but everything will come clear soon."

When Gehrke asked whether other departments were being cut, Marquardt said anthropology would be going as well.

"If ever there was a breeding ground for atheists, it's anthropology. It makes no sense to have a department like that in a Lutheran university."

To which Gehrke responded, "Not in a fundamentalist university anyway. You realize you're ripping the entire church body apart to enforce your views, right? Where does that arrogance come from? Whatever happened to Saint Paul's idea that we see through a glass darkly, that we know God only in part now, that we will know God more fully on the other side of the grave? Where's your humility?"

Marquardt said he believed what Paul said. It's in the Bible, after all, and there are plenty of things in this world he didn't understand. But he also was humble enough to take the Bible at its word when it speaks clearly about topics like homosexuality, the subservience of women, and the necessity of belief in Jesus as the way, the truth, and the life.

"You're the arrogant one, Dr. Gehrke. You and yours are the ones making faith more complicated than it is. You're the ones with the historical criticism and the nuances and the notion that science takes precedence over God's Word. You're free to believe and teach all that, of course. Just not at Oberhausen University. Now, our business here is over. I expect to receive your signed documents soon. Have a good day." Marquardt and the HR rep stood to remove all doubt that the meeting was finished.

Once the announcement was made, throngs of students and faculty flooded the Oberhausen quadrangle in protest. They had signed up for Oberhausen, not Oral Roberts University or Bob Jones University or Liberty University. Getting rid of the theology department, the anthropology department, and Hillman Gehrke were major steps toward fundamentalism and killing the academic integrity they cherished.

"Gehrke must not go! Gehrke must not go!" they chanted. Then, as the evening wore on: "Marquardt must go! Marquardt must go!"

Marquardt watched demonstrators from his office. He was unmoved.

"The Lord will see us through this turmoil," he thought to himself. He waited until the crowd dispersed before leaving to walk to his home on the other side of campus.

* * *

The next morning, Marquardt scheduled a meeting with Oberhausen's provost, James Waldschmidt, who held a doctorate in education from the University of Iowa. Waldschmidt was highly respected in the academic community and often spoke at provost conventions.

After sharing coffee and pastries, Marquardt got down to business.

"So, Jim, what are your thoughts about our accreditation being suspended?"

Waldschmidt hesitated before responding, unsure that he could be candid with the new university president. Finally, he said he thought it was a serious situation, and Oberhausen needed to do whatever it took to convince the Higher Learning Commission that the issues it raised were being addressed and remediated.

"I have some different thoughts," Marquardt responded. "Jim, do you know how many schools of higher education are under some kind of suspension right now?"

Waldschmidt said he had no idea. Marquardt had done the research, and the number was north of forty schools that, for one reason or another, had been suspended and threatened with loss of accreditation.

"That's a lot of schools, Jim. Maybe they're as disgusted as I am that this so-called commission is poking its nose where it doesn't belong. Here's what I think we ought to do. Put together a team to contact all those schools. Ask them whether they wouldn't be interested in supporting and becoming part of a new accrediting organization, one we could all trust and respect.

"I've even got a name for it. The American Association for Academic Authenticity. We'd get to name the standards we want to be judged by. We'd have a hand in who gets to serve on accreditation teams. And, I believe, the dues we would pay to be part of the new organization would be far less than what we pay now. Imagine the headlines we could create when we receive a Quadruple A rating from the AAAA. Problem solved, right?"

Waldschmidt slowly shook his head.

"Dr. Marquardt, I need to point out it would take years for a new accrediting agency to gain the respect already enjoyed by the Higher Learning Commission. It would never happen if the AAAA were seen as nothing but a sham organization ginned up by colleges who couldn't be accredited any other way."

Marquardt's eyes narrowed and his nostrils flared, just for a second, as Waldschmidt opposed his thinking, but he composed himself. He told Waldschmidt he could be seen as a pioneer in academic circles, coming up with new approaches to accreditation.

"Besides, these days, most people don't pay attention to the ins-and-outs of accreditation. They don't know one accreditation agency from another. As long as we can say we're accredited—just a bullet point on our recruiting materials—we'll be okay. Come on, let's see if we can make this happen."

Waldschmidt agreed to think about Marquardt's idea and get back to him with a more detailed analysis. When he returned to his office, he called his wife to tell her their lives were about to change. He would be looking for a new university home.

Inside Headquarters

After Haller won the CLCA presidency, he never thought he would be greeted warmly at CLCA headquarters. He failed to anticipate, however, just how thoroughly he would be frozen out.

His administrative assistant, Betty Neeb, was cordial enough. He quickly learned she wasn't even Lutheran. She'd been in the job for twenty years, and Haller's predecessors had liked her lack of involvement with their denomination. In her Baptist congregation, no one lobbied her to pass along ideas to her boss. No one pumped her for inside information about the ins-and-outs of the CLCA. She did her job well, collected her paycheck, and went home. Haller had his doubts about the purity of her doctrine, but he didn't get into such topics with her. He saw the wisdom of having her a step removed from his denomination.

He learned just enough about her to have a working relationship. She was well-groomed, nearing sixty, and she had a son, a daughter, and two grandsons, ages ten and eight. Her husband worked as a telephone lineman. Haller's chitchat with her consisted mainly of talking Cardinal baseball—the St. Louis team had a sizable following in Iowa—and asking, on occasion, "How's the family?"

Betty, it turned out, was the only person at CLCA headquarters who would say more to him than "Good morning, President Haller" or "How are you, President Haller?" They didn't really care. When they passed him in the hallway or got caught on an elevator with him, they tried their best not to make eye contact.

Haller had failed to consider the reality of headquarters, namely, that most people who worked there were hired, not elected, and his control over them was limited. They were holdovers from the previous administration, and they had no loyalty to his priorities or his agenda. Instead, they obstructed him at every turn.

When Haller wanted to revise Sunday school materials to be more Bible-oriented, he was told it would take time to line up a new team of writers, editors, and illustrators. When he tried to change the direction of overseas missions to devote less money to food and more to Bible tracts in foreign languages, his staff told him long-term contracts were in place with food vendors, and they couldn't be canceled. When he proposed creating a review panel to check the orthodoxy of congregation pastors, he was advised that such an initiative would have to originate with the congregations because they, not headquarters, held power in the denomination. Truth be told, the professionals at CLCA headquarters didn't share Haller's vision for the church, and they weren't about to jump on the "pure doctrine at all costs" bandwagon.

Haller convened a meeting of George Spurgat, his general counsel; Tom Weisheit, his human resources executive; and Harold Kreiss, his public relations man, to see what could be done. Each of them tried to postpone the meeting. When they couldn't, they sauntered into his office individually, with Spurgat arriving about fifteen minutes late. Usually, tardiness would be an inexcusable trespass when a president called a meeting, but none of them seemed to mind violating corporate etiquette when Haller was involved.

The bags under Haller's eyes were pronounced. He hadn't slept well in days, but he was fueled by a heavy dose of caffeine and a heavier dose of outrage.

"Look, I'm the president around here," he told the executives assembled around his conference room table. "What can I do short of firing these people to get some cooperation? And can I fire them without repercussions? Can I bring in my own people?"

Spurgat explained that Iowa was an at-will state, which meant an employee could be fired for any reason or no reason at all. There were limits, however. Employers still had to follow state and federal laws governing protected classes, such as race, national origin, gender, sexual orientation, age, religion, disability, and pregnancy. Religious employers sometimes had more latitude in these areas. If Haller got serious about firing people, it would be best to review each affected employee on a case-by-case basis.

The human resources executive cautioned that firing large numbers of people could make it difficult to recruit their replacements. Workers weren't inclined to sign on with an organization seen to be quick to fire its employees.

"But I wouldn't be quick to fire people who did their jobs the way I want them to," Haller responded. "I just need people willing to bring the Bible and pure doctrine back into the church." In addition to having his law degree, Spurgat was an ordained CLCA minister. He looked away and rolled his eyes. Haller noticed.

"What? You're not on board either? Who exactly can I rely on to get done what I was elected to do?"

Spurgat said he was there to provide the best advice he could to Haller and the church. His advice was that Haller might be within his rights to fire people, but it might be best not to exercise those rights, at least not on a grand scale.

"I'm hearing I'm within my rights, legally, to do so, right?"

"Within limits, yes. But again, if you decide to fire people, I recommend that we review them on a case-by-case basis."

The HR executive said it would be customary to offer severance packages to people if they're being let go. There would be financial implications. "We'd have to think those through," he said.

"So, Harold, you've been quiet. What's your assessment of the public relations issues we might face?"

Harold put his hand over his mouth. He shook his head for a while before he answered.

"First, don't forget, just about everyone who works here has deep ties to this church body and lots of friends within it. People will be shocked if there's widespread firing. Those who are fired will be asked about it, and they won't hold back. They'll be bitter, and they'll vent. And there will be a tide of vitriol within the church unlike anything we've ever seen. Keep in mind that not everyone agrees with you that there's heresy in the church, and not everyone cares.

"Your media coverage will be horrible. You'll be portrayed not as a churchman trying to restore pure doctrine but as a dictator using heavy-handed measures to cram an agenda down the throat of the church. I can't see any good coming from this."

Haller fumed. "Well, I can," he said. "I have plenty of people rooting for me to clean up this church, and they'll applaud me for doing it. And I'm going to do it! So, either figure out a way to help me, or step aside. All of you think about it. Let me know how we can make this work. And by the way, if people don't agree there's heresy in this church, or they don't care, then they don't belong in the CLCA." With that, he waved them away.

The three shook their heads as they walked together back to their offices.

"God Almighty," Kreiss said. "He's going to do it, and he'll open the gates of hell when he does."

* * *

As he went on his morning runs, the president of the CLCA felt as though all of Des Moines had ganged up to throw him into solitary confinement. That, coupled with the deterioration of his family, which he couldn't discuss with anyone, meant he was haunted by a loneliness unlike any he had known. He needed kindred souls around him, even if just for a few days, to buoy his spirits. It was time, he thought, to resurrect his small band of compatriots, the Reformation Restoration Alliance.

Haller gave Betty a list of ten men. He told her to call the men to find a time they could all get together for three days in Des Moines.

"Tell them we'll pay for their travel, food, and lodging. They're valued advisors of mine, and I need to convene them."

When Betty asked how the expenses would be paid, Haller told her to tap his presidential discretionary fund. She hesitated. Finally, she asked whether a meeting like this would be a legitimate, justifiable use of the fund.

"It's discretionary!" he bellowed, a bit annoyed. "I can use it any way I want, and this is what I want. Now, I expect you to get it done."

"Yes, sir." Betty acquiesced, but her tone somehow signaled not just deference but doubt and just a trace of defiance.

And so it came to be that the Double R A reunited for the first time since Haller's rise to power.

The confab of the collared began with cocktails on a Tuesday evening at the Hotel Fort Des Moines, a four-star property described as a "curated time capsule." Since its founding in 1919, it had played host to Elvis Presley, Johnny Cash, John F. Kennedy, Lyndon Johnson, Barack Obama, and even Nikita Khrushchev. The hotel surrounded its guests with vast expanses of mahogany and marble, combining contemporary sophistication with the opulence and splendor of the Roaring Twenties.

Haller spared no expense for his friends, who drank Manhattans, vodka tonics, and beer at In Confidence, the hotel's speakeasy-styled bar. His buddies gathered around Haller, slapping him on the back and teasing him about how fast and how far he had risen. Someone started a chorus of "For He's a Jolly Good Fellow." Haller chose not to tell his friends how unjolly he had become.

They all avoided mentioning Haller's son, remembering how Caleb had spoken out against his father at the church convention. One of the group, however, asked how Martha was adjusting to life in Des Moines. Haller grimaced while he thought of a response, taking a few extra seconds to polish off his glass of scotch.

"She's well," he finally said, "but she hasn't spent much time here. She decided to pursue a course of studies in Cape Girardeau, with my blessing, of course. I saw her just the other day." He didn't mention that he'd tried to stop her from going to college. He didn't mention he'd seen her only through the window of her father's house. He didn't mention that they hadn't exchanged a word in more than a year. He didn't mention she had started divorce proceedings against him. Instead, he called the socializing to an end.

"We have a lot of work ahead of us tomorrow. I want all of you to get a good night's sleep. We'll reconvene promptly at eight in the morning."

* * *

The hotel staff made sure to have an ample supply of coffee, bagels, and doughnuts on hand. After the obligatory prayer, and the Triple I Salute, Haller spelled out what was on his mind.

There had been more backlash than he had anticipated against his efforts to restore the church to purity. Congregations were leaving, students were outraged, remittances to the national church body were plummeting. As he had promised, he wanted this group to serve as advisors, and he needed their advice. What could be done to fix the situation?

"Well, have you prayed about it?" one of the group asked.

Haller became testy. Of course he had prayed. So far, the answer that had come to him was to convene this group. So, instead of raising questions about his spiritual practices, how about coming up with some ideas?

The church needed to mount an advertising and social media campaign, someone said. It's time to attract new members. Make the pitch that anyone looking for a church that's faithful to the Bible, that has roots going back to the 1500s, that understands what it takes to get a person's thoughts lined up with God's thoughts, needs to join the CLCA.

Heads started nodding in agreement, sure that their church had what it took to get people on the good side of God. Haller said the plan might work, but it would take time, and he needed big ideas that would work now.

The group grew quiet as they struggled to find workable ideas. Finally, Luke Geisler, the pastor from Camanche, Iowa, spoke up.

"Okay, here's a big idea. Sell the Cape Girardeau seminary."

The group let out a collective gasp. Every man in the room had graduated from the seminary. It held a place of honor in all their hearts.

"Unthinkable," someone muttered.

"Who would even want to buy it?" another asked.

"You never know until you put it on the market," Geisler said. "Years ago, we had a small college not far from us that shut down. The state of Iowa bought the campus. It uses the dorms as transitional housing for the homeless. Some of the buildings are now administrative offices, and state and county employees throughout Iowa come to the campus for training. It's worked out well. The state paid millions for it back then, and I'm guessing you could get a lot more for the seminary now."

But where would we train pastors? someone asked.

"Look, Oberhausen is going through some big changes," Geisler said. "I'm guessing a lot of students are going to be leaving, especially if we don't iron out the accreditation issues. You'll have enough space there to accommodate the seminarians and their professors. And you'll get some efficiencies too. You'll lose the expenses that come with running a seminary campus. And anyone from headquarters having business with the seminary can take a short drive over to campus instead of having to make the trip from Des Moines to Cape Girardeau. I think it would work."

Haller put the idea on his list as worthy of consideration.

"How are we going to replace the congregations that left us, and more important, how are we going to replace the remittances they sent?" he asked next. "We've tried asking congregations to increase what they send to the national church body. Almost universally, we're hearing they're barely scraping by and have nothing more to send. I'm not sure I believe that, but that's where we are."

No one had a solution to the problem. After several hours of discussion, someone offered this thought:

"Maybe a reduction in the size of the CLCA is what God wants. Think about what we hear in scripture. 'Many are called, but few are chosen.' 'Small is the gate and narrow the road that leads to life, and only a few find it.'

"God isn't worried about numbers. He's worried about true believers staying true to pure doctrine. We should just listen to him and let our church become smaller. The economics will work out. God will provide us with enough resources to sustain the church at a size he wants it to be."

Haller liked the idea. He would be the president of true believers. The hypocrites and the heretics could go elsewhere.

The next two days were spent fleshing out the group's ideas, figuring out a workable size for the CLCA, and discussing who might be engaged to sell the Cape Girardeau seminary. Haller remembered he knew a high-powered real estate professional. If he could repair the damage to their relationship, he might persuade him to take the assignment.

The following week, when his administrative assistant told him the Reverend Otto Haller was on the line, Eric Richter was more than delighted.

"Tell him I can't take his call right now, but set up a time for us to talk."

Frank LaRussa

Hillman Gehrke didn't know a good labor relations lawyer, but his friend, Andy Detter, did. He invited Gehrke to Chicago to be introduced to Frank LaRussa, one of the best around. Andy and Anna were happy to open their home to Gehrke for a few days.

The sky threatened to unleash a torrent of snow as Gehrke landed at O'Hare. It was shaping up to be another brutal winter in the Windy City. Gehrke tried as best he could to shield himself from the chilly winds as he waited for Detter's BMW to pull into the passenger pickup area. When his ride finally arrived, he loaded his suitcase into the trunk and climbed into the front seat next to Detter, hustling to avoid being chided to "move it along" by airport police.

Conversation had to wait a couple of minutes until Gehrke's teeth stopped chattering, so Detter used the time to provide an update on Caleb and Ashley.

"Ashley's finding her way at the *Tribune*. They've started her as a general assignment reporter. She might be covering a fire one day and an orangutan arriving at the zoo the next. They've promised she'll get to report on social justice, but like anyone starting out, she has to pay her dues. She loves it.

"Caleb's doing well at DePaul, and he's getting a head start on what he believes might be his life's work, putting together all the pieces for what he wants to accomplish. He's exploring the idea of helping the poor build and own tiny houses. He's convinced the School of Architecture, the one founded by Frank Lloyd Wright, to have their students develop a collection of tiny house model plans that could accommodate anyone from a single person to a family of four or five.

"He's been talking with the Department of Housing and Urban Development, as well as the state of Illinois, to see whether they might provide financing for several pilot projects. And he's lobbying Chicago for land somewhere to build an initial ten to fifteen houses. It looks as though he'll have his career ready to launch as soon as he graduates, and he'll be able to use all this to write his thesis. So, in a word, the kids are all right."

Gehrke politely let Detter update him but then revealed he'd already been filled in. He talked just about every day with Caleb's mom, so he knew all about how Ashley and Caleb were doing. Detter's eyebrows rose in mock surprise, and he smiled and nodded his head.

"Anna and I thought you might have something going with Martha. If you don't mind my saying so, that's an interesting little web you're tangled in, what with her divorce still pending. I hope it works out for the two of you."

Once they arrived at the Detter home, Anna greeted them with hot chocolate and pumpkin pie, and the three visited together in the living room. As proud owners of a Frank Lloyd Wright home, the couple made sure, as far as possible, to keep the home as the architect intended, even using the furniture he had designed.

The Detters pressed Gehrke to talk about his most recent battles with Haller and Marquardt, but the professor wanted to delay that conversation.

"I want to hear what's going on away from Oberhausen and Des Moines. How are congregations and pastors reacting to the rise of Otto Haller? What's happening with your congregation? What kind of future do you think the CLCA has?"

Anna said her friends couldn't believe a petty, loathsome, small-minded dictator had been elected president. Like Anna, they had grown up in the church. They preferred order and harmony to chaos and mudslinging. Most of them had no idea who Haller was or where he had come from. When they were directed to GodsTruthIsMyTruth.com, they were shocked by what they read and saw.

At their congregation, a group of members agitated almost immediately to leave the national church, and their pastor supported them. About two thirds of the congregation voted to leave, but the meeting turned sour.

"A sizable contingent wanted to stay, simply because they could trace their family roots back to the founding of the CLCA," Anna said. "They couldn't imagine not being part of it. And then there were those who truly believe heretics are taking over the church. They wanted to support Haller. 'He alone can restore purity,' they think. Our congregation left, and we're staying independent of any national denomination, at least for now. We lost a lot of members, though, who transferred to congregations that decided to stay.

"We'll be fine. Most of us sticking with our congregation are pretty affluent. I'm not sure how other congregations will fare. A lot of them are small, and I think they'll have a hard time attracting new members. There aren't many people wanting to join a church so gung-ho about a heresy hunt. My prognosis is the CLCA is going to decline, and quickly."

Oberhausen wasn't going to do well under Marquardt, Gehrke said. He told the Detters about his meeting with the newly appointed Oberhausen president.

"Why would you simply eliminate the theology department from a university with such a strong theological tradition? Why would you shut down the anthropology department on the premise that 'it's a breeding ground for atheists'? I'm sure Marquardt's starting to worry about finances, but a pending shortfall is just an excuse for getting rid of me and my kind, not a reason. These are the moves of an ideologue, not an academic.

"Any thoughtful professor or student will see the clown show that Oberhausen is becoming. They'll leave as soon as they can, and good luck recruiting their replacements. I'm sure things will play out the same at the seminary in Cape Girardeau. It'll take years, maybe decades, to reverse the damage being done by the present regime. I'm not sure the schools have that long."

The next morning, Gehrke and Detter met LaRussa in the Loop for a late breakfast at Miss Ricky's, a homey, laid-back spot with soft, comfortable chairs. The lawyer was known as a courtroom brawler, so the companies he went up against almost always settled before a judge and jury could hear their case. He came equipped with lots of flash—a Rolex, Gucci loafers, and a pinky ring on each hand. No wedding ring. His clothes smelled of cigar smoke. Gehrke figured a man like LaRussa might find domestic life a bit confining for his tastes.

The trio gave their breakfast orders to Wendy the waitress, who studied a few blocks away at the Art Institute of Chicago. Then they got down to business. LaRussa had little time for chitchat.

"So, professor, what's going on with you? Let me see those documents."

There were lots of head shakes, grunts, and an occasional guffaw as he reviewed the pages. Finally, he said:

"So what do you want, Doc? You want to stay with this school, or take 'em for a ride? I can make either happen."

No way would he stay, Gehrke said. He wanted the full measure of what Oberhausen should pay to terminate his career in the church. He wanted to get rid of a nondisclosure clause or anything that would keep him from saying what must be said about the power politics that would ruin his church. And he wanted to be able to give his colleagues good advice once they got called into Marquardt's office.

"The only advice you need to give them is have them call me," LaRussa said. "I'll take care of them the same as I'm taking care of you. No charge. You want to know why? I'll tell you. First, Andy here is a good friend of mine, and I'm happy to help out. Second, this won't take much of my time. Once their lawyers hear I'm on the case, they won't let their client jerk your friends around, and they won't put up much of a fight. Of that, I'm sure.

"Tell you what. Leave these documents with me. I'll work them over, make sure you get the best deal possible. You sign them, take them back, and hand them over to this Marquardt guy and his so-called lawyers. Tell them to sign, or you'll see them in court. You'll get what you want."

So, it's come to this, Gehrke thought. It's all about power, and money, and making other people kowtow to your will. It wasn't a game the theology professor ever thought he would have to play, but if he had to, he was certain he had the right players on his team.

The rest of the meal, they just talked football. Gehrke was a lifelong Packers fan. Detter and LaRussa rooted for the Bears.

LaRussa rolled his eyes. "Jeez, I can't believe I'm doing this for a Packers fan!" he joked. "Good thing you're a friend of Andy's here."

As they left the restaurant, Gehrke told Detter he'd find his way back to Oak Park later. He wanted to spend some time at the Art Institute and take care of some other things.

* * *

There was only one painting Gehrke wanted to see, American Gothic by native Iowan Grant Wood. He'd come across many reproductions and photos, of course. The painting was legendary in Iowa because it paid tribute to the small town of Eldon. Now he had bragging rights. He could tell the Iowans he lived with that he'd seen the real thing. After emerging from the museum, he summoned an Uber to take him to the University of Chicago.

News travels quickly in academic circles. As soon as he heard Gehrke was being let go, Ted Robertson, dean of the university's Divinity School, was on the phone. The two theologians had been in the same class at Harvard.

"Hillman, has a year gone by that I haven't tried to recruit you? Sounds like it's time for you to take me seriously. Get your butt over here to Chicago, and let's talk."

Robertson—bearded, balding, and bespectacled—had remained one of Gehrke's closest friends for decades. The two men had done casual rowing together on the Charles River during their time in Massachusetts. They had enjoyed their classroom debates, always cordial, always stimulating. And, important to Gehrke, Robertson knew and fondly remembered Laura, the wife Gehrke had lost just three years after their wedding.

Gehrke admired the soaring Gothic structures as the two men toured the campus. Eventually, Robertson steered his friend to Grounds of Being, the on-campus coffee shop in the basement of Swift Hall, home of the Divinity School. The shop's slogan: "Where God Drinks Coffee."

"You know, Hillman, if you come here, you'll be joining an institution that has been home to some of the world's great theologians. Paul Tillich taught here. Mircea Eliade's memorial service was held right here on campus. And

I'm sure you resonate with Martin Marty, who has to be the most respected, most influential Lutheran of our lifetime, right?"

Gehrke knew he'd be moving to Chicago, but as he sat conversing with Robertson, he felt surprised by the sense of mourning that came upon him. He started to realize all the CLCA had meant to him, all it had offered him.

The upstarts who had taken over couldn't possibly realize what they were destroying, could they? For generations, people like Gehrke had been rooted in the church. They drew nourishment from it. They learned to live, to laugh, and to love within its embrace. They came to understand the importance of compromise and tolerance. They grew into a community. They shared a spirit that lived, and breathed, and moved among them. They cared about one another and, increasingly, about the world around them.

Everything they knew about life had been informed by the church. As each generation took over from the previous generation, they became the drivers and caretakers of the church.

He, Hillman Gehrke, was infused with the church. He absorbed its spirit as a child. He gained profound insights into his faith during his seminary years. When he lost his wife, the church rallied to help him work through his grief and regain his life. He and his were the church. He believed it with every fiber of his being.

Now, barbarians had taken over the church he loved, unleashing a spirit that, left unchecked, would transform a community of living faith into a cult of unbending ideologues. Some people would be disappointed that Gehrke wouldn't put up more of a fight, but he was choosing to do as Jesus had counseled his disciples. He was shaking the dust off his feet, walking away from where he was no longer welcome.

Robertson kept talking as Gehrke's attention wandered.

"Hillman, have you heard a word I've said? Are you interested? Do you want to come join us?"

Gehrke realized he'd been burrowing deep into the tunnel of thought that had overtaken him. He looked up at his longtime friend.

"Yes," he said, absentmindedly. "Yes, I'll come. I've just been wondering whether I'll ever be able to find another community to replace Oberhausen.

It's more than a university to me. It's my community. It's a home for me."

"It was a home, but it's being destroyed by storm troopers," Robertson replied. "You'll see. Come here, and we'll do everything we can to create a new home for you. By the way, we haven't discussed tenure. You will be tenured from Day One, just in case you wondered. And I've checked what Oberhausen pays its full professors. We'll pay you thirty percent more."

"Okay, now I'm starting to feel at home," Gehrke smiled.

Before he headed back to the Detters' home, he made a call.

"Martha, I want you to start thinking about something. I want you to start thinking about moving to Chicago in the next few months. We'll work it out so you can continue your studies here."

She would. She promised.

"And Martha, see if you can get me a copy of that police report you told me about. It might come in handy somewhere down the line."

* * *

Shortly before Thanksgiving 2028, Betty Neeb presented Haller with a packet of material that had been mailed to his office. She chose not to open it. It was marked "Personal and Confidential." She pretended not to notice it was from Young & Young, a family-law practice in Cape Girardeau.

Haller had been able to keep Martha's divorce petition quiet. Rumors circulated, of course, but no one had the courage to ask him about it directly. He chose not to attend the court hearing to avoid being recognized. Thankfully, the *Southeast Missourian* had never made it a practice to scour the courts for notable divorce proceedings, and Martha had no interest in publicizing the event.

As he reviewed the material, he became angry. Why couldn't Martha just be a dutiful wife, he wondered. Why couldn't she just be happy being a minister's wife, and the wife of a highly elevated minister at that? He hadn't done anything wrong, he told himself. He was a victim. His wife and his son were the rebels in their now-fractured family.

He was being asked to sign his marriage away and return the papers promptly. He reviewed the allocation of assets, which included almost nothing since the Hallers had never owned a house. Martha could have their car, he thought, and fine, she could have half their savings and half his pension when the time came to collect it.

He considered throwing the whole packet in the trash. From what he had read, though, the divorce would proceed whether he signed the papers or not. He might receive some momentary satisfaction by not signing, but he also had learned that things could get more complicated if he didn't. Complications caused delays, and delays left open the possibility that the divorce could become more visible.

He signed the papers, put them in an envelope he addressed, and asked Betty to take care of putting it in the mail. With one stroke of the pen, he became a single man for the first time in more than thirty years. A single man who continued to wear his wedding ring. A single man with a secret he hoped would not come to light.

A Seminary for Sale

Haller began his conversation with Richter by apologizing for the temper tantrum he threw when they had last been together. No need for apologies, Richter said. In his world, things often got much more contentious much more quickly, and a little rudeness was an everyday occurrence. Besides, he thought, the smell of money makes it easy to be gracious, and the CLCA was throwing off a bouquet of pleasant aromas.

The real estate strategist suggested that he and Haller meet in Cape Girardeau so he could gain a better understanding of the commercial potential of the seminary campus. It was only a five-hour drive from Indianapolis, and he'd be happy to make the trip.

Haller arrived the evening before Richter amid cold, blustery winds and wisps of snow. He drove his rental car past the home of Martha and her father several times, resisting the urge to knock on the door and plead for a new start that he knew wouldn't occur. He sped up once he saw Martha looking out the window. If she recognized him, he worried, she might call the police, and he didn't want to risk having another report filed about him.

He invited the seminary president, Charles Hermann, to dinner at Celebrations, one of the few fine-dining spots in Cape. Hermann previously had been a campus pastor and a religion professor at Southeast Missouri State. He had been selected to replace Randall Bertram after the row over Bertram's refusal to deliver course syllabi to Haller. Like almost all CLCA ministers, he had graduated from the seminary in Cape Girardeau. He was known to be orthodox. He was about to receive a doctorate in theology from Notre Dame, so his academic credentials were solid. He lived in town, so many professors already knew him, and the church saved a little money by not having to relocate him.

Hermann knew he would be called on to snuff out heresy on his campus, and he was willing to tackle the issue. He was determined, however, that any of his accused professors would receive due process. It was the principled way to proceed. He was prepared to tell Haller just that if the topic arose.

A bottle of merlot had already been opened when Hermann arrived at the restaurant. Haller, sitting in a dimly lit corner, had taken the liberty of ordering red wine, assuming Hermann would order steak or another red meat in a restaurant known for American cuisine and barbecue. Hermann normally stuck to iced tea, but to honor the generosity of his host, he indulged in a glass of wine.

He was five years younger than Haller, so they hadn't crossed paths in their seminary days. Even so, they had studied under some of the same professors, and they had walked the same halls and lived in the same dormitories, so they could share their reminiscences of Martin Luther Seminary.

"Let me tell you the reason for my visit," Haller said as they dug into their main courses.

"Honestly, I'm a little afraid to hear," Hermann said. "I'm still just settling into my job. So far, all things considered, we have a peaceful, placid, collegial campus. I hope you're not wanting to disturb that, at least not right now."

Eventually, there would have to be a reckoning, Haller said. The impure would have to be culled from the pure. But he didn't think that would happen for at least another year. The Theological Magisterium needed time to articulate the many heresies to be forbidden in the CLCA.

There was, however, another issue the seminary could help address. National church finances had been declining rapidly, and the seminary would be called upon to do its part to help.

Hermann looked puzzled. He had become familiar with the financials at the seminary, and he knew it wasn't generating any extra cash.

"That's true," Haller said, "but you have an asset that could prove to be valuable to the CLCA."

"I can't imagine what that would be."

"Real estate! We want to sell your campus."

The color drained from Hermann's face. He hadn't been president for even a year, and his fiefdom was being taken from him. Professors' jobs would be lost, he protested. And where would future pastors be trained?

Haller assured him everything would work out. There's space available at Oberhausen. We can move the seminary professors and students to the Des Moines campus, he told Hermann.

"So, you're asking me to give up my presidency? If I'd known it would come to this, I wouldn't have taken the job in the first place."

Haller said the seminary would have space on the Oberhausen campus but would be independent. Hermann would still be seminary president. They could even arrange things so seminarians would have separate dorms and classrooms. They'd have to share the library, the cafeteria, and the gym with the rest of the campus, though.

"This would be a logistical nightmare," Hermann protested. "I can't begin to imagine the thousands of details that will have to be worked through."

"Yes, the devil is in the details, and salvation comes by getting all the details right," Haller said. "The first detail is figuring out whether your campus is even marketable. A real estate professional, Kurt Richter, is coming tomorrow to help us figure that out. He's a political consultant as well as a real estate expert. His firm is wired with government types here in Missouri, and some of them might be interested in taking the campus over. People call him Gearshift because he has a real talent for helping people shift gears and change course. You'll be joining us as I show him around. And not a word of this to anyone, understand?"

* * *

Heads turned when Richter drove his Bentley into the seminary parking lot on the morning of Monday, January 15, 2029. Martin Luther King's birthday, the radio personality trumpeted on the conservative Sirius channel Richter usually tuned into. Someday, he promised himself, he'd look into how it was that a Black man had come to be named for a white, German, 16th-century monk.

After an early lunch in the seminary cafeteria, the three men took a walking tour of Martin Luther Seminary. Richter nodded approvingly as he toured dormitories, offices, classrooms, a chapel, a library, a cafeteria, and a gymnasium. As a bonus, the campus contained thirty-two single-family homes to accommodate faculty members and their families. Seventeen faculty members chose to take advantage of the housing, and the seminary rented out the rest to community members.

Richter raved about the beauty of the campus. With its faithfully executed Gothic architecture, visitors might think they were at a small, prestigious European university. Seminarians could feel they were walking in the footsteps of Luther, even if they resided 4,500 miles from the reformer's University of Wittenberg.

"Why did the denomination choose to build its only seminary here?" Richter asked. "Little old Cape Girardeau wouldn't have occurred to me as a prime location."

Haller asked Hermann to explain.

"A lot of Lutherans came to Cape Girardeau from northern Europe in the 1800s," the seminary president said. "The farmland supported corn, soybeans, and livestock. The woodlands and the Mississippi River felt familiar, like home, so the Lutherans warmed to the area. Eventually, as our ancestors established a life for themselves over several decades, they spread into Missouri, Michigan, Illinois, Iowa, Wisconsin, and other parts of the Midwest. Today, the CLCA is all over the world. But we've always had a soft spot in our hearts for this part of Missouri. It made sense to put the seminary here. It's a good place to inject CLCA blood into the veins of our future pastors."

Haller chimed in. "All of us pastors have gone through Martin Luther Seminary. Charles, me, even the traitors like Gehrke. I wasn't treated so well here, but even so, I have some good memories of the place."

When the tour was finished, Haller dismissed Hermann so he and Richter could talk business.

"I think you're on to something here," Richter assured Haller. "I've had my staff do some research. Did you know that more than a hundred colleges have closed since 2021? Some are in big cities. Some, like the seminary, are in smaller towns. Those who have sold their campuses have averaged proceeds of about $50 million. I have no doubt we could sell the seminary, and you'd have some financial breathing room as you sort out the turmoil in the church."

Haller felt defensive about the "turmoil," but he bit his tongue. There was no denying that the CLCA's once tranquil waters were anything but calm.

Richter said his associates had been scouting for possible buyers, and if the church contracted with Richter and Rolfe, the agency probably could have a workable deal on the table in six months or less. Provisions for using the campus until the move to Oberhausen was completed could be arranged.

The real estate professional said his company was interested in more than just representing the church in the seminary sale. It wanted to enter a partnership with the CLCA.

"We're aware that a number of congregations have left, and a number of others have been weakened as members transferred elsewhere," Richter said. "It's just an unpleasant fact that a number of congregations will have to sell their property. If we do a good job for you in selling the seminary, I'd like to ask that you position us as the real estate agency of choice for CLCA congregations that would need our services.

"No congregation would have to do business with us, of course, but we would offer terms so attractive that they'd see the advantages in coming to us. And if you'd do that, we would take on the sale of the seminary for a commission of just one percent. Normally we would get three percent and the agents for the buyer would get three percent. They'll still expect their three percent, but we'd be saving you two, or probably a million dollars or more on top of the $50 million you'd gain from the sale."

"You still belong to Concordia Indianapolis, right?" Haller asked. "You're still a member of a CLCA congregation?"

"Full-fledged, and I'll be staying that way, even though you've squeezed the bland right out of this church body!" Richter smiled.

Haller said he thought could sell the arrangement to his board, especially if the real estate professional was a CLCA member. He held out his hand to shake on the deal, and the two men headed home.

On the way back to Indianapolis, Richter called his office and asked several associates to gather around a speakerphone.

"Folks, I want you to set up a new company. See whether the name Heavenly Hospitality LLC is available. I think we have a nice opportunity coming our way."

Gehrke's Farewell

G ehrke scheduled a meeting with Marquardt once he returned to Des Moines. He suggested it would be a good idea for Marquardt to bring along Oberhausen's HR rep and whatever lawyers the university was using for advice on his termination.

The theology professor walked from his office to Marquardt's with the chilly Des Moines wind following him. Once he entered the administration building, he took a few minutes to warm up. The cold often made him shiver, and he wanted to be as calm and collected as possible before coming face to face with Marquardt and his minions.

His executioners had gathered around a meeting table in Marquardt's office. When he entered, each of them pretended to be deep in paperwork. They kept their heads down, trying to let Gehrke know they would deal with him when they were ready, and not before, so Gehrke took the lead. He placed an envelope on the table.

"I've signed the documents you'll find here," he told them, not caring whether they looked up or not. "They've been drawn up by my lawyer, Frank LaRussa. I have no desire to speak with any of you again. Any concerns you have can be addressed directly to him. You'll find his contact information in the envelope." With that, he turned and left.

One of the lawyers let out a soft whistle. He couldn't fathom that Gehrke could afford LaRussa, widely known as the top labor lawyer in the country. His rate was easily $1,400 an hour.

Marquardt's face grew red as he pored over the terms. Gehrke was asking for three years' salary—triple the severance pay he had been offered—and there was no non-disclosure agreement in the document. The document also made clear that he would not lose his pension or his inclusion on the clergy roster.

"Preposterous!" Marquardt screamed. "I'll never agree to this. Heretics don't get to negotiate the terms of their termination. I'll lie down in the street and get run over by a bus before I'll sign this."

If you take on LaRussa, you'll wish you hadn't done so, the lawyers declared. They knew of CEOs who had died by suicide or heart attacks after run-ins with LaRussa.

Marquardt was unfazed. He ordered the lawyers to get Gehrke back in his office, but when they called, as he promised, Gehrke told them to contact his attorney.

The Chicago lawyer said he had nothing further to say except he would see them and Marquardt in court if they didn't sign. He reminded them that Gehrke wasn't being dismissed over theology. The courts would be more than happy to hear this case because it involved labor law, not internal church struggles. LaRussa reminded Oberhausen's lawyers that he had never lost a case. If they wanted to head to court, he and Gehrke would be seeking quintuple severance pay and compensation for Gehrke's legal expenses, which would rival Mount Everest in their height, width, and mass. And there would be no non-disclosure agreement. None of this was negotiable.

"And tell Dr. Marquardt I'll be representing any other terminated faculty member who wishes to use me. And why wouldn't they?"

Marquardt's lawyers advised him that Oberhausen could easily end up spending far more in legal fees than what the university would pay Gehrke, even at triple the amount originally offered.

"This is ridiculous," Marquardt said. "This man needs to suffer. He can't be walking out of here with enough money to retire! I won't sign."

Again, the lawyers told him that signing was the prudent thing to do, financially. Grudgingly, Marquardt picked up his pen, signed the documents, and commanded his defeated team to leave his office. He then told his administrative assistant to contact Gehrke.

"Tell him he is not to step into an Oberhausen classroom again, effective immediately. Tell him he has to vacate his office by the end of the week."

* * *

That afternoon, as he was beginning to load papers and books into cardboard boxes, a cadre of students came by Gehrke's office. There were more bodies than the small space could accommodate, so the students asked their professor to come with them for coffee in the school cafeteria. On the walk over, several well-wishers stopped the group to pay their respects to the ousted theology professor. Some vowed to continue the good fight for him. Others teared up as they said goodbye.

It was mid-afternoon, so the cafeteria was not crowded. Gehrke felt a tinge of melancholy as he realized he might be in the room for the last time. He had enjoyed so many conversations and friendly arguments there. He had counseled more than a few students through personal or family crises. He had celebrated birthdays, work and marriage anniversaries, and academic achievements with his colleagues. For a moment, he resented that his life was being upended so suddenly. Then, he realized as much as he might miss Oberhausen, he was being spared the school's inevitable turmoil. It was time to bury the university he had once loved, separate from the autocracy it was becoming, and open the next chapter of his life.

Once they gathered around a table, the group asked Gehrke what would become of him. He said he'd be fine, and an announcement about his future would be forthcoming in the next few days. He was more worried about them and all the other students at Oberhausen, he said.

"This suspension of accreditation is a big deal. I hope you all realize that. Unless the school is accredited, your diplomas won't be worth the paper they'll come on. You might as well be home-schooled.

"You'll have a much more difficult time getting into graduate school, if you can do so at all. You might not be able to find the kind of job you're hoping for. If I were you, I'd be looking to transfer as soon as I could. For the moment, accreditation hasn't been revoked, but if things don't change, it will be, probably sooner than you think."

One of the students asked whether Gehrke would recommend schools to consider. He said the students should be looking for the schools known for excellence in their chosen fields. Oberhausen has many wonderful, highly qualified professors, he said, and the students were right to enroll. But the days of getting a good education at Oberhausen were quickly ending.

"If you came here because of the school's religious orientation, don't be afraid to look at state-run and secular colleges and universities. It would be good for you to be exposed to the wider variety of people you'll find there. The sooner you emerge from the catacombs of Oberhausen and the CLCA, the better."

One of the students, an anthropology major, said she'd already been exploring other options. She planned to apply to one of the best universities in the country.

"Which one?" Gehrke asked.

"The University of Chicago."

Gehrke smiled. "Well, you never know. Maybe our paths will cross again someday. How about you, Brent? What are you thinking?"

The young man hesitated, scratched his head, and then said: "I'm just going to cogitate on it for a while. Something will come to me."

Everyone laughed at the words Gehrke had said so many times before. After a round of hugs and tears, the group dispersed. Gehrke headed back to his office to finish packing. He asked his department head whether the boxes could be shipped to him.

"Just tell me where."

"Send them over to my place. But I'll let you in on a secret."

"What's that?"

"Soon, I'll ship the boxes to Swift Hall at the University of Chicago."

"Whoa! You're kidding. That's big news. Congratulations."

Gehrke said an announcement would be made in a few days. Until then, he swore the man to secrecy.

* * *

A few weeks after Gehrke left, the American Association for Academic Authenticity announced its formation with a news release. Thirty-two colleges and universities were canceling their affiliation with the Higher Learning Commission to join the AAAA. The new organization would be based in Hannibal, Missouri. Initially, it would be headquartered on the campus of Hannibal-LaGrange University, one of the first members of the new organization.

"This is an accreditation agency for the 21st century," proclaimed the executive director, Nancy Bauer, Ph.D. "The schools joining our organization are among the best in the nation. They've decided they want to be held to even higher standards than those enforced by the HLC. We anticipate many other schools will be joining us over the next few years once they see what we have to offer."

The news release popped up on the computer screen of Lucy Rosenkoetter, the education reporter for the *Des Moines Register*. She smelled a story once she noticed Oberhausen was on the list of founding schools.

"This is just bizarre," she told her editor. "I can't imagine anyone accrediting Oberhausen right now. They're closing down their theology and anthropology departments. They're letting go of some of their best faculty, including Hillman Gehrke, who's a nationally respected theologian. Their accreditation has been suspended by the Higher Learning Commission. There's a story here, for sure."

Rosenkoetter called Marquardt's office to request an interview. She learned he was in Germany to meet with other university presidents in Hamburg. Could she interview the school's provost, James Waldschmidt?

"He's not available," she was told. "He's taken a leave of absence."

Rosenkoetter took a closer look at the schools of the AAAA. Great Lakes Christian College in Lansing, Michigan. Nazarene Bible College in Colorado Springs. Northwestern College in Oak Lawn, Illinois. Southwestern Baptist College in Bolivar, Missouri. And a collection of other schools even more obscure. Oberhausen definitely was keeping company with a basket of less-than-stellar institutions.

A little more research on her part revealed that every school joining the

AAAA had been suspended from accreditation within the past year. She also learned about accreditation mills, which award accreditation without having government authority or recognition from mainstream academia to operate as an accreditor. She couldn't believe the highly respected Oberhausen University was affiliating with what clearly was an accreditation mill, yet the conclusion couldn't be avoided.

"There's plenty of them out there," said a source at the Higher Learning Commission. "The American Bureau of Higher Education. The Education Accrediting Association. The Higher Education Accreditation Commission. The National Accreditation Association. Probably a hundred or more in all."

"So, if Oberhausen wanted to go that route, why not just sign up with an existing organization? Why go with something brand new?"

"You'd have to ask them, but maybe they have more control if they get in on the ground floor of a new agency. Of course, any school concerned with legitimate accreditation wouldn't want control. Accreditation is all about submitting to the discipline of education and being held accountable for the job you're doing. Schools that use accreditation mills don't care about either of those things."

Rosenkoetter made one last call to see whether she could find anyone at Oberhausen to discuss the American Association for Academic Authenticity. She couldn't.

She had reported briefly on Hillman Gehrke's leaving the school and had his cell number.

"I didn't know Marquardt and Oberhausen would want to join a bogus accreditation agency, but I'm not surprised," Gehrke said. "Any serious professor or student should simply walk away as soon as possible. Marquardt and Haller are turning the school and the church body into a clown show. It's a sad time in the history of the CLCA. The saddest."

When Rosenkoetter's story was posted, it wasn't alone. Newspapers in other towns with members of the newly formed AAAA also figured out the ruse. A spate of stories appeared nationwide. As quickly as the organization was announced, it was discredited.

When Marquardt learned of Rosenkoetter's story, he called her from

Germany, chiding her for not waiting to publish until she interviewed him.

"What gives you the right to make a judgment about the AAAA anyway?" he shouted.

"I didn't make a judgment. I wrote a story. Your fellow educators made the judgment. I have to tell you, though, this doesn't look good for your institution. Maybe you should rethink what you're doing."

"You stick to journalism, if that's what you call what you do. I'll stick to education. And one more thing. I forbid you to talk with Hillman Gehrke about anything relating to Oberhausen." With that, he disconnected the call. He and his wife had a banquet to attend in Hamburg. Mrs. Marquardt was having a marvelous time.

Rosenkoetter broke out laughing. "I'll talk to anyone I damn well please," she said to no one in particular. She vowed to keep a closer eye on Oberhausen.

"Queeg Has Left the Building"

Nine cardboard boxes sat in one corner of Haller's office, filled with the syllabi he had ordered ten months earlier. They had remained untouched. As much as he wanted to start pressing his heresy campaign, he had more urgent problems to tackle. The number of congregations leaving the CLCA had grown to more than a thousand, including many of the denomination's largest contributors. Remittances to the national church body had fallen by forty percent. Enrollments for both Oberhausen and Martin Luther Seminary were projected to drop by more than twenty-five percent in the next school year.

Haller figured any defections by congregations probably were over by now, and most congregations were choosing to stay within the CLCA. Many applauded Haller's anti-heresy campaign. Most figured goings-on at the national church body had little effect on them, day to day; they might not be happy with the direction of the church, but they saw no point in expending energy and resources on the legal and logistical steps needed to leave. Sermons would be preached, babies would be baptized, couples would be married, and bodies would be buried whether they belonged to the CLCA or not. If they chose to keep more money at home and give less to the national church, what's the worst that could happen? They'd be kicked out? Not likely, but if so, who cared?

It was this lukewarm attitude that most frustrated Haller. He had counted on a tsunami of support once he took office, with money and troops aplenty overflowing to wage his war. The Reformation Restoration Alliance had done a good job of getting sympathizers elected as delegates to the national convention, but the delegates didn't truly reflect the church body. Most members couldn't be rallied to Haller's cause because, at its heart, the CLCA was still the bland CLCA, a sea of tranquility, the Dead Sea of Christianity.

Maybe Haller was right. Maybe most members were Bible literalists. But regardless, most members didn't like gut-wrenching controversy. Most members just hoped Haller's crusade would eventually go away, and calm would be restored. Most wanted nothing more than to attend Sunday services and share coffee and doughnuts afterward.

Haller and his friends in the Reformation Restoration Alliance, it turned out, suffered from the Dunning-Kruger effect. They believed they were smarter and more capable than they really were. They didn't have the skills to recognize their own incompetence. Most of them had done a decent job of running a congregation, but they didn't know what it took to administer a denomination with international reach. They believed they would be the saviors of the CLCA once they restored pure doctrine. It was quickly becoming clear that, if left unchecked, they would be destroyers, not just of alleged heretics but of the whole church body.

In June 2029, Haller convened Spurgat, Weisheit, and Kreiss for a strategy session. John Mueller, the vice president of finance, was also summoned. Haller tried opening the meeting with the Triple I Salute, offered with his elbow planted on the armrest of his chair. When it wasn't reciprocated, he rotated his arm to place the three fingers on his face, pretending he had meant all along to scratch it. None of these church executives was a pure doctrine loyalist, it turned out. They were holdovers from the previous administration, and they weren't easily removed from their positions. As good Lutherans, they gave great deference to authority, but in the case of Haller, they doubted whether his authority flowed from anything other than some unsavory political machinations. As good family people, they didn't want to walk away from their paychecks unless their consciences felt violated beyond redemption. And while they were close, they weren't there yet. Of course, consciences often have a way of making accommodations when livelihoods are on the line.

The CLCA president opened his meeting. "First of all, I'm happy to tell you the work of the CLCA Theological Magisterium has taken off. We now have documents in place with rulings on everything from the inerrancy of scripture to the abomination of homosexual marriage; from abortion to the evils of diversity, equity, and inclusion; from communism to communing with non-CLCA people. We have the tools we need to purge the church of the heretics among us."

Spurgat spoke. "Well, that's quite an accomplishment, Otto." His tone signaled he was damning with faint praise. No one else offered a comment, so Haller moved on.

He provided an update on the plan to sell Martin Luther Seminary, which Richter had assured him was progressing nicely. It looked as though the state of Missouri wanted to replicate Iowa's success in using an abandoned campus to provide transitional housing for the homeless. The final details were being worked out, and the church should realize proceeds in excess of $50 million. Mueller said that amount would fall to about $35 million after paying for commissions, closing costs, and the expenses of moving the faculty to Oberhausen and making modifications to accommodate a seminary.

"Okay, $35 million," Haller huffed. "It's still a sizable amount of money."

The people in the room supported the sale, reluctantly, because they knew the church needed the cash to meet obligations and ease financial pressures. They had all cautioned that the sale would provide only temporary relief. They also had heard from numerous pastors upset by the sale of the campus they held so dear, and the group was finding it difficult to soothe their displeasure.

Haller acknowledged more would need to be done to ensure long-term stability for the denomination. He once again raised the option of firing his non-supporters at church headquarters. And for the first time, he revealed to his fellow church officers the idea of shrinking the membership of the denomination.

"I believe it's what God wants," Haller said. "We'll be a church body of true believers who fully support pure doctrine. The economics will work out—God will see to that—and the first step to make things work out is to fire the people who don't support me. The savings will be substantial. It's one of the many ways God will provide for the faithful church he wants.

"I'm dictating that congregations not fully committed to pure doctrine must be removed from the CLCA. The longer they stay, the more likely it is they'll adulterate our teachings, and that's a sure road to hell for the members of the CLCA."

The usually milquetoast PR executive, Harold Kreiss, rolled his eyes and shook his head, not bothering to hide his irritation. "You're going to force congregations to leave? You going to tell them they're headed to hell?"

Haller nodded unapologetically. "You know what scripture says. 'The truth shall make you free.' This is the truth, and if people hear it, maybe it will be a wake-up call for them."

"More likely, it will be an insult, and you don't keep people on your side by insulting them. Tell them that, and they'll wish they had left yesterday. We can't afford to lose any more congregations."

Mueller kept sighing deeply.

"You have to realize the way we're structured financially. We're loaded with fixed costs like insurance, salaries, and depreciation. We have mainly illiquid assets, like buildings, which are difficult to sell quickly. Once you start trying to pay for fixed costs by selling illiquid assets, like the seminary, the university, and the headquarters building, you're committing to a downward spiral. Ultimately, you have to declare bankruptcy and cease to exist. A diplomat would call what you're proposing imprudent. A realist would call it unsustainable. An economist would call it mad."

"You're all forgetting one thing. The Lord will provide. Discuss is over. I want to reconvene in one week, and I want you to present me with plans to make these ideas work. Make it happen. I'm going home."

* * *

The four church executives stayed in the meeting room after Haller left, stunned into silence. Finally, Mueller spoke: "Commander Queeg has left the building, and he failed to find the strawberries." Despite the gravity of the situation, they couldn't stop themselves from breaking into laughter.

They discussed whether there was anything short of murder that could dislodge Haller from his post. One of them suggested pulling out the CLCA constitution and bylaws, which contained a whole section on expelling the president of the church from his position. Ten causes for removal from office were named. Of them, the group thought the second one, a breach of fiduciary responsibilities, offered the best hope of banishing Haller.

"The man has done nothing but cause turmoil both before and since he entered office," Mueller said. "We're losing millions of dollars because of him. And now he's talking about actively telling congregations to leave the church? There's a strong case to be made that the man is not upholding his fiduciary responsibilities."

Reading further into the document, however, disheartened the group. The procedures for dislodging a president were complicated and cumbersome. The district presidents had to be told, as a group, which charges were being anticipated. Then, formal charges had to be committed to paper. The accuser had to meet face-to-face with the president to present the charges. The district presidents had to be reconvened to agree the charges were substantiated. And on and on and on. The process could drag on all the way to the next church convention. The odds were good that Haller could be voted out, but by then, he could have destroyed the denomination.

"What this church needs is a twenty-fifth amendment," the HR executive said, referring to the U. S. constitutional amendment outlining procedures for senior government leaders to accelerate removing a president in the event of incapacitation. "Remind me to submit a proposal to the next convention, assuming the denomination is still around to hold a convention."

The group decided to slow walk Haller's plans so they could buy time until they could figure out how to derail them altogether.

"Meantime, say your prayers," Kreiss counseled. "And God help me, I'm not above praying for an aneurysm, a heart attack, or a run-in with a bus to solve our problems."

The group pretended to look horrified.

Real Estate Plans

Eric Richter determined it was worth his while to travel to Minneapolis. Over the course of two weeks, four panicked pastors had called him, requesting his assistance in disposing of their congregations' assets.

"Let's meet at Monello," he told them. "Breakfast is on me." The four men showed up in their collars, excited to be dining at one of the city's premier restaurants. Richter wore his navy blue Ferragamo suit and a red power tie.

Things were playing out as he suspected they would. The state of Missouri bought the seminary for $50 million, so Richter and Rolfe pocketed a half million from the sale. As Haller had promised, the denomination endorsed Richter's firm as the agency of choice for all of a congregation's real estate needs. Calls were coming in on a regular basis from around the country. Only Haller knew that Richter's advice had played a significant role in generating the controversies that were roiling CLCA congregations.

It was Richter, after all, who suggested to Haller the idea of sending out a questionnaire virtually guaranteed to stir up trouble within congregations. Many congregations had the good sense to throw the questionnaire into the trash can. For those that didn't, however, an atmosphere of distrust followed as soon as laypeople started putting their pastors' orthodoxy to the test.

If a pastor refused to submit to the questionnaire, some of his members took it as *prima facie* evidence that the minister harbored heretical views. The congregation was forced to take sides, with some defending and some condemning the minister. Sometimes, the pastor asked to be placed on a call list, hoping to be hired by a congregation wise enough to see through the hell of heresy hunting. Other times, one faction or another left the congregation. Either way, the situation caused serious financial difficulties.

"My congregation just can't make a go of it anymore," one of the pastors explained. "Many members left once this disease of smoking out heretics took root. I've never even had a chance to discuss the issues involved. We've not been able to come together as a congregation to study the issues. People just left, and no one is coming in to take their place.

"I've cut staff to the bone. I've taken a ten percent pay cut. We often turn off the heat during the week, which puts us at risk of frozen water pipes. But it's not enough. The remaining members of the church council have directed me to do what it takes to liquidate our assets, pay off our building loan, and say goodbye to our congregation. I hope to find a congregation wise enough to avoid these hellish battles."

The other three ministers had similar stories. Richter let each of them speak in turn, recognizing the psychological importance of letting a man tell his own story, even if was virtually a carbon copy of every other story in the room. He told the men his firm, Richter and Rolfe, could help. "Thank God," one of them muttered. Another looked as if he was on the verge of crying. All four of them let out a breath, and their bodies relaxed as they hadn't in weeks.

Richter said he had studied the neighborhoods of each congregation. For two of them, he thought the best bet would be to find another congregation that had outgrown its facilities. "They still exist," he assured them. "Usually, they're non-denominational. They've developed a core of members excited about what they're doing. They're riding a wave of optimism, and they're willing to take on debt to expand. I'm betting we'll find buyers like that for your congregations."

The third congregation was just steps away from a relatively new, private Christian high school of about three hundred students. Richter thought he could convince the principal of the school of the wisdom of buying the church's sanctuary and its nearby gym. Overnight, the school could have a chapel and could expand its physical education programs.

As for the fourth congregation, Richter said the location was well situated for commercial purposes. He revealed to the group his new brainchild.

"Full disclosure," he said. "Several partners and I have begun a business called Heavenly Hospitality. We're aware, of course, of the turmoil within the CLCA. I'm a member of a CLCA congregation in Indianapolis, and my pastor keeps me informed week to week of what's going on. I thought one way to help would be to start Heavenly Hospitality.

"When the circumstances are right, we offer to purchase a congregation's property. Then we modify it to be part chapel, part banquet facility, and part meeting spaces for groups of ten to twenty-five or so. It's a one-stop shop for modestly sized weddings and receptions. Groups like Rotary Clubs can meet there. And we add a coffee shop, selling beverages well below the ridiculous Starbucks prices. We figure it brings people our way and exposes them to the full range of our services and facilities.

"We've only built one so far, in Kansas City. It's working out better than we projected. We think Grace Lutheran here in Minneapolis would be a perfect addition to the Heavenly Hospitality family. And who knows, if you gentlemen stay in the area, you might be performing some of your weddings at Heavenly Hospitality. You can tell families we'll give them a ten percent discount if they use a CLCA minister, either active or, uh, formerly with the denomination. And if you bring weddings our way, we'll give you a slice of the action as well."

Richter struck a deal to buy Grace Lutheran's property. Within two years, Heavenly Hospitality Minneapolis was generating revenue of two million dollars a year. The company went on to build out more than a hundred Heavenly Hospitality locations throughout the United States. Richter retired a happy, wealthy man, made rich by Heavenly Hospitality and real estate commissions from selling church buildings throughout the nation.

When they became empty nesters, he and his wife left their congregation in Indianapolis to move to Florida. He began worshiping on Sundays at the end of a golf club or in front of a big-screen TV watching his beloved Indianapolis Colts. As he often reminded himself, controversy can be the breeding ground of opportunity. Or, as the CLCA came to learn, it can be the incubator of destruction.

Telltale Hands

If you're a minister, it's difficult to find someone to tell your troubles to. It's also difficult to be held to account. Most people avoid having to tell their pastor he's being a jerk.

The CLCA had a way to address the problem. The denomination created a kind of buddy system. Ministers were paired with one another in symbiotic relationships. They could, in confidence, discuss any problems they were having, personal or professional. If necessary, one minister could blow a whistle if he saw weaknesses or transgressions in the other.

Haller, since he had been excluded from the CLCA roster, never had such a relationship. If he had, it's possible that GodsTruthIsMyTruth.com would never have been created. His zeal for purity might have been tempered and its sharp edges blunted. Instead, he gravitated toward a few ministers who reinforced his worst tendencies.

So, it came as a surprise to him when, so early in his presidency, the Reverend Paul Koenig requested a meeting. The avuncular Koenig, ten years Haller's senior, had gone bald years ago, and his stomach had picked up a generous layer of fat. He had been a parish pastor for much of his career. For a dozen years, he had presided full time over the denomination's Iowa District, which, like the national church body, was also based in Des Moines. District presidents were elected in their districts, not at the national convention, so a number of them, including Koenig, didn't support Haller's heresy hunt.

Koenig had come to know many of Oberhausen's professors because the district was home to the university. He enjoyed spending time there. His association with the university, he believed, kept him growing intellectually, and his exposure to students kept him young. He tried to live by the motto: "Be curious, not judgmental." Like many people, he attributed the saying to Walt Whitman, but one day, he became curious and learned no one knew exactly who came up with it.

He explained at his first meeting with Haller that, by virtue of their offices, they were paired with one another in a clergy coupling. "You can confide in me, and I in you," Koenig said. "If anything is weighing on you, I'm happy to listen to you, counsel you, and pray for you. And if necessary, I'm here to speak truth to power. Yours is a lonely job. Let me make it a bit less lonely."

Haller nodded. He thanked Koenig for coming by and said he appreciated the visit. But he made sure it was over in less than half an hour.

Koenig sent occasional emails to check in on Haller, who acknowledged them but never requested counsel, guidance, or just a quick meeting for coffee. Then one rainy, lightning-filled day in August 2029, this email came:

"Otto, a matter concerning you has come to my attention. It requires that we get together immediately. I'm writing not just as your clergy partner but as the district president responsible for disciplining and correcting you. I will be at your office tomorrow at nine a.m."

Haller felt his stomach start to churn. He bit his lower lip, and his shoulders tightened. He thought about not coming into the office. He considered telling Betty to schedule back-to-back meetings for the entire day. He thought about saying he had a doctor's appointment that couldn't be postponed. He realized, though, that eventually he would have to take the meeting. He decided to just get it over. And what could Koenig do to him, after all? He was the president of the entire church body. He had the power, not Koenig.

The rain continued the next morning when Koenig appeared. The two men shook hands. Over a cup of coffee, they shared pleasantries and discussed recent events in the church. Haller asked Koenig whether he had come to talk about issues around defecting congregations, the seminary sale, or the accreditation flareup at Oberhausen. All troublesome topics, Koenig said, but not within his purview.

"There's a matter of personal integrity I want to discuss," he said. Haller's mind started racing, searching to guess what Koenig might know about him.

"So, what are they saying about me now? What kind of slander? Who's accusing me of God knows what? What are they saying I've done?" His heart started racing.

Haller couldn't bring himself to look directly at Koenig. His grip on his coffee mug tightened as he became increasingly tense. Finally, after more than a minute, Koenig spoke.

"Otto, put down your mug and show me your hands." Reluctantly, the younger man obliged.

"Now can you guess why I'm here?" Haller shook his head, but he knew.

"That ring on your finger is a lie, isn't it? You're not married. You haven't been for several months. Yet you've led the church to believe you are. The CLCA has never had a divorced man as president of the church body, as I'm sure you know."

"It's not my fault I'm divorced," Haller said. "It's not my fault my wife decided to become a feminist. It's not my fault she chose to divorce me."

"I don't want to get into the inner workings of your marriage. I'm sure it was complicated. But there's an even more pressing matter. You weren't honest with the church. You went on pretending you were married when you weren't. Maybe the church could have lived with a divorced leader, maybe not. But it can't abide a man who lies about something so basic.

"So, I'm here today to ask for your resignation. We can give you a severance package. We can help you save face if that's what you want. When we make the announcement, we can say you needed to resign because of matters of a personal nature that you wish to keep private. I can't promise the real story won't emerge, but it won't be because the church revealed it."

"And what if I refuse? What would happen?"

Koenig asked Haller to produce a copy of the constitution and bylaws. They reviewed the whole complicated process together.

"It would culminate in taking a vote of the congregations. Each congregation would get one vote, regardless of its size. It would take sixty percent of the congregations to vote to remove you from office."

Haller said he liked those odds, especially now that so many of the big city, heretic-sympathizing congregations had defected. Koenig told him to think things through. If a public process were to begin, more than just the divorce and coverup would come out. His estrangement from his son would be recounted in great detail. His physical skirmishes with his ex-wife and her father would be revealed. And who knows what innuendoes and half-truths would find their way into the conversation? Haller should know better than most how difficult lies and smears can be to discredit.

"What makes you think I've had physical skirmishes with my wife?"

Koenig said the matter had been investigated thoroughly. There were witnesses willing to testify about such skirmishes.

"There's even a police report about your throwing your ex-father-in-law to the floor when you pushed past him to try to get to Martha. Nothing good can come from a prolonged review of your home life."

Haller's nostrils flared. "Who told you about the police report? That was supposed to be buried. For that matter, who told you about the divorce?"

Notification of the divorce had come from the Missouri District president. He had heard rumors. He checked with the court to verify them. Koenig wasn't at liberty to say how he received the police report, he said, but he had a copy, and he verified it was real.

"Supposing, just supposing, I decide to step down. Would I have a pension? Would I have health insurance?"

The insurance could be kept in force for nine months, Koenig said, but no, there would be no pension. Haller hadn't been on the clergy roster long enough to vest, and he wouldn't be able to remain on the roster. Any pension arrangements with Ebenezer Lutheran, the congregation in Frohna, would be in force, of course.

The CLCA president felt cornered. He asked to have a couple of days to think about his options, even though he had none. And so he resigned.

The day of the announcement, a dozen supporters gathered outside the CLCA offices, flashing the Triple I Salute, chanting "Holler for Haller."

The man, briefcase in hand, came out to greet his followers. He surveyed those who gathered. Inwardly, his heart was broken by how few people came. Somehow, though, he believed his time in ministry had not yet ended. He would find a way back into the lives of the people who believed in him.

* * *

Gehrke wasn't scheduled to begin his duties in Chicago until a month before Fall Semester 2029. He had three years' salary in the bank, and he was in no hurry to leave Des Moines. He could visit with friends, research and write a couple of papers commissioned by academic journals, and pack up his apartment at his leisure. He even ratcheted up his physical fitness regimen and took up pickle ball. Life had given him an unplanned sabbatical, and he was more than happy to take it.

Every time she had a three-day weekend or a break, Martha flew into town. Gehrke met her at Des Moines International, and the two of them would melt into each other's arms as soon as she cleared the gate. She would sometimes protest that Gehrke shouldn't be footing the bill for so many flights. Invariably, he would laugh and say: "Don't worry about it. They're all courtesy of the largesse of Jeremiah Marquardt."

At first, she chose to stay in hotels rather than at Gehrke's apartment. She needed time after her divorce to adjust to being single, she explained. She didn't want to proceed too quickly with Gehrke. By the time of her fourth visit, she agreed to start staying in Gehrke's guest bedroom. Over the course of several months, they settled on a more amorous accommodation that worked for both of them.

In May, Gehrke suggested spending a Saturday at Gray's Lake Park. There had been some rain earlier in the week, but park visitors posted online that walking trails were in good shape and easy to navigate. Martha packed a picnic lunch, and they headed out.

Gehrke didn't own a dog, but as they explored the park, almost every dog they encountered approached him as if he were an old friend. Martha was a bird watcher and was delighted with the waterfowl along the lake.

As they were walking hand in hand, Martha suddenly froze.

"What's wrong?" Gehrke asked.

"You see that guy up ahead? Is that who I think it is?"

A distant runner was approaching the couple. His face hadn't come into focus, but even so, Martha knew him by the way he carried himself. She had lived with him for decades.

"Hillman, can we just get off the trail for a bit? Hide behind some trees or bushes? He frightens me."

"Look, Martha. Right now, you and I have a chance to show this cretin he has no power over us. He caused some havoc in your life, some in mine. But if we want him to be done with us, we have to show him we'll stand up to him if he ever tries to mess with us again. Let's stay on the trail."

Martha found it difficult to speak, but she nodded her assent. Then she braced herself for the confrontation about to occur.

As he ran, Haller was looking down, still stewing over the events that had robbed him of his presidency. But he looked up when he came within forty feet of the couple and slowed to a walk. He couldn't believe his eyes.

"Well, well, well," he said as he neared the couple. "I should have known. Is this who you're 'writing' for, Martha? Did you go to college to learn to write or just to get away from me so you could start shacking up with this heretic . . . this horny, horrible heretic?"

"Leave her alone, Haller. You're not her husband. She and I never even talked until Caleb and Ashley's wedding, and Martha never did anything to violate her marriage vows. If you hadn't abused her, or if you had shown you were sorry for the pain you caused her, she probably would still be with you. But you didn't, and she's not. So leave her alone."

"Oh, Mr. Knight in Shining Armor! Sir Heretic the Hero! So, what's the deal, Gehrke? I get you booted from Oberhausen, and you decide to humiliate me by hooking up with my wife? Well, let's take this a little further. I can arrange to get you totally booted from the clergy roster. I can get you totally defrocked. I can get friends of mine to file ethics complaints against you for breaking up my marriage. And just like that, your pension vanishes."

Gehrke stepped closer to Haller. Martha had never seen Gehrke's eyes look so cold and hard. He started jabbing Haller in the chest.

"Give it a try, but let's get one thing straight, Haller. I didn't break up your marriage. Martha didn't break up your marriage. You broke up your marriage. You were a jerk in seminary, and you're a jerk now.

"You know why? Because you've turned your heart into a hard rock of pure doctrine covered by a thick glaze of biblical inerrancy. And I have to tell you, friend. You missed the biggest lesson in the Bible. You missed learning how to love. And that's a hell unlike any other. Try to learn before it's too late, because I promise you, your hate will keep you in your own personal hell."

Haller felt his heart racing. To get away from Gehrke, he stepped back, turned away, and stood in front of Martha.

"What's your story? Harlot takes up with heretic? In all the time we were married, I never imagined you would have any use for a man like Gehrke. What happened to you anyway?"

As Martha started to speak, Haller raised a hand with the intention of hitting her. In an instant, Gehrke grabbed Haller's wrist, twisted his arm, and drove him to his knees. Haller cried out in pain.

"You're not getting up until you promise to walk away from us and never bother us again. You're nothing but a sad, little man, Haller, and it's time to get out of our lives. You understand?"

Haller whimpered and then nodded. Gehrke released him, took Martha's hand, and the two of them continued on their walk. Haller proceeded the other way, eventually fading into the distance.

A short time later, Martha stopped, stood in front of Gehrke, and gave him a long, grateful hug.

"We're done with him, right?" she said.

"We're done with him. Right."

A Reckoning at Oberhausen

Jeremiah Marquardt stood before his bosses, the Oberhausen board of regents. Like him, they believed in the "inspired, inerrant, infallible" platform. Like him, they had come to Oberhausen to clean out heretics. Like him, they were quickly learning their job was more complicated. During their brief time in office, they had faced blowback from staff firings, student protests, accreditation snafus, and an imminent drop in enrollment.

Most of them were exasperated with Marquardt for not keeping them apprised of major actions. Still, they stood by him. He was one of the orthodox clergy, after all. Sometimes, they reasoned, a man in Marquardt's position had to step on a few toes to make progress, if progress was what you call the basket of controversies he had put together.

In 2013, the university built a special room just for board meetings, equipped with the finest audio-visual paraphernalia. Its décor was sleek, simple, and Scandinavian, meant to point to the future, not the past. This edition of the board seemed out of place.

Marquardt cleared his throat several times as the group came to order. He kept looking at the letter in his hands, occasionally wincing. After leading the regents in the obligatory prayer, he shared the letter's contents.

"Gentlemen, Travelers, the company that provides our directors and officers insurance, is indicating it will not renew our policy when it expires. You'll recall we carry this insurance to protect us all from personal losses in case we are sued by faculty, staff, students, parents, alumni, vendors, anyone who might claim that our actions have caused them harm. Whether a plaintiff would win or not, our individual legal expenses could be considerable, and a judgment in their favor could bankrupt us. The policy is very important.

"The company says we have strayed so far from generally accepted management principles that we are no longer an acceptable risk."

Marquardt listed the specifics that concerned the insurers, including the manner in which Hillman Gehrke was dismissed, the dissolution of the theology and anthropology departments, the suspension of accreditation by the Higher Learning Commission, and the "pay to play" accreditation by a body not respected among academics. Any one of these actions could provoke a lawsuit, and probably would, Travelers said. Any one of them could have been handled much more professionally. And any one of them holds the seeds of more risk to come.

Board members asked whether another company would be willing to provide the coverage. Marquardt had been exploring the possibilities, but so far, no one had stepped forward. Travelers was well respected for its ability to assess such risks, and if they wouldn't take on Oberhausen, no one else would either.

One of the lay board members, Steve Stubenrauch, a loud, burly mountain of a man, owned a construction firm in Omaha. Without D&O insurance, he said, he would have to resign from the board. He couldn't take the risk of having his personal assets taken because of some suit against the university, legitimate or not. Once a suit gets in front a jury, who knows what might happen? His comments frightened the other board members into wondering whether they would also have to resign.

Reluctantly, Marquardt revealed a plan Travelers had presented to him. The company would be willing to renew Oberhausen on probation if the university agreed to a major revamping of its governance and operations, including:

-Hiring a reputable management consulting firm to help institute best practices for operating a university.

-Renouncing any involvement with the American Association of Academic Authenticity.

-Asking the Higher Learning Commission for readmission, even if only on a suspended basis, and doing everything possible to regain full accreditation.

-Consolidating Martin Luther Seminary into Oberhausen to simplify operations.

"The next two points are hard for me to discuss," Marquardt said. "One will be challenging to implement. The other will be personally difficult for me, but if it's what you want, I will bow to your wishes."

Travelers noted that after decades of declining financial support, Oberhausen received almost nothing from the CLCA. So, why was the CLCA so involved in Oberhausen's operations? Why was the university's board elected by the church body in convention, and why should church officers have so much say in how the university operated, including who served as president?

"The company says we should break ties with the church and establish a new, independent nonprofit organization that will own Oberhausen. It wants to see a board that will establish and periodically review a vision, mission, and purpose for the university; oversee governance; appoint the president and establish performance criteria for the position; exercise fiduciary responsibility; establish criteria for board members and elect board members and officers; and represent the broader public interest in higher education. There are some other stipulations, but those are the highlights."

The board didn't want to commit to the idea, and it wasn't sure it would be acceptable to the church. Marquardt said he had become resigned to the necessity of what Travelers proposed. Unless some radical measures were taken, he had become convinced that Oberhausen's future was in jeopardy, and the danger was imminent.

"Which brings me to the final point," Marquardt said. Travelers believed it would be best for all involved if Marquardt stepped down as president of Oberhausen. His handling of Gehrke was botched, after all, and his leadership role in establishing the American Association for Academic Authenticity revealed a lack of judgment.

"I'll always believe Hillman Gehrke and his kind should be banished from Oberhausen and the CLCA. I don't regret using whatever means I had at my disposal to get rid of him. But Travelers believes things could have been handled better. They've told me I don't have the experience, or the credentials, or the judgment to lead a major university.

"I understand I was brought to the school by a man who has been shown to have his own shortcomings. I took the job thinking it would be a crowning achievement for my career and a good last step before retirement. I wish I could be proud of my brief time here, but honestly, I'm not. My decisions have been driven more by emotion than thought. And so, I willingly tender my resignation."

The board members with ministerial backgrounds had all studied under Marquardt in Cape Girardeau. They thought highly of him and had wonderful memories of his teaching abilities. They hesitated to accept the resignation.

Lay board members, those like Steve Stubenrauch, had been elected because they also held to the Triple I precepts. But they knew when changes needed to be made. Stubenrauch moved—with sadness, he said—to accept Marquardt's resignation. Once the motion received a second, the group spent a few minutes expressing their admiration for Marquardt and their regret that things had come to this. Then, by a vote of nine to four, they sent him away.

Lucy Rosenkoetter at the *Des Moines Register* got wind of the story before the university issued an official news release. Marquardt, as expected, refused to speak with her, but the Oberhausen provost, James Waldschmidt, had returned to campus and took her call.

"I'm sure Dr. Marquardt had good intentions during his brief time at Oberhausen, and I wish him all the best," Waldschmidt said. "We've suffered some setbacks, but they're nothing we can't overcome. Now that the worst of our controversies are behind us, faculty, staff, students, parents, and alumni will rally to our side. We think our future is bright."

Six months later, after an extensive search, the board selected Waldschmidt as the school's next president. His colleagues at Oberhausen and throughout academia praised the selection. Travelers, assured that the school was in good hands, agreed to continue its directors and officers liability policy on a probationary basis. Any long-term relationship would come only when the university could break free of its ties with the CLCA.

In 2030, the church and the university came to an agreement. Oberhausen, after absorbing the Cape Girardeau seminary, would become independent of the CLCA. It would continue to train pastors for the church.

The church could specify requirements for its ministerial candidates, and a church certification board would ensure they met the requirements, much as a hospital might test a nurse before offering employment. Oberhausen professors, however, would have the freedom to teach as they saw fit.

This arrangement was accepted by both the church and the Higher Learning Commission. After making a number of other administrative adjustments, Oberhausen's accreditation was restored in 2031, and the university remained as a Travelers client for many years.

Marquardt and his wife returned to Cape Girardeau. They joined the congregation once headed by Ed Schroeder, Martha Haller's father. Occasionally, Marquardt would lead a class at the congregation. He had learned to prefer classes that emphasized ethics or Lutheran history. He steered away from harping on the "inspired, inerrant, infallible" Bible, having learned the controversies the topic could provoke.

Haller's Sermon

The unmarried Otto Haller, for the first time since graduating from seminary, held no office in a congregation or church body. Once he was forced out of the CLCA presidency, he asked his friend and pastor, Herb Sellmeyer, if he could take the pulpit one Sunday at Gethsemane, the congregation he had joined in Des Moines. Sellmeyer acquiesced but quickly regretted his decision.

Haller opened in the name of the Father, and the Son, and the Holy Spirit. He asked the Lord to bless the words he was about to speak.

Then, he spent half an hour portraying himself as a victim of a church conspiracy. There were ministers just looking for an excuse to depose him, he said. They found it when they discovered his wife had recently divorced him, glossing over how he hid the divorce from the church.

"They told me I could resign by saying it was for personal reasons. They told me they wouldn't mention my divorce. But two days later, my enemies let it leak. So now you all know. But let me tell you how it really is.

"Now, my wife . . . okay, my ex-wife . . . I thought we had a perfect marriage. She took care of me, she raised our son, I brought home the money, what there was of it.

"But then, she decides to be a feminist. She leaves our home to go study, of all things, writing. You know what that great basketball coach, Bobby Knight, said about writing? He said, 'We all learned to write in second grade. Most of us moved on to other things.' Imagine. Going to college just to learn to write. Sad.

"So, I get elected president of your church body. I didn't campaign, but if people wanted me, what could I do, right? So, I move to Des Moines. She doesn't come. She stays in Missouri to study . . . writing."

He shook his head and raised his palms toward the sky.

"Writing. Can you believe it? Writing. Whatever. It is what it is. So, one day, I'm sitting in my office, and my admin, Betty . . . you gotta love her, Betty . . . one day Betty brings me this envelope. It's marked 'personal and confidential.' Betty doesn't open it, bless her heart. It's the divorce papers. Did my wife, correction, ex-wife, write them? No, a lawyer wrote them.

"I didn't want a divorce. I never asked for a divorce. She did, and she wouldn't even talk to me about it. So what was I going to do? Force her to stay married? I didn't want to be married to a feminist, but God doesn't like divorce, right? So I would have stayed married. But I couldn't force her to stay with me. So I signed the papers.

"I was going to tell the church, you know. I was just looking for the right time. But before I could do it, someone uncovered the divorce papers in the Missouri courts. So now it looked like I was hiding something. But I wasn't. I was just looking for the right time. They asked for my resignation, so what was I supposed to do? I gave it to them. But I'm not a bad person. I'd ask for forgiveness, but for what? I didn't do anything wrong.

"I still believe in everything I've always believed in. Pure doctrine. The Bible. The inspired, inerrant, infallible Bible. I'll always believe in it. All of you should too."

He stepped away from the pulpit but then returned.

"Oh, uh, I hope God blesses all of you, now and forevermore." He took his seat near the altar but not before making the sign of the cross and flashing the Triple I Salute to the congregation. More than a few returned the gesture.

Sellmeyer felt relieved that communion wasn't being offered that Sunday. After Haller's self-serving "sermon," Sellmeyer could not have allowed Haller to distribute the elements with him.

After the service, Sellmeyer walked outside to greet his congregants. He didn't wait for Haller, who came anyway.

A sizable group gathered around Haller comfort him.

He addressed his followers, almost in a whisper. "Let me ask you something. Do you think there's merit in an online church? If I were to start one, would you all join in on Sunday mornings? Think about the convenience. I'd talk about God and the Bible within the framework of pure doctrine. I'd give you what you needed, unadorned by political correctness, wokeness, social justice, scientific conjecture, or any nuance. Just the Bible, plain and simple. Would you join me?"

Not wanting to offend their regular pastor, the group hesitated to yell out "Yes!" But they smiled and nodded their heads.

Not long after, Haller reclaimed GodsTruthIsMyTruth.com from the young minister who had been its caretaker. He added a new tab called Online Lutheran Church, where each Sunday, he would appear at 10 a.m. central time to preach on some Bible text. He simultaneously appeared on YouTube, Facebook, Roku, and Apple TV. His sermons were archived at all his internet outlets.

Some people emailed him to ask how they might practice communion without attending a traditional congregation. Haller had an idea.

"You need a pastor to consecrate the elements. Then, when I offer communion during the webcast, you can join me. So, here's what we can do. For $40, plus shipping and handling, I'll send you a bottle of wine and a box of communion wafers that I've already consecrated. It would be no different from having an elder go to a recuperating person's home with wafers and wine that a pastor has consecrated. With the consecrated elements in your home, when we get to the part of the webcast where I celebrate communion, you can join in. Just make sure you keep the wine refrigerated so you can use it from week to week. And don't use it for anything else."

People were all too happy to send him the money, and he made a profit on the markup. As people ran out of wine and wafers, it became a recurring source of revenue, a nice little supplement to the donations coming in.

Before he became president of the CLCA, Haller never took money from the proceeds of GodsTruthIsMyTruth.com, which were mushrooming as he gave it his full attention. Now, because it was his one and only ministry, he felt justified in drawing a salary from the website.

Haller had a logo designed that featured a cross next to a hand configured in the shape of the Triple I Salute. As his online congregation grew, he changed the name from Online Lutheran Church to Online Christian Church and then to Online Evangelical Christian Bible Federation. The Triple I Salute attracted worshipers who took it to mean something beyond the intended "inspired, inerrant, and infallible" mantra.

Haller's "doctrinal purity," it turned out, had special appeal for zealots. They were attracted by Haller's resurrected "Holohoax" rants, his calls for laws against same-sex marriage, his strong stance against abortion, his support of *laissez faire* capitalism, and his belief that home schooling was the best way to transmit righteous values to the next generation.

People began requesting that he make personal appearances in their communities. For any group that could pull together $10,000 plus travel expenses—and there were many—Haller found room in his schedule to visit their town.

After a couple of years, he moved from Des Moines to a nineteenth-century home in St. Louis's Soulard neighborhood, in the shadow of the Anheuser-Busch brewery and just a couple of miles from Busch Stadium. The neighborhood, built in the era of 1800s beer barons, felt like home to him. As he took his runs, he noted the shuttered Catholic and Lutheran church buildings dotting the area, and his chest swelled with pride that he had found a way to keep old-time religion alive in the 21st century.

He occasionally attended a Cardinal game, sitting alone, eating a hot dog. On these occasions, he traded his collar for a Cardinal T-shirt and cap. He kept to himself. To those around him, he seemed lost in thought, failing to react even when his team turned a double play or hit a home run. People couldn't know he was remembering earlier times, better times, times he missed, times he had shared with Caleb as father and son.

For a while, he tried visiting his old congregation in Frohna. They were cordial, but they had moved on. They knew that Martha had divorced him, and they suspected he was to blame. It took only a couple of visits before he stopped coming.

Haller never reunited with his son. He never remarried. He lived alone, free of heretics, free of friendships, free of the obligations of being in relationships. In the dark of night, his computer kept him company.

When he died, he left his money to Bob Jones University, believing it to be the standard bearer for what had become his brand of Christianity. As time progressed, Haller felt more of a kinship with its fundamentalism than he did with his Lutheran roots.

Haller had made a connection of sorts with his people. When he went on the road, he could talk with them about the Bible, and God, and pure doctrine, but neither he nor they wanted to talk about his life and his loneliness. Certain people, those who had trouble coping with an increasingly complex world, clamored for his brand of purity. They had no idea what a sad, lonely life it could create.

A Denomination Fails

After Haller's forced resignation from the CLCA presidency, the church body's board faced a difficult problem. Until the denomination could meet again in convention, the board had to name an interim president. Like Haller, they had ridden into their offices on the Triple I platform. They wanted to select someone with Haller's doctrinal convictions but without his baggage.

Seeing how quickly the church fragmented and nosedived under Haller, they divined that other skills might be needed. Also, Travelers informed them that, like Oberhausen's board, they would be without directors and officers insurance unless they made a prudent leadership decision.

They reviewed candidates within the Reformation Restoration Alliance but quickly saw they were strong on pure doctrine but weak on just about any other skill a president would need. They also were hemmed in by the constitutional requirement that any president of the church body had to be on the clergy roster of the CLCA.

After a marathon session, one board member had an idea.

"He's not really one of us, but whoever we appoint will hold the position only until the next convention. I think the best choice for now would be George Spurgat. He's both a lawyer and a CLCA clergyman. He's been at church headquarters for two decades. We may not agree with his theology, but he's intelligent. He's not controversial. He'd be a perfect caretaker until we can regroup and elect someone else."

When he was approached, Spurgat shuddered, and he felt a hard thudding in his chest. He knew just how desperate the CLCA's situation was, and he doubted anything could be done to turn the situation around. Only a sharply developed sense of duty made him consider it.

"I have no interest in spearheading a heresy hunt," he told the board. "Your man Haller wreaked havoc on this church, and I have serious doubts we can bounce back. If I agree to take the job, I want the freedom to do the things needed to give us a chance to turn this situation around. It can't be done by beating the bushes for heretics. Frankly, I'm not sure it can be done at all. I'll try, but if and only if I'm given a free hand."

The board consented to his demands. Spurgat launched a tour of the CLCA's traditional pockets of strength, asking pastors who still cared about the church body to bring influential lay people with them to day-long seminars. There he showed the financial and membership data detailing just how desperate the situation had become.

His immediate priority was to secure the pension and health insurance plans of ministers and workers who had given their lives to the church. It wouldn't be fair to have these foundations of their lives fail them, especially when so many of them were nearing retirement.

The CLCA subsidized a number of mission congregations who needed financial support. Spurgat wanted to continue to help congregations in inner-city neighborhoods. Their members relied on them for food, clothing, and rent subsidies to make it through life.

"As far as I'm concerned, anything else the church does can go by the wayside if necessary," he told the groups that met with him. "We've always said congregations have the power in this church. Now they're going to have to decide whether they want to support this obsession with heresy or move on to things that will be more . . . productive. I'll just remind you that Jesus said to feed and give drink to the hungry and thirsty, clothe those who need garments, welcome strangers, care for the sick, and visit those in prison. Hunting heretics wasn't on his list.

"He had his problems with some religious leaders. Scribes and Pharisees. He rebuked them for emphasizing the letter of the Law while being blind to the spirit of love. Frankly, I think this preoccupation with uncovering and banishing heretics is about as pharisaical as anything I've ever seen in a church. I hope you pray about it. I hope it stops. I hope we can find a better way to live together."

After Spurgat completed his tour, more money came in, but it wasn't enough to reverse the CLCA death spiral. Many congregations wanted to find a higher road, but many wanted to keep purifying a church that had lasted a hundred fifty years. As the financial resources dried up, the denomination ceased to exist.

Those congregations that didn't close down simply carried on independent of any church body. If they did their job well, if they preached the Gospel of love, if they offered hope, they survived and sometimes thrived. If not, they perished.

Hillman and Martha

In the summer of 2030, after the school year ended, Martha Haller moved to Chicago. The Detters provided her with lodging, giving her and Hillman Gehrke time to work out the details of how they would live their life together once they married.

They spent the summer walking hand in hand almost every day, getting Martha used to the fast pace of Chicago life. Hillman coached her in riding subways and the L. She learned how to study the peculiarities of her fellow passengers—sidelong glances only, Hillman instructed. By observing their antics, from pickpocketing to fighting for seats, she learned the basics of surviving on public transportation by avoiding suspicious characters.

She enjoyed feeling the wind as it came off Lake Michigan. She and Hillman laughed as they looked at their distorted images in the Bean in Millennium Park. They spent many mornings strolling around the University of Chicago, taking time to study the Gothic architecture, stopping for morning coffee at the Grounds of Being in Swift Hall.

Students would stop to say hello to Dr. Gehrke, who had quickly developed a reputation as an excellent lecturer who cared about his students. When a colleague would walk by, Hillman would say, "Gene, come here. I want you to meet my fiancée, Martha. I can't believe she's agreed to marry me."

One morning, Ted Robertson, dean of the divinity school, came searching for a latte. He had been out of town, so Hillman hadn't been able to introduce him to Martha. When he walked in, the couple were holding hands under their table. They both rose as Ted joined them. After some chitchat, Ted told Martha that Hillman had been his best friend since their time together at Harvard's Divinity School.

"I imagine Hillman told you about Laura, his first wife. She had an amazing smile. She had a great heart. When she died, Hillman was devastated."

Martha, coming from modest circumstances in Cape Girardeau and Frohna, didn't care to hear about how wonderful Hillman's first wife was. She had more than a bit of insecurity about marrying a nationally recognized theologian and scholar.

"Here's the thing, Martha. Whenever I'd ask Hillman why he hadn't married again, he would tell me he hadn't met anyone who could measure up to Laura. When he started seeing you, all he could talk about was your courage, your love for your son, your thirst for knowledge, and your ambition to become not just a writer but a real voice the nation might listen to. He told me about your advice to your son. 'Explore what you need to explore.' He's delighted that you're following your own advice.

"Believe me, he wouldn't fall for just anyone. God knows he's had his chances, but until now, no one interested him. He loves you deeply. I have no doubt. I'm so pleased you two have found each other."

Martha smiled and shook just a bit as a tear rolled down her cheek. She was so grateful that Hillman had been speaking so warmly about her. Otto never had.

She considered enrolling in the University of Chicago's writing program. As the wife of a professor, she could have gone for free. She worried, though, that even if she earned her degree totally on merit, people might think Gehrke's colleagues had mollycoddled her as they evaluated her work. After researching several programs, including the ones Caleb mentioned at Columbia College, she chose to enroll at Loyola University. Her first order of business, however, was to write her wedding vows.

"Today, Hillman Gehrke, before God, before our friends, and before my son, Caleb, and my daughter-in-law, Ashley, I pledge to you my abiding love. I have come to know you as a man of great intellect, great humor, and above all, great love. You make me feel protected, seen, and appreciated. I had no idea a relationship like ours was possible. I love you, Hillman, and I will be with you until my final breath. I thank God for you every day."

After living alone for most of his adult life, Hillman was overjoyed to have found Martha.

"Dearest Martha, I had given up on finding a life partner, and then, like an angel, you came into my life. From the moment I saw you, from our first dance together, I knew you were something special. Life hasn't always been easy for either of us. We've seen suffering, we've seen heartache, but we've always survived. Now, we have each other to walk with for the rest of our lives together. God has blessed me with the gift of you. I'm so grateful, and I will stand by you forever."

* * *

The couple scheduled their wedding for August 2030. Given their backgrounds, it seemed inevitable to their friends that they would marry in a congregation of the former Confessional Lutheran Church in America. The idea, though, did not appeal to either of them. For much of their lives, the church had been a source of hope, comfort, and fellowship. Events of recent years, however, had made them both wary of having anything to do with the remnants of the denomination.

Increasingly, Hillman and his University of Chicago colleagues—the Christian colleagues—had been congregating on Sunday mornings in the home of Ted Robertson and his husband, Vinay Gupta. The worshipers were more than happy to leave behind the trappings of denominational life, the bureaucracy, the slowness to adapt, the pressured finances, and above all, the politics. They were working out a model of ecclesiastical life that looked more like the early church—meeting in people's homes, caring for one another, engaging in community service projects, learning from one another, and avoiding the kinds of hierarchies that drew such a sharp line between clergy and laity. Everyone's gifts and everyone's contributions to the community were valued and appreciated.

So it came to be that at two p.m. Saturday, August 24, 2030, Hillman Gehrke and Martha Haller stood before a small gathering of friends at the home of Ted and Vinay. Officiating at the ceremony were Caleb Haller and

Ashley Detter, two humble members of the priesthood of all believers. After the happy couple said "I do" and kissed one another, the four embraced and began life together as a tight-knit, loving family. Ashley couldn't stop smiling, and Caleb was delighted with his new stepfather. His heretic-hunting days were over, nothing but a distant memory.

Epilogue

In 2035, the Rev. Dr. Hillman Gehrke was invited to write about his long career in the Confessional Lutheran Church in America, and his dismissal from Oberhausen University, for the website TowardACompassionateChristianity.com. *His article is reprinted here.*

* * *

For most of my life, the CLCA was my anchor and my home. Its ministers and schools taught me about the God I worship. It provided a community of colleagues and friends who enriched me and comforted me, especially after my first wife died just three years after we married. It gave me a place to sort truth from lies and to seek help when confronted with things that puzzled me.

With the CLCA, I had a tradition to stand on, kick against, and test the many bogus, half-baked ideas and movements floating around during my lifetime. Ayn Rand and her objectivism, Vladimir Putin and his oligarchs, and Donald Trump and his loyalists all failed to stand up to the scrutiny I learned to give them through my CLCA education.

Slowly, almost imperceptibly at first, a sinister spirit crept into the denomination under the cover of righteousness. A small group of ministers raised up the idea that an "inspired, inerrant, infallible" Bible was the foundation of the Christian faith. Those of us who questioned this proposition, who believe faith and church are rooted instead in the love and sacrifice of Christ, were branded heretics.

For most of the denomination's history, we could have conversations about this fundamental disagreement. We could adjourn these conversations when we reached an impasse, and we could agree to reconvene at a later date. We could continue to talk, and maybe we could find compromises and areas of agreement. We could continue in a spirit of collegiality and respect. We could honor the Lord we all worship by treating each other with love, just as we had done since the founding of the CLCA more than a hundred fifty years ago.

Instead, the "inspired, inerrant, infallible" contingent chose to demonize those of us who believe scripture can withstand an examination using historical and literary criticism. I think it's apparent that it took far more than six days to create our planet, but those who commandeered the CLCA didn't. They chose to interpret the first creation story in Genesis literally; I don't. That doesn't stop me from trusting in the love of God, the sacrifice of Jesus, and the strength of the Holy Spirit as the source of knowledge and wisdom about how people can have life and have it abundantly.

We disagree on our approach to biblical interpretation. This doesn't, however, make my opponents doctrinally pure, and it doesn't make me a heretic. Any time someone claims to be "pure"—doctrinally, ethnically, or morally—the sin of arrogance has a fertile breeding ground, and the lust for power can be fed.

There was nothing God-pleasing about the smear tactics and the power politics used to take over the CLCA. The spirit of divisiveness could not have come from the Lord of love. The lust for control could not have been rooted in the humility we as Christians are told to seek.

Over the past two decades, our nation and our world have been roiled by power seekers who use unethical strategies and tactics to create chaos. Once chaos reigns, they assure frightened people that they and only they can restore order. They then proceed to grab power, enforce their dogma, and take away people's right to question and argue even small points. When it happens in government and society, it's oppressive and unjust, and people can be persecuted by those who hunger for power. When it happens in the church, it's oppressive and unholy, and people's lives can be turned upside down by the spiritually arrogant.

Today, the CLCA has ceased to exist, and that's a shame. The ugliness that infected the denomination has done more damage than just tearing down a church body and its structures. It has bred cynicism among many, members and non-members alike, about church and religion altogether. It's impossible for a church to be taken seriously when it espouses a sentiment like "they'll know we are Christians by our love" and then lets loose bully squads and strong-arm enforcers within its ranks.

People ask me how I've been affected personally. I'm not one to say I'm spiritual but not religious. I am spiritual. I am religious. And I want to be part of a community of believers bigger than myself. I want to be in a church.

I've been slow to affiliate with another denomination, although I might someday. Instead, my wife, Martha, and I worship with a small group of other Christians. We take turns hosting one another in our homes. So far, we've enjoyed not having to deal with the trappings of denominational life—the bureaucracy, the finances, the slowness, and yes, the politics.

That's not to say I'll never again be part of a denomination. Size can be important in addressing needs like disaster relief and world hunger. Size creates the strength needed to build universities and social service agencies. Size makes it easier to collaborate with other Christians and other faiths to address societal issues.

But to join another denomination, I would have to be convinced that it cares about both righteousness and justice. I'd want it to be committed to a seeking for truth about the God who asked us to love both the divine and the people all around us. I'd want it to fight for justice in issues such as race and economic inequality. I'd want it to embody a spirit of humility and openness, not a spirit of arrogance and self-righteousness.

Right now, I'm learning to live with ambivalence. I'm at one of those in-between moments, hurt by a denomination I once loved, sad to have seen its demise, and unsure and praying about what my next step should be. I'm just going to cogitate on it for a while. I'm sure an answer will come to me.

What Others Are Saying

Survivors of ecclesiastical warfare will recognize familiar character types, political strategies, and toxic scenarios in this story, all of which remind us that church people are as subject as anyone to the seduction of having control, acclaim, wealth, and the power to get rid of those with whom they disagree. Every church, and perhaps everyinstitution and nation, has heretic hunters, and as this story discerns, the zealots among them generally prove themselves the most destructive heretics of all. The church's true and only treasure is the gospel of Jesus Christ, not patriarchy, rectitude, or even orthodoxy.

Frederick Niedner
Senior Research Professor in Theology
Valparaiso University

As a former politician, I witnessed firsthand how certain politicians used the word of Christ to justify inevitably un-Christian ideas and ideals. I wondered, "How did those politicians get to such inaccurate dogma?" Reading Peter Faur's *The Heretic Hunters*, I can now see how they got there. *The Heretic Hunters* is, as the subtitle reads, a parable for our time. At times heartbreaking, at times frustrating, *The Heretic Hunters* also shows that love can and will trump hate. A must-read for anyone trying to make sense of the times we are in.

Lorenzo Sierra
Former Arizona State Representative
Author, *Fight Like Hell: Love, Politics, and the Will to Live*

The Heretic Hunters gets at the raw edge of faith—what happens when belief curdles into fear, when doctrine is turned into a weapon. But what stays is the quiet instinct of love and how it can still survive the noise of institutions obsessed with control. It's about what happens when a person must choose between trusting what they've been told is infallible and trusting what their inner self knows to be true.

David Martinez
Author
Bones Worth Breaking

While the Christian community confesses that is the one, holy, catholic, and apostolic church, it has experienced numerous ecclesiastical conflicts and consequent interdenominational and intradenominational divisions. This fictional account is reminiscent of a major conflict within a North American Lutheran church body during the mid-twentieth century.

The personalities of the main characters, the theological debates, the quest for ecclesiastical political power, the passion for what is perceived as truth, the diverse interpretations of Scripture, the family and communal dynamics, and the broken relationships that result from conflict are explored expertly, realistically, and believably in the storyline. The paradoxical nature of the church, whose members are simultaneously saints and sinners, thus becomes readily apparent. The novel will capture the attention of its readers and will remind them of the multifaceted and complex dynamic that is operative in human relationships within the church and beyond. Thus, the story actually serves as a "parable" for any time.

Kurt K. Hendel
Bernard, Fischer, Westberg Distinguished Ministry
Professor Emeritus of Reformation History
Lutheran School of Theology at Chicago

Discussion Questions

The Heretic Hunters is a story of fracture and faith—of people caught between loyalty and conscience, tradition and transformation. Inspired by real theological tensions but imagined for our time, the novel invites readers to wrestle with sacred questions: What does it mean to belong? Who decides what is true? And can love survive when doctrine becomes a weapon?

Whether you're reading in a book club, a church group, or on your own, these questions are meant to open space for honest dialogue. They explore the characters' journeys, the theological undercurrents, and the evolving role of denominations in a polarized age. There are no right answers—only deeper questions.

Theological Reflection

1. *"When church becomes a blood sport, can even love survive?"* How does this question echo through the novel's events and relationships?
2. Hillman Gehrke champions inclusive theology, interfaith dialogue, and moral courage. In what ways does his character embody the values of Christianity?
3. What does the novel suggest about the nature of heresy? Who defines it, and how does that definition shift across generations or power structures?
4. Salvation is a recurring theme. How do you define salvation—for individuals, for institutions, or for faith itself?

Denominations and Power

1. The novel portrays a denomination unraveling under ideological pressure. What parallels do you see in today's religious landscape?
2. How does the use of social media in the story reflect real-world dynamics of influence, polarization, and spiritual branding?
3. Otto Haller uses smear campaigns, power politics, and later, authoritarian governance to try to achieve his goals. Do you see parallels to life in 21st-century America?
4. Otto Haller represents theological certainty and institutional control. How do his beliefs and actions shape his life, his family, and his denomination?
5. What role should denominations play in shaping moral discourse today? Are they still relevant, or are they being replaced by looser spiritual networks?

Character Exploration

1. Martha Haller moves from silent suffering to active resistance. What drives her transformation, and how does it reflect broader themes of spiritual awakening?
2. Otto Haller and Hillman Gehrke have far different beliefs about the nature of God, Christianity, and salvation. Do you side more with Haller or Gehrke? Why?
3. Does it seem right that, toward the end of his life, Haller came to identify more with evangelical Christianity?
4. Choose a moment when a character faces a moral crossroads. How did the character's decision shape your understanding of courage, compromise, cowardice, or conviction?

About the Author

Peter Faur, a native St. Louisan, was the religion editor of *The St. Louis Globe-Democrat*, where he worked from 1977 to 1982. Before then, he served as a staff writer for *The Lutheran Witness* and as editor of *The St. Louis Lutheran*.

He spent most of his career in public relations, working in telecommunications, chemical manufacturing, brewing, and copper mining. His work won several Gold Quills from the International Association of Business Communicators and a Silver Anvil from the Public Relations Society of America.

Faur holds a bachelor of arts degree in education with minors in theology and psychology from Concordia University, Chicago; a master's degree in journalism from Kansas State University; and master's degrees in business administration and management from Fontbonne University in St. Louis.

His first novel, *Red Metal*, told the story of a battle between a copper-mining company CEO and a hedge fund manager.

From 2006 to 2020, he served on the board of the Arizona Center for Nature Conservation, which operates the Phoenix Zoo. Today he is a member of the policy committee of Lutheran Advocacy Ministry Arizona.

His pastimes include writing, reading, running, and movie-going. He and his wife, Pat, have lived in Phoenix since 2003 and attend La Casa de Cristo Lutheran Church.

You can connect with me on:

- https://peterfaur.com
- https://www.facebook.com/peter.faur
- https://www.threads.com/@peterfaur
- https://bsky.app/profile/peterfaur.bsky.social

www.ingramcontent.com/pod-product-compliance
Lightning Source LLC
Chambersburg PA
CBHW050251110726